Viking Clan

Book 22 in the Dragon Heart Series

By

Griff Hosker

Contents

Part One
Gift from the gods

Prologue

Many men, especially those who lived beyond my lands, thought that when I made Sámr Ship Killer my heir that I had sowed the seeds for the destruction of the clan. They thought there would be division and strife amongst my family. That was not so. My son, Gruffyd, and grandson, Ragnar, were happy for my great-grandson to lead the Clan of the Wolf. I had spoken with them both. Each had their own reasons for approving my decision. For Ragnar, it meant he could be a father and, in the fullness of time, a grandfather. He could enjoy that which my son, Wolf Killer, had not enjoyed, a family life. For Gruffyd it meant he could sail the seas and raid. His son, Mordaf had not been to sea with me as much as Sámr. He envied the adventures and the tales which Sámr had told upon his return. Gruffyd and his son Mordaf had been captured in Om Walum and that had changed him. My son had told me he did not wish to be Jarl of the Clan of the Wolf. Part of me wondered if Gruffyd wanted to begin a new clan. Hrolf the Horseman had done so. The Clan of the Horse, so we heard, was growing and had their feet firmly planted in Frankia. I was not as close to Gruffyd as I was to Ragnar and his son. A man did not bemoan such things. He lived with them.

We had buried Rolf Horse Killer and Olaf Leather Neck. There were now just three Ulfheonar left to follow me. There would be no more once we had passed. My great-grandson was too young, yet, to lead the clan and I had no intention of leaving the Land of the Wolf, but I needed the Ulfheonar to help me teach Sámr Ship Killer how to lead. All four of us had lived longer than most warriors. Haaken One Eye, like me, had been on the earth for more than sixty-five summers. None of us knew any warrior who had lived that long. We had to make the most of our time.

I knew what my task was. I had to make Sámr the leader of the clan. I had failed the last time I had tried to do so and merely driven Wolf Killer away from me. I would not make the same mistake again. Haaken One Eye agreed to live with me at my hall where we could teach Sámr all that he needed to know. Rollo had a family, a life beyond my walls but there were other Ulfheonar who had been wounded. They could help me to train my great-grandson. Karl Word Master and Cnut Cnutson both lived within my walls. They could aid us.

My great-grandson and his new bride lived across the Water in my old hall. We had rescued Aethelflaed from Danes who sought to use her to rule the East Angles. Many people thought that Vikings took their brides by force. Nothing could be further from the truth. Aethelflaed had chosen Sámr. Baldr Witch Saviour and his bride, Nanna, also lived in that rambling old hall. It had been my first home and had plenty of room. Baldr was the start of Sámr's hearth weru. He would need a band of warriors who would protect him as he led the clan. I could not go to the Otherworld until he had.

Chapter 1

My hall was large and rambling but the household at Cyninges-tūn was small. There was just Uhtric, Atticus of Syracuse and Germund, the lame warrior we had brought back from Miklagård, who lived in my hall. The slaves and servants had their own quarters. They were closer to the palisade. It suited everyone. They did not worry about disturbing Jarl Dragonheart and I enjoyed the peace of a hall with just old men within it. I was comfortable with the two old men and the Greek. It was familiar to me and I liked familiarity. Sámr would sail across the Water each morning to begin his training. It helped hone his ship skills. Baldr wanted to come with him but I insisted that he stay at the hall and watch the women. I wanted Sámr to learn to be confident sailing the small boat across the water. Sailing was one of the skills he needed. He had to be able to read the wind and feel the current. The Water was benign. The ocean was not. Each night when he left, I would be able to go back to the comfortable world of my hall. I could play chess with Atticus and drink the strong wine I liked. I could watch the fire and I could remember.

When Uhtric died the balance and harmony of my home were ruined. I should not have been surprised. He had been with me since Erika had been alive. Yet I thought he would always be there. He was familiar and another link to my past. When he became ill Kara, my daughter and chief volva, came to see him but she could do nothing for him. She told me that it was just old age. She told me that he would die. He had looked after my home and kept my hall ready for me whenever I sailed to sea. He and Germund were the ones who chopped my wood and prepared my food. Germund was almost like a brother to Uhtric. Atticus the Greek had less in common with him but, as the three of us sat with the old man as he began to slip away, he was tearful. He was a Greek and they were not as stoic as Vikings. I was sad and I hoped that there would be a place in the Otherworld for Uhtric but I did not know.

My oldest servant had been silent for a little time and I wondered if he had drifted to the Otherworld. His eyes opened as he gripped my fingers, "Jarl Dragonheart, I have a boon to ask. I am dying or else I would not be so bold and I expect you to say no but I must ask anyway."

I smiled. That was Uhtric's way. He never wished to be a bother to anyone. "Old friend, ask."

"I would like to hold the blade that was touched by the gods before I die. I know that I am not a warrior but I have lived most of my life in the shadow of that sword…"

I stood. "Of course." It hung on the wall. I sent Germund to fetch it and the old Roman sword I had taken from the cave in the land of the Walhaz I put the hilt of the sword that was touched by the gods in his hands and laid the other along his body. The ancient sword looked battered and weary but it had saved my life in the cave in Om Walum when I had fought the witch. I wondered if it might do the same for Uhtric.

When his thin, blue fingers gripped the hilt of Ragnar's Spirit, a smile came over him. "I feel power racing through my body. I feel…" His head drooped to one side although his eyes remained open and the smile was fixed upon his face. He was dead.

Atticus put his ear to Uhtric's mouth and shook his head. "Did the sword kill him?" Atticus was a man of logic and science but since he had come to the Land of the Wolf, he had observed things which he could not explain.

"Perhaps. I think it was Odin. The sword in his hands meant he could take him to Valhalla. Uhtric was not a warrior but Valhalla needs servants to serve ale and mead."

"But he was not Norse."

"I am not Norse. My father was Saxon and my mother of the old people. Odin does not mind for he is the Allfather to all men. The sword gained him entry."

"And why did you put the old blade upon his body, lord?"

I took both swords from Uhtric and closed his eyes, "In truth, Germund, I know not why save that I heard a voice in my head tell me to do so. I never ignore such voices. I saw the power which this sword held when I fought the witch. She called the blue stones, Odin's stones. They may help his passage to the Otherworld. It may be that as the sword is from the old people of this land, it seems to have powers which are as great as Ragnar's Spirit. I know not. It is done and now we must put my old friend in the ground." I hung the swords back on the wall. "I tire of burying friends." Rolf and Olaf were still raw scars in my heart.

Even though he was not Norse we buried him the way all the dead of the clan were buried. We dug a grave and lined the outside with stones to make the shape of a boat. Dressed in his best we carried him to the grave. He had lost much weight in his last months of life and Sámr, Atticus, Germund and I easily managed to carry him to his resting place. We laid him on his side and brought his knees up to his chin. We placed around him all the things he loved. We buried the spice chest and the key. He had felt proud that he was in charge of the spices. We had none left for we had neither traded nor raided the hot lands for some time. The knife he used to carve meat was placed with him as was the wooden cross he had kept in his sleeping chamber. He had been a follower of the White Christ. Since the death of my second wife, Brigid, he had worshipped in secret. We had no priest to say Christian words over him. He would have to do with mine. When all was placed around him then each man in the village put soil upon him until he was covered. Then we covered the grave with the turf we had cut to make the grave. Atticus sprinkled the seeds of wild thyme upon the turf. It was a herb which Uhtric had loved and some of the seeds would take. As the years went on the grave would become a blue and green haven for bees and that would please Uhtric who loved their honey.

After I had said words over him, Atticus mumbled some Latin. Atticus was a Christian too. When all was done, we went to the house of the alewife, Agnete. I had bought two barrels of beer and the men of my town would celebrate Uhtric's life. In my clan, everyone was valued, slave or lord. It made no difference. I stood with Haaken One Eye, Aðils Shape Shifter, Atticus, Germund and Sámr. Kara and her daughter Ylva came over to speak with me.

"Father, will you take another servant?"

I shook my head. "No, Kara. I am too old to get used to another in my hall. Atticus and Germund can see to my needs." He nodded. "You have no plans to die have you?"

He laughed, "I will do my best, lord, to outlive you although that would be a prodigious feat."

"Good." I noticed that Aiden was not with his wife and daughter. He had been unwell for some time. Turning to Kara I said, "Aiden is no better?"

She said, simply, "He is dying. We three know that. In your heart, father, you know it too. If he had been well, he would have travelled to Om Walum with you to rescue Gruffyd."

I shook my head, "If Aiden goes then the only friend I have left from the old days will be Haaken."

Ylva linked her arm through mine, "Grandfather, there are new friends to replace them. There is Sámr and me also. Do not dismiss us so lightly."

I squeezed her arm, "And I do not. It is just that I shared experiences with Aiden that can never be replicated."

"Then remember those days. My father is not unhappy for he is going to the Otherworld." She reached up and put her palm on my forehead. "You will hear his voice here. He will be with you always."

Kara took Ylva's arm, "Come, daughter, let us go and minister to your father. We will leave these warriors to drink and celebrate Uhtric.

He is at peace now and in the Otherworld." She smiled at me, "He is content."

Haaken One Eye did not like to dwell on maudlin matters. He looked at Sámr and said, "Well, Sámr Ship Killer, we had best begin your training. None of us are getting any younger and I yearn for action. What say you, Dragonheart? Should we not raid with him? That is the best training in the world!"

I laughed, "Aye I know but while it is still winter and cold grips the land, let us give him skills that he will need. Rollo Thin Skin can teach him to use the sword and the spear. Haaken can teach him how to make up songs and Aðils Shape Shifter can show him how to disappear in plain sight!"

"I can do that, Jarl Dragonheart, but remember that my days of raiding are ended. I have a wife and a family. I am happy to give you this month but when the new grass shows then I will be back to my farm."

"Then we begin Sámr's training with you. Winter is always the hardest time to hide anyway." I turned to Sámr. "I give you to Aðils Shape Shifter for the next seven days. That will give Haaken, Rollo and me the opportunity to plan the rest of your training."

Sámr looked serious, "I am ready, great grandfather. I know that I bear a great burden and if I am to fill your boots then I must change." He tapped his heart and his head, "In here and in here." He went with Aðils Shape Shifter to his home up Lang's Dale. Haaken went back to his wife to make arrangements to come and live with me. He was away but one night. Haaken knew the importance of my task and was keen to make a start.

I found I missed Uhtric more than I cared to admit. I had woken, each morning when I was in my hall, to Uhtric. Germund tried his best but he was a warrior. Uhtric had always been my servant. He knew my ways. Sometimes he knew I wanted the steam hut before I did. He knew I did not like to talk before I ate. He knew which foods I liked. His porridge was something special. With a mixture of fruit and nuts, depending upon the season and flavoured with honey, it was something I could never have again. I was a warrior and not a cook. Germund was not Uhtric and so I ate different food. It unsettled me and distracted me from the work of training Sámr. It was fortunate that Aðils had him for those few days. I am an old man and old men have strange fantasies. I began to wonder if there was a curse upon my land. I had had my son and grandson kidnapped by a witch and two of my closest warriors had died. I was glad when Haaken One Eye returned and my hall seemed less empty.

The thought of a curse became stronger when Ylva summoned me to Aiden's side. My galdramenn was dying. Uhtric had been in the ground

9

for just three days. Aiden's wife and daughter seemed remarkably calm about the impending death. They led me into his hall and the chamber Aiden and Kara shared. It was lit by some of the candles we had taken from the churches of the White Christ. The room was bathed in a soft golden light. It was when I saw Aiden's face that I realised why they appeared so unconcerned. He looked content. For the last weeks, as the illness from within him had consumed his body, he had looked pained. Now he looked peaceful. I had left Haaken and the others outside. They could speak with him but I needed words with him first. He smiled as I entered.

"Dragonheart, it is good that you have never changed. A man can read your thoughts by simply looking at your face. This is not a time for mourning but to rejoice. I leave this pain-wracked body and I go to join the spirits. I will still enjoy this valley of ours and the Water of Cyninges-tūn. I will watch over my oldest friend, my wife and my daughter."

"I do not want you to go. I have lost too many old friends already." I know I sounded like a petulant child but I could not help it.

"The sisters have spun and your thread is a strong one. I knew when the healer in Miklagård opened up your body that you would live longer than most of us. Only Ylva will outlive you."

I had a sudden and chilling thought, "Sámr!"

"I have not dreamed his death and he will lead the clan when you go to Valhalla."

"Then I go to Valhalla?"

"Even without your sword Odin would welcome you but fear not, the sword that was touched by the gods will be in your hand." He coughed and I saw a spasm of pain. "I have not much time. Dragonheart, old friend, I have a request. It is strange that it is almost the same request which Uhtric made. I would be buried with the old sword you found in the bottom of the cavern in Walhaz."

I frowned. I had thought the old rusted blade was a link to my past. I was reluctant to give it to Aiden and at that moment, I heard the voice, in my head, of my mother, *'Let it go!'* "Of course."

He nodded, "When you told me the tale of the cave and the stones then I began to see that I had been blind all these years. Ragnar's Spirit is a powerful weapon. It is a weapon of war. That old and rusted one is the sword which holds power. You took it from the ground. It needs to be returned to the ground."

"I will fetch it."

He shook his head and held out his hands for Kara and Ylva. They seemed to know what was coming, "I need it not now. I am no warrior.

10

There is no place in Valhalla for me. Odin does not need a galdramenn. The Land of the Wolf needs me. I just needed to know that you would let it go. I will watch over it until it is needed again." He gave a smile. "Farewell, wife. I will see you soon."

Kara leaned over to kiss him, "You are the only man I would have married. The sisters chose well for me."

"Daughter, you know what you have to do? We have placed a heavy burden upon your shoulders."

"I am the daughter of the greatest galdramenn to walk the earth and the most powerful volva. If this task is not meant for me then who?"

He nodded, "Farewell, Dragonheart. My life has been fulfilled walking in your shadow. Know that from now, until the end of your days, I will be your shadow but a shadow that you cannot see, only hear." His eyes closed and there was a soft sigh. He died. I could not believe it had happened so quickly. It was almost as though he had chosen his own moment to pass on. There was barely time for a goodbye.

I had no time to speak even if I could have forced words beyond the lump in my throat for the most remarkable thing happened. I swear that Aiden's body lifted from the bed upon which he lay. The candles all flickered as though a breeze had blown through the chamber. That was impossible for the doors were all closed. Then the body slowly sank and Kara and Ylva folded his hands across his body.

"It is done, father. My husband is in the spirit world. The warriors may come and see his body then we must bury him. Fetch the sword and have a boat made ready. He will be buried close by my mother."

I walked out, stunned. I barely saw my men. I just nodded and said, "You may go within." I walked to my hall and Atticus stood looking worried. "Have two boats brought here to the quay. Fetch some mattocks and spades. We bury Aiden."

I went to the wall and took down the old rusted blade. I felt its power as soon as I touched it. I had never used it as a weapon and yet I knew that it had power. It was almost the same power as I felt when I held Ragnar's Spirit. I wrapped a fur around my shoulders and left my hall. I walked to the quay with the sword in my arms and waited for the two boats to come across the water.

Arne the Fisherman and his son, Leif, tied them to the wooden quay. "Jarl?"

"Aiden has died and we go to bury him. We shall not need you for it will be the Ulfheonar who buries him." They nodded and moved to the side as Haaken, Cnut, Germund and Karl carried Aiden's body towards us. The people of Cyninges-tūn came out to watch in silence. Ylva and Kara walked behind.

11

Atticus hurried from my hall with tools. He placed them in the boat and then clutched his cross as the body bearers walked passed him. We placed Aiden's body in one boat and Kara and Ylva climbed into the other. We rowed across the Water. It was still as I could remember. The air itself seemed to be holding its breath. Old Olaf's top was shrouded in cloud but I saw that there were some shafts of sunlight to the west. We ground ashore on sand and shingle that formed the eastern shore of the Water. We dragged the boats on to the beach. Ylva and Kara went to my wife's grave to touch it. After a few moments, they nodded and pointed to the ground next to it. We took the mattocks to loosen the soil and then the ones with the shovels removed it. There was no turf here. It was too rocky. We would have to dig turf from elsewhere to finish it. The stones we removed we placed to the side. They would form the outline of the grave.

When it was deep enough Kara said, "That is sufficient. Fetch my husband."

Germund and Haaken carried Aiden, who did not weigh as much as he once had. They laid him reverently in the grave. Ylva and Kara rearranged his body so that his knees were under his chin and he was on his side. They placed some of his maps with him along with his red jewels and leather satchel with his potions, salves and spells. Ylva turned to me and held out her hands. I gave her the sword and she laid it along his body. The hilt was close to his head. We arranged the stones around the side. Kara then took a shovel and placed soil on the corpse. We did not have the village to help us and the grave took longer to fill. That gave me time to reflect upon the life that had been Aiden's. The only death which might affect me more would be Haaken's. I could barely think of a time without Aiden. He had been instrumental in returning my wife and children when they were captured. He had been into the darkness that was the witch's lair on Syllingar and he had been in Din Guardi, beneath the sea. There were so many adventures that we had shared and I could not envision life without him. He had been as much a part of my life as Haaken or Ragnar's Spirit.

I was still remembering when Kara said. "You may go now. Ylva and I will finish the grave. We will walk around the Water back to the hall. We need to speak."

One did not argue with a volva and we sailed the two boats back to the quay. After we had tied them up Haaken One Eye said, "Let us send the wizard on his way properly. Let us broach the ale barrel!"

Atticus had anticipated us and he had the horns and the ale ready. There was also food bubbling away on the pot. If it was cooked by

Atticus then it would be heavily flavoured and honeyed. That was his way.

When we had spoken of Aiden and remembered him Haaken One Eye said, "When Sámr returns he will be unhappy that he missed the passing of Aiden."

"And that is part of the learning. A leader cannot be everywhere at once. He was not needed. I will tell him."

I said, "Rollo will teach him how to use the sword. I have skills but Rollo is younger and has greater strength. His broad back and oaken arms will harden Sámr."

Haaken shook his head, "There speaks brawn! You can impart those skills in the twinkling of an eye. Sámr will still be learning to be a singer when he is a grey beard. However, Dragonheart, I know what you mean. If he is to lead the clan then he needs to raid and give commands."

"I know. I plan on visiting Erik Short Toe to get my drekar ready."

Karl Word Master shook his head, "*'Heart of the Dragon'* is old, Jarl. Why not take one of the younger drekar?"

I had thought about that. It was true my drekar was the oldest vessel we had but I wanted Sámr to sail and command that vessel. She did not have many voyages left in her. Sámr would commission a new one when he became a little older. "She will serve my great-grandson and I want him to have the best around him. Erik Short Toe will tell me if there is a problem." The Norns were spinning but my mind was filled with Aiden and Sámr. I did not hear them.

Chapter 2

I waited until Sámr returned from Lang's Dale before I left. Atticus would teach Sámr chess, Rollo the sword and Haaken the songs. We spoke of Aiden. He seemed to understand my urgency. He was now a husband. He was a man. He had spent a week living with an Ulfheonar who had changed once he had married. Aðils Shape Shifter had withdrawn into himself for the sake of his family. Sámr was of my blood and he could not do that. He had to share himself with his family and the clan. We spoke at length the night before I left.

When I reached Whale Island, I discovered that my son, Gruffyd, and his son, Mordaf, had gone to raid the Franks. They had heard of the success of Hrolf the Horseman and wished to emulate him. They had taken many of Ragnar's men too. Gruffyd and his family had moved his home west of Whale Island. He had found a piece of high ground not far from the beginning of the High Divide. He had made himself a stronghold. Almost losing Mordaf in Om Walum had changed my son.

Before I visited Erik Short Toe, I spoke with my grandson, Ragnar. He could not believe that we had had two deaths in such a short space of time. Like me, his initial reaction was that it was a curse.

Shaking my head, I said, "I thought so too but Kara has explained it to me. Aiden had been ill for many years and was in great pain. He chose to die. He chose to die when he did to make the painless for me. He knew that I grieved over Uhtric." I shrugged, "It was the way his mind worked."

"Aye, he was the cleverest man I knew and it is good that he has the old sword with him. It came from the earth and is now returned." I nodded. "How goes the training of my son?"

"He has been with the Shape Shifter. None can ever be as good as Aðils but so long as he has Ulfheonar skills then I will be happy."

My grandson looked worried, "You would not make him Ulfheonar?"

"No, and besides, that path is chosen for you. I do not see that in Sámr. Olaf and Haaken will give him more skills and then we begin the real training. We raid."

"Would you have me with you, or Ulla War Cry?"

"Would you wish Ulla War Cry to come?" I saw the answer on his face. I smiled and shook my head, "You have chosen a different path for your feet. It is good that you are the jarl who brings peace and harmony to the southern side of the Land of the Wolf."

"And where do you raid?"

I had thought about this and already made a decision. "Your son needs to learn to be a navigator. I am lucky. Erik Short Toe learned from Josephus and he has more skills than any other captain. His sons are not as skilled as him. Sámr Ship Killer will need to be his own captain. I would sail to the hot lands further south." I thought of Uhtric. He had been buried with the spice box. I smiled. "We need more spices and we have not raided there for some time."

"Yet others have. They may be ready for you."

"True, and if they are then that will temper the steel that is your son. If we wanted an easy life then we would raid the Picts or Hibernians. We know that those who live in the hot lands are fierce warriors."

He looked at me and studied my face, "You do not have the death wish, do you? I know you have endured many deaths but your people need you still."

"Sámr is not yet ready to take over as leader. I am not yet ready to die. He is now married and I would have him have children of his own. The clan needs our blood to ensure its survival."

"Then I will have some of my hearth weru travel with you."

"No, for I think that Sámr will choose those who sail with him. It is a skill he will need when he leads the clan."

I saw the disappointment on Ragnar's face but he nodded and said, "Will you be double-crewed?"

"Perhaps."

"The seas are more dangerous these days. We still have many ships which visit Whale Island and their captains talk. The Saxons have ships. They patrol their waters. A single ship with just forty or so warriors aboard risks being taken." I nodded. "Do not forget the Danes. When you went to Lundenwic and the Land of the East Angles you killed many Danes. They bear grudges. Your sword draws enemies like honey draws ants."

"If I was to worry about every Dane I have upset, I would lock myself in my hall and never budge!"

"And Syllingar; what of that island? The witch in the cave of Om Walum will have more reason than ever to wreak her vengeance upon you. I do not believe that the witch has forgotten you and there is no Aiden to sail with you."

"Ragnar, the web is already woven and the threads entwined. You choose to stay here in the Land of the Wolf. You are content not to venture beyond our borders. I am happy with the decision. Sámr is a Viking. He will sail whether you wish it or not." I looked at him. I knew how to look into a man's eyes and determine what he was thinking. I was not a galdramenn but I knew how to do this. "Do you wish to sail with us? You could help to teach your son."

He shook his head, "We both know that I am not the leader that you are or my father was. If I am honest, I do not think that Gruffyd is either but he still tries to be another Dragonheart. His new home is intended to be a stronghold such as yours. The witch and the horrors he endured there means that he will look to fight easier enemies. You have never chosen the easy way. Sámr does not want to be Dragonheart but he wants to lead. You and the Ulfheonar are in a better position to teach him." I looked into his eyes and saw that he spoke what was in his mind and I nodded. "You are disappointed in me?"

I shook my head, "A man can never be disappointed in those of his blood. When I was younger, I made that mistake with your father. We became estranged and I still grieve for those undone years. You are Ragnar and you have chosen your path. I am content."

I left Whale Island and visited, briefly with Raibeart ap Pasgen at Úlfarrston. I was pleased to see that he had strengthened its defences. "It is good to see you, Dragonheart."

I saw that he was no longer the lean young warrior who had become a Viking by choice, if not by birth. He had filled out and now there were grey flecks in his hair. "How goes your world, Raibeart?"

He smiled, "I trade more than I raid. Since you appointed Bergil Hafþórrsson to be Jarl of Dyflin trade has been brisk and my sons are traders, not raiders. You visit with Erik Short Toe?"

"I need my drekar for a raid."

"He has made the shipyard a prosperous place." He nodded towards the river, "He does well considering the river has such a dangerous entrance."

I knew what he meant. At high tide, it was not a problem but at low tide, the shipyard became sealed by sands and shallows. It was said that a man could walk from Úlfarrston to the northern shore. Erik and Bolli serviced ships and built others. They were happy in their world. I bade him farewell and headed up the river.

Raibeart was right. There were many more houses than there used to be and the drekar were all either tied up or drawn on to the bank so that the shipwrights could work on them. This was all due to Erik Short Toe. He had brought his family here and shared the settlement with Bolli Bollison. Erik Short Toe was no longer the ship's boy who had sailed with Josephus and me to Miklagård. He was now a grandfather. His joints were stiff and his hair almost gone and yet, as soon as I arrived, his face broke into a smile, "You want me to prepare the drekar!"

"You are galdramenn!"

16

"No, Dragonheart, but you and I do not do as others do. We do not visit and chat. We are not old friends talking to each other. When you come to see me then you need me to sail."

I was suddenly sad that he thought that way. He was right, of course, and that merely made it worse. I nodded, "We will remedy that this day. I do need the drekar but not for a month or so. If you and your wife will have me, I will stay with you for a few days so that we can make up for lost time."

"You are more than welcome but I do not want you to feel that you need to. I am always happy to stand at the steerboard and watch you lead." He led me into his hall which was close to the river and the quay where he worked on his ships. "And we can have long talks while the rowers rest and Ran takes us across the ocean. Come, wife, we have a guest, fetch ale!"

His sons had moved out and Erik lived comfortably with his wife and slaves. His wife brought us ale and then left us. I saw a small ship's boy helping her. I had not seen him before. I wondered if he was a grandchild. "I need you to teach Sámr how to be drekar captain."

He nodded, "I can teach him to navigate and use a compass and hourglass but we both know that being a captain of a drekar requires other skills. Only you can do that."

"And that is why we sail to the hot lands. We two will watch over Sámr and guide him. Josephus guided you and you shall guide Sámr. It is *wyrd* that we will sail close to the land where Josephus was most comfortable. He made you the captain you are today."

"But who made you what you are?" I said nothing. He drank more ale and stared into the fire. "We both know who it was. It was the Gods, it was Odin when he struck your sword with the lightning. The power went not only into the blade but into you. As soon as you had the sword then the clan grew stronger. You were chosen. That is why men follow you when it seems that our course takes us towards disaster. Odin watches over you."

It was good to talk to an old friend and we spent all afternoon and into the early evening talking about the voyages we had taken and the people we had known. We only stopped when the food arrived. We ate alone for his wife knew that we needed this time. Like all Viking women, there was something of a volva in her. The food was good. It was a fish stew. Erik lived so close to the sea and knew the fishermen so well that he was offered the freshest of fish. The good food and the fine ale helped me to forget all of my troubles. The dead became a distant memory for Erik and I had only spoken of the good things in our lives. I found I envied Erik Short Toe. He had all that he wanted close to hand and he answered

17

to no one, save to me. I made an annual demand but other than that he was free to do as he wished. Odin had chosen me but he had laid a burden upon my shoulders.

We looked over *'Heart of the Dragon'* the next day. We already knew that she was an old drekar and now she looked it. The sun had bleached her deck as white as snow. There were the marks of battle along her gunwale. Although there was no weed on her hull the strakes down the steerboard side looked a little worse for wear. Erik ran his hand down the gunwale, "I fear, Dragonheart, that this will be the last voyage of *'Heart'*. We can replace the ropes, yard and mast. We can fit a new sail but her heart is old. If the worm is not in her yet it will be soon. We had her out of the water last year and we coated her keel but she will suffer if we have a northern storm."

"Then it is good that we sail her in warmer waters. She only needs one more voyage. Sámr can commission his own drekar but for this lesson, he will need *'Heart'*."

Erik patted her affectionately, "Aye, well she can do that." He looked up at me. "And how do we deal with the witch at Syllingar? We have no Aiden to aid us now."

I nodded, "I have given this thought. We do not go near to the islands of Syllingar. We intend to raid the hot lands. They are well to the south of us. Once we pass the land of the Walhaz we sail due south until we are many leagues from Syllingar."

"The empty ocean?"

"Remember that Josephus did so. He was not afraid. We do not sail west. We will not risk sailing off the edge of the world. We sail south. When the air becomes warmer then we turn east."

He smiled, "Then I will find all of Josephus' old charts. This will be an adventure for Haaken to sing of."

The two of us went over every part of her. I gave Erik coin for he would need to make purchases. I was not going to take a chance with Sámr's life. There would be enough dangers on the voyage without risking a weakness in a ship. I stayed for two days with Erik. We were both getting old and who knew when we might meet again? As we parted, he said, "I will make copies of the maps and give them to Sámr when this voyage is over. Mine had Josephus' hand all over them and, as such, are precious to me."

I was away for some time and by the time I had returned to Cyninges-tūn Sámr had finished his work with Aðils Shape Shifter. I noticed a change in Sámr immediately. He seemed to move more smoothly. When he was in my hall his were the footsteps I did not hear. Ulfheonar learned to make as little noise as possible and to move with the maximum economy. Aðils had done what I had asked. Sámr was sad to have missed the passing of Aiden. I wondered if Aiden had chosen his moment of death so that it would affect fewer people. That would have been typical of Aiden.

The four of us, Sámr, Rollo Thin Skin, Haaken and myself ate in my hall. Atticus served us. I would have used one of Kara's servants to help but Atticus seemed aware that soon he would be alone in the hall when we went to raid. He wanted time with me. I told them of the drekar and my plans.

Haaken seemed to be particularly pleased, "Good. The heat of the sun will be good for my old bones."

Rollo picked at his teeth with a sliver of wood, "Aye but wearing mail in a hot country is more tiring."

"We will be at sea. We need not wear mail then."

They bantered for a while. Haaken was a positive warrior. Every horn was half full. Olaf Leather Neck had been the opposite. Rollo's closest friends had been Rolf and Olaf. They were dead and he had changed a little to become more like them. It was as though the clan needed the balance. Sámr smiled at them both. He knew them well and was fully aware of their strengths. He turned to me, "I am young to lead, Dragonheart."

"And you will not be leading yet. This voyage is like the making of a sword. Just as we heat a blade and beat it, plunge it in water, or even blood and then repeat the process, so we will do that with you. When the sword has been tempered then it can be used in battle. You will watch and learn. Erik has his son making you your own compass. One of the things we seek on this voyage is an hourglass for you. Erik has one but a navigator needs his own."

He nodded, "Did my father not wish to sail with me?"

I would not lie to him, "No, for he is at one with his land. Nor did Gruffyd. Your grandfather, my son, Wolf Killer, took your father away from my home when he was young. They built a home on the edge of our world and it cost him. Ragnar is close to your grandmother and safe at Whale Island. He is content. It is why he will not lead the clan. The leader of our clan needs to be hungry and without fear. That is why it will be you."

He nodded, "Atticus has taught me more than chess. He has begun to teach me to read Latin and Greek." He shook his head, "It is slow work but I can now decipher some of the squiggles." I smiled. Aiden knew how to read but I had never had time. It was good that Sámr could read. "Atticus wishes to come with us."

"And you know that he should not. He is no warrior and any help he might give us would be offset by the fact that we would need to watch him and protect him from harm. When you lead you choose your crew carefully. The crew will be your choice. There will only be Haaken and me on the ship who are Ulfheonar. Many men will wish to follow. You choose carefully. This is all part of your training."

"I know. I have skills with the sword. I can track but I need to know how to use a shield wall and how to raid. I will choose carefully. Baldr Witch Saviour is an obvious choice but what of Aethelflaed and Nanna?"

"They could stay in the hall but I do not think that they would be happy there."

"No, Dragonheart, for they would be isolated."

"If they come here then Atticus and Germund can watch them and Kara and Ylva can teach them the ways of the clan."

He brightened. "Then I am happy. We will begin on the morrow to choose the men we will take for I am anxious to get to sea. The sooner we sail then the sooner we can return." He looked over at Baldr who was laughing with Haaken. "It is *wyrd* that we will be taking Baldr back close to the place we found him on the ship in the Blue Sea."

"Never forget the Norns. Their threads cover this world. They are paths to follow and they are there to ensnare. Let us hope that this is not a trap."

Sámr's days were taken up in selecting the men who would follow him. He had many offers. I was pleased that he chose the right men. He also learned how to use the compass on the still and calm Water. Here features were fixed. At sea, they were not and a sailor relied on the sun, the moon and the stars. At night his wife would feed him and comfort him for she knew he would soon be leaving. Her captivity in the land of the Walhaz had made her stoical. It was almost as though the Allfather had been preparing her for a life amongst Vikings.

Ylva and Kara had been spinning. They had used some of Aethelflaed's hair as well as mine and Ylva's to weave a piece of material. It was sewn into Sámr's tunic. I had my necklet of blue stones and Sámr had his spell. My daughter was giving us all the help she could. Our mail was repaired. Half of the crew who would be coming with us had mail. It was the younger ones who wore leather byrnies. I had a new shield made and my helmet was strengthened. The blow to the stones had not damaged them for Odin had been watching over me but it did not do to take things for granted. We were sailing in warm waters but we were well provided with sealskin capes and boots. In our hold were goods for us to trade should we need to. We were Vikings. Trading and raiding went hand in hand.

We headed down to Whale Island at Harpa. The wound in my leg had ached in the winter but now, with new grass underfoot, the discomfort lessened. The wound was a reminder of my mortality. Aethelflaed and Nanna wept but Ylva and Kara put their arms around them. They would offer them comfort. We were heading for another adventure. Would this be my last?

Chapter 3

Most of the men marched, with Sámr, to Whale Island. Haaken and I rode. We were the oldest and the only two Ulfheonar. It was right and proper. When we reached the port, we found that Gruffyd and Mordaf had returned. They had raided the northern coast of the Franks. This time the Norns had been in a kindly mood. The winds were favourable and the enemies predictable. The drekar had come back laden with animals, pots, slaves and treasure. It explained his slow return. Hearing that I was due he had waited to speak with me before he returned to his new stronghold.

He was more relaxed when he spoke with me. He was coming out of the dark tunnel which had been his meeting with the witch. He had needed the success of this raid to recover his confidence. Mordaf had been blooded. His first voyage had been as ship's boy and it had not gone well. This time he had been ship's boy but he went ashore and used his short sword for the first time. He was making small steps but he was becoming a warrior.

"We will raid the Franks again, father. The Danes and those who follow Hrolf the Horsemen often raid and the best Frankish warriors are dead. They build strongholds away from the river. I spoke with Danes who believe that Hrolf will rule the land soon. He has done well. I heard that Ragnar Hairy Breeches is gathering men for a raid next year on Paris!"

I nodded, "It is why Sámr and I raid further south. We do not wish to emulate Hrolf nor try to rival him nor do we wish to be close to a Dane like Hairy Breeches."

Gruffyd looked hurt. "I do not wish to take any honour or glory from Hrolf. I wish to make a name for me."

I smiled to take the sting from my words, "You are easy to take offence, Gruffyd. I was not criticising you. I was explaining why Sámr will take a different path. Baldr is like a blood brother to him and he knows the hot lands. This is *wyrd*. I am pleased that you and Ragnar have found your own paths. Sámr still seeks his."

I saw that Gruffyd was a little embarrassed by the words he had used to me. His mother had always been oversensitive. She had looked for meanings beneath the words. That had never been my way. What I said came from the heart. He nodded, "I was sorry to hear of Uhtric and Aiden's deaths. Uhtric helped to raise me and Aiden was like an uncle to me."

22

"Aiden chose his time to die and Uhtric was just weary. He was old but he will be in Valhalla. When I die, he will be waiting to serve me a horn of ale."

"He was not a warrior." I heard the doubt in my son's voice.

I said, quietly, "It was Aiden who told me that he would be in Valhalla. I believed Aiden."

While Ragnar and Astrid awaited their son, I went aboard my drekar. Haaken had two slaves carry our chests aboard. They were placed at the steering board with Erik's. We would not row. As we secured them to the sides Haaken said, "I can hear Brigid's words in Gruffyd's voice. Do you not fear that Sámr and Aethelflaed's children might have the same affliction? They are both Christians and both princesses."

"It may be but it was neither Sámr nor me who made the decision. It was the Norns. You were lucky, Haaken, and given a Norse bride and an easy life."

"I had all girls!"

"And that was chosen for you but you have to admit that Anya gives you an easy life."

He smiled, "Aye. She never minds me sailing the seas and is content with the farm." He sat on his chest and looked north. "Will this be the last time I see Old Olaf?"

"Neither of us knows that. Now that Aiden is gone who will dream our deaths? This is better. When death comes it will be as it was for Olaf Leather Neck and Rolf Horse Killer. It will be swift. I have seen the other side. I have peered into Valhalla. It does not frighten me."

The men began to board. Sámr would not be among the first. He had goodbyes to give. Haraldr Leifsson led the men from Cyninges-tún. Sven Tomason, Einar and Snorri Cnutson were with him. Siggi Eainarson, Lars Long Nose and Arne Ship Sealer were close behind. Then came my more experienced warriors, Beorn Hafþórrsson, Benni Hafþórrsson, Haraldr Leifsson and Ráðgeir Ráðgeirson. The ones who came after, I knew by sight but not by name. They were the younger warriors like Baldr and Bergil. They would be Sámr's oathsworn one day and I would get to know them as we sailed.

Erik Short Toe and his son Arne came back from the prow where they had been erecting the canvas shelter. I had not asked for it but they were making a shelter for Haaken and me to rest when we reached the hot lands. "*'Heart'* is eager to sail, Jarl Dragonheart. Can you not feel her tugging to be away from the land? She was not happy when you did not take her to find Atticus."

23

I patted her gunwale, "I am sorry, my lady. It was remiss of me." I felt the wood beneath my fingers and it felt alive. "It is good to stand on her deck. It is as though I can feel Bolli Bollison in her timbers."

Erik nodded, "Arne go and fetch my compass and hourglass." As Arne ran off, he asked, "Does Sámr know how to use the compass?"

"After a fashion. He has yet to use it with an hourglass."

"Then this voyage is perfect. There is more sun to the south. Josephus did not like the northern seas. Too often he did not see the sun for days upon end."

I nodded, "And we are well provisioned? I do not want to put in to raid before we reach the warmer seas. I would have us just disappear."

"We have provisions for over two moons. We have hooks and lines. We have a spare sail to catch rainwater." He pointed up at the yard, "We have a new sail. Ylva and Kara wove an eye for the wolf. We have a red wolf on the sail."

"Not a dragon?"

"Ylva came with the spell. She said that she and Kara had dreamed and both saw a wolf on the sail. A red wolf instead of a red dragon." I was content. My daughter and granddaughter knew their business. Erik said, "And now, if you will excuse me, it is time to prepare for sea." Arne brought him the beautifully carved box with the hourglass and compass. "Arne, go and tell Sámr that we sail. The time for goodbyes is gone. The tide waits for no man."

"Aye, father."

Astrid was tearful as she parted from her son at the quay. I saw that Ulla War Cry had a face which showed that he had had words with his father. I would have taken him but I respected Ragnar's wishes. Haaken stood ready to advise Sámr if he needed it. I just sat on my chest. I saw Sámr turn and wave as the gangplank was removed. We were still tied up. Erik would warp us away from the quay but Sámr needed to assign oars. He looked at me and I smiled. Haaken moved towards him to offer advice but he shook his head.

He took a deep breath and spoke, "Ráðgeir Ráðgeirson, you and the older warriors take the oars by the stern. The rest of us will take our lead from you." Ráðgeir Ráðgeirson smiled and nodded, "Haaken One Eye, if you would give us the beat?"

Haaken nodded, "Aye, Sámr Ship Breaker "

The crew all liked Sámr. All had chosen to be with him. I knew of captains who had left with men on board who made life hard for them. That did not happen on my ships. The smaller, lighter men and those with no experience sat at the prow end. Sámr and Baldr sat behind

Haraldr Leifsson and Sven Tomason. Once they were ready, they raised their oars.

Erik nodded, "Arne set us free from the land."

Arne shouted, "Ship's boys!"

They each ran to a rope and began to pull in the ropes that those on the land had untied. They began to coil them. I recognised one as being the boy I had seen in Erik Short Toe's home. He looked smaller than the rest.

"Steerboard side, push us off!"

As one they pushed out their oars until they reached the wooden piles and they pushed. We slowly moved away from the quay. Erik nodded to Haaken One Eye who shouted, "Oars out!" I saw him glance to the skies as he did so. This was the first time that Olaf Leather Neck had not given the command. Haaken had a spear in his hand. He began to bang on the deck. "And, row!"

Beorn Hafþórrsson, Benni Hafþórrsson, Haraldr Leifsson and Ráðgeir Ráðgeirson were at the front of the rowers, closest to the steering board. They were the strongest men in the clan. They rowed to Haaken's rhythm. The others followed them. Haaken kept the beat steady and slow as we edged out into the channel which would lead us to the sea. Erik had his hand on the steering board. Once we lowered the sail then Sámr's lessons would begin. The ship's boys ran to the sheets. They no longer had to lower the sail from the yard. They were able to haul it up. It was for that reason that we had brought eight ship's boys. It was more than we normally brought but all had bows and slings. We could leave the drekar defended when we raided. Arne took charge of the boys. They had practised, of course, but not while the ship was moving and that was always more difficult. He had sailed many times with his brothers and his father. When Erik left the sea then Arne would take over.

Erik knew the waters like the back of his hand and he made minor adjustments until he was satisfied. We were heading south and west. "Arne, raise the sail!"

Arne cupped his hands. The eight boys were all watching him. "Haul now!" When they had practised it, they had been still and Erik had told me that the sail had risen in one swift movement. This time, however, one of the boys, Erik, the one I had seen in Erik Short Toe's home, lost his footing as a wave struck the side of the drekar. The hoisting of the sail was more ragged than Arne would have liked. There would be words.

Erik Short Toe shouted, "Oars in!"

25

I did not mind the delay in raising the sail for as it became taut the wolf seemed to come alive. The eye appeared to move. I knew that it would inspire fear in our foes.

Sámr and Baldr placed their oars on the mast fish and then Sámr made his way to us. Although he had rowed before I saw that his hands were more than a little raw from the oars. He would learn and his skin would harden. He brought with him his compass. Erik nodded approvingly. The sun was visible in the sky. Arne hurried to us for they had finished securing the sheets. He took out his father's compass and the hourglass. The sand had all run to one end. Arne turned it and then aligned the compass with the sun. Sámr had practised but he watched Arne nonetheless. The whole of the voyage was a lesson. He watched as Arne made a mark with the piece of charcoal. Each captain used his own notation. I had spent time with Sámr. He knew what to do and he made his mark. I saw the sigh of relief when Erik nodded. I kept my face impassive but I was proud of him. He had done it right.

Erik waved him over. "Come, Sámr, take the steering board with me so that you may feel *'Heart'*."

Everyone knew what a responsive ship we had but until you touched the steering board when the ship was under full sail then you did not know how responsive. Erik pointed out the direction he wanted Sámr to take but he kept his hand on the steering board. I watched the sand slip through the hourglass. It was half empty when Erik took his hand away. A short while later there was a flap from above. Erik put his hand on the board and made a slight adjustment. He pointed to the sail which was now full and bye. "Listen, for the ship will tell you when you need to move the board."

"But I was following the course!"

"Aye but the wind has shifted. You were looking ahead. Look ahead and up. Two eyes are good but three or four are better. I will take over now for it is almost time to take another compass reading."

I confess that Erik was being more patient than most captains. He had learned from the best. Josephus had been not only the best captain I had ever seen but the most patient. Haaken brought me a horn of ale over, "So far he is doing well, Dragonheart."

"He is but there are many leagues to go. He can still see the land. When we enter the Unending Sea then we will judge him better."

Haaken nodded, "And when the crew fights?"

"I am on board and no one will expect him to lead."

"And this time you have but me to watch your back."

I smiled at him, "We have not moved far since we defended those walls at the home of Prince Buthar. I am content Haaken. Many have tried to kill us. We are battered, bruised and broken but we endure."

I knew that Sámr was exhausted as the light faded and we headed south between Man and Mercia. Half of the ship's boys would sleep and the other half would watch. Arne would take over the middle watch but Sámr would have to stay by the steering board to watch Erik. We would not land until we spied Bardsey Island. There we would have a safe anchorage and puffins to eat. We would push on between the lands of the Hibernians, the Saxons and the men of Man. Until we reached the Unending Sea then they would be the greatest danger. Haaken and I slept.

My sleep was dream-filled. It was a sea of faces which rose and fell like waves on the water. Some were friends and many were foes. It was as if the Spirit World was trying to tell me something but I could not discern what. Had Aiden been there then it might have been a different story. He would have dreamed the same dream and he would have told me what it meant. It was like sailing without a compass. I did not know what was true and what was false. I woke in the middle of the night. The crew were all asleep save for Arne and four ship's boys. I made water. I guessed that was what had woken me up.

I nodded to Arne as I went to the leeward side. When I had been younger making water had not seemed to be a problem. Now it almost ruled my life and I hated it. Part of the reason was that once I was awake, I found it hard to go back to sleep. When I had done it, I went over to Arne. "How goes the night?"

"The wind has veered a little and the sea is a little livelier. By my estimate, we are approaching the channel between the Angles' Sea and the land of the Hibernians."

"Then I will watch with you."

The night was black but I had been on these seas for more than fifty years. I knew what to look for. The regular and deep swells told me that we were not close to the coast. Few ships sailed at night and even fewer raided. We would be alone on the sea. Of course, dawn was a different prospect. Welsh ships would set sail just before dawn broke. Most would be merchants but there were increasing numbers of pirates and ships seeking to stop trade. Once we had sent our knarr far and wide to trade. We had lost many and whilst we had punished those who had done it the very act of taking our ships had made us draw in a little. Now we did not use knarr to trade as much as we once had but our drekar, which could carry less but which could defend themselves.

I watched the sky begin to lighten and went to Erik Short Toe. I shook him awake. When at sea Erik was like a cat. He napped. He was awake instantly, "There is trouble?"

I shook my head, "No, but dawn will be upon us soon. I was going to rouse the men. Better to be safe than sorry. The wind is still with us and we can sleep during the day."

"You are wise." He looked at Sámr, "He is doing well but there is much to learn."

"If he learns no more about sailing than he has done already then I shall be happy. I knew less than he does when I was much older. We have two months to turn him into a sailor. We both know that the first hours have gone well. That cannot last."

The ship's boys roused everyone. They left Sámr and Baldr until last. He was not happy when he saw that everyone else was already up. He came over to me, "I need no special treatment, Dragonheart. I should be woken with the others."

I smiled, "That is just the ship's boys being thoughtful. Do not be angry with them. Besides, there was nought to fret about."

Dawn came and the seas were empty. Had we seen a sail then I would have been worried. Few ships risked the seas at night and any that did so were, like us, predators. We ate bread, cheese and salted meat. Later we would eat the pickled fish or the raw fish that the ship's boys would catch but while we had bread which did not need soaking in ale to make it edible, we would eat the food of the land rather than the food of the sea. With the ship's boys keeping a lookout, the crew, dressed just in tunics and soft leather shoes, enjoyed the sun which kept the rain clouds away. The seal-skin capes and heavy cloaks, along with the seal-skin boots, would still be in their chests until they needed them. Some men threw bones and gambled but most used their knives to carve bone. Once we might have carved the tusks of the walrus and narwhal but we had long ago learned that they could be sold to the followers of the White Christ. Some believed that the narwhal horn was the horn of a unicorn while their priests had the walrus tusks carved into crucifixes. I had never had time for such indulgences. This voyage would be different and I wondered if I might carve something. I had an idea for a bone wolf.

All thoughts were driven from my head when the peace of the morning was shattered by Erik, the ship's boy, who was the mast top lookout. "Ships to steerboard!" His hand pointed to the south and west. It was Hibernian pirates and they were hunting."

Chapter 4

All eyes were on me but I remained silent for I was willing Sámr to make a decision. I would give him until the count of ten to shout his orders. I had reached five when he shouted, "Arm yourselves! Prepare for battle!"

I saw Haaken and my more experienced men nod. It was the right decision. Running away, blindly, would be disastrous. Arne was roused to join his father at the steerboard. He carried his father's helmet and sword. There were no passengers on a drekar. When he reached him, he waited a moment to let the sand run out and then turned the hourglass. I went to my chest. The wound in my leg had healed but I was not confident enough to move around too much or too quickly. I donned my sea boots. The soft leather slippers did not afford enough grip on the deck. I did not bother with my helmet. I just slipped my mail coif over my head. I took out Wolf's Blood and Ragnar's Spirit and fastened them to my belt. Finally, I took out the warrior bands and slipped them over my wrists. They were not an adornment. They protected my forearms.

I then went to the steerboard side and pulled myself up on to the backstay. I saw the ships now. They had no masts and were rowed. If we intended battle then we would have taken down the mast but there was little to be gained from fighting Hibernian pirates. Conan Mac Finbarr had told us of these pirates. They lived on the western coast of Hibernia. The farming there was unpredictable and they prowled the seas between the land of Gwynedd and Hibernia. The Mercian occupation of the island of Ynys Môn in the Angles' Sea had merely given them more victims and more opportunities. Conan Mac Finbarr had told me that they packed their boats with men for their plan was to capture any ships they attacked. Knowing that gave us an advantage.

Haaken had also donned his seal skin boots and coif. He was strapping on his sword when he joined me, "A little test from the gods eh?"

"It could be or, more likely, it is the Norns." I stepped back down onto the deck.

The three Hibernian ships were spreading out across the sea. One would get ahead of us while the third would stop us from turning around. That would be the biggest mistake we could make for we had the wind. I saw that the experienced men had not bothered with their helmets and none had donned their mail. The newer, less experienced men had their leather, metal studded byrnies and their helmets. The extra weight would not impair them and might afford some protection. The Hibernians did not use bows effectively. It was their numbers which made them dangerous.

Haaken asked, "What would you do?" He nodded at Sámr who, along with Baldr, was making his way from their chests at the bow end.

"I would turn to sail towards the one at the fore of the three ships. He is the leader. The wind is with us and if we destroyed him then the wind would take us from the others. They might be strong men rowing their boats but we both know that there is a limit to the distance a man can row."

"Then let us hope your great-grandson has your mind."

Sámr reached us and looked up at me. He smiled for I had an impassive expression on my face, "You have a plan, great grandfather, and you are waiting to see if I can replicate it."

"Of course, and you have a plan, have you not? Those hours enduring defeat after defeat to Atticus over the chess board have taught you something."

He nodded, "They have, although it was when we played fox and ducks with the pawns which has given me the battle plan. There is little to be gained from fighting pirates. This is the work of the Norns to test my mettle. We try to outrun them. *'Heart of the Dragon'* has a clean hull and a new sail. The wind favours us."

I nodded, "A good plan. And if it fails? If the Hibernians close the gap?"

"Then we take out the first ship for that will be the leader."

I saw that all eyes were on us and Erik Short Toe was looking expectantly at me. "Tell Erik what you intend and make your dispositions."

He nodded but I saw the nervousness in his eyes. I had been the same when Prince Butar had entrusted me with an attack for the first time. "Erik Short Toe, take us south and east. Let us show these Hibernians our stern."

"Aye, Sámr Ship Killer."

"Ráðgeir Ráðgeirson, bring Beorn Hafþórrsson and Benni Hafþórrsson to the steering board. You will guard the Dragonheart and Erik Short Toe."

Ráðgeir Ráðgeirson looked happy to be given such an honourable task.

"Haraldr Leifsson, take the men of Cyninges-tūn to the bow and guard it. The rest of you will be with me. Ship's boys, take your bows and harass the enemy. I have a silver penny for any boy who kills their helmsman!"

As they all rushed off to their positions and Erik adjusted the steering board Haaken said, "I can see that he has your mind. It is unlikely that the boys will hit the helmsman but arrows descending from on high will upset him and discourage him." He took out his sword and his seax. "I hope my fate is not to die at the hands of some hairy-arsed barbarian! I have survived witches and skull takers. Such an end would not befit a poet of my stature!"

Ráðgeir who had returned with Benni and Beorn laughed, "Do not worry, Haaken One Eye, you can always talk them to death."

I saw that the three of them had not brought their shields. The Hibernians were not known as archers and two weapons doubled our chance of success. Beorn Hafþórrsson carried a double-handed axe. He had taken it in the land of the East Angles when we had fought the Danes. He was a big man and could wreak havoc amongst half-naked Hibernians.

The ships were clearer now. They were lower than we were and so overloaded that had the seas been a little rougher they would have risked being swamped. The three ships were racing through the water. Although they had no sails the wind was aiding their rowers and the leading Hibernian looked likely to reach us. It was obvious that Sámr was right. This was the leader. He had a red pennant flying from his masthead. I could not make out the design. He had the better crew of the three and that might prove to be his undoing for there was a gap between him and his consorts starting to open. They were the better rowers. That lead would only extend the further we sailed. We ploughed on and, inexorably, the leading Hibernian closed with us. I saw Arne turn the hourglass.

Sámr came back. He came alone. I was standing close to Erik. Sámr, after looking at the three ships, said, "They will catch us." We were on a converging course. If we turned away then we would lose some of the wind and they would draw us in.

"Aye, Sámr Ship Killer, what would you have me do?"

He looked at me as Erik spoke and I said nothing but I was willing him to come up with the right answer. He rubbed his chin. I smiled. I did that when I was thinking. He looked at the second and third ships. He nodded, "The wind is from the north. Turn, Erik Short Toe, and take us across the leader's stern. Hopefully, the ship's boys can disable him and, if not, then we fight him."

"Aye! Prepare to come about!" The shout was for the ship's boys. Two of them were perched precariously on the yard. Arne took out his bow and strung it.

31

Our drekar leapt forward. The three Hibernians took a few precious moments to react. The leading one was but ten lengths from us. The second and third were more than twenty lengths away. The pirate with the red pennant turned. Already he had given us the advantage. If we turned back on our original course, we had a chance to outrun him but Sámr had made the right decision. He had thrown the bones and gambled that we could hurt the Hibernians and then escape.

I smiled, "May the Allfather be with you!"

The course change was not dramatic but the Hibernians were not as well drilled as our crews and we saw that some of the oars on the second and third boats collided with each other. They slowed and the gap between them and the leader grew. We ploughed on, almost skating over the waves. The wind-aided us now and we sailed faster. I saw that we would reach the ship with the red pennant in a very short time. Sámr was at the mast and a decision needed to be made. I had seen that the Hibernian had turned his bows slightly. Instead of crossing the stern, we would sail along the side of the ship. I turned to Erik, "Take out one bank of oars."

He grinned, "Aye, Dragonheart."

He adjusted the steerboard slightly. The Hibernian was approaching at an angle to us. He thought we were trying to cut behind him and he turned so that he was bow on to us. It meant he could turn either way. As we made our move, I saw Sámr look up at our masthead. He knew we had changed course. Erik needed no instruction from me and when we neared to within two lengths of the Hibernian, he put the steering board over to run down the Hibernian leader's steerboard side. Even though the Hibernian pirate had the best crew there was a delay in the reaction of his crew. It was crucial.

Arrows flew from our masthead and prow as the ship's boys loosed their arrows. The helmsman was protected by shields but two of those who were protecting him were struck. I thought for just a heartbeat that our bows would collide. We would have survived for our ship was well made but it would have meant we needed to repair it. Then I saw that we would miss. Our bow crashed and cracked through oars. I saw shards of wood fly into the air and heard the screams of men impaled on broken oars. The collision slowed us slightly. Our drekar seemed to shudder. I heard orders being shouted aboard the Hibernian and then, as our bow passed their stern, grappling hooks were hurled. They meant to board us. Although they had been hurt their leader was relying upon the other two ships to come to his aid.

I drew my weapons. As the hooks bit, our men ran to try to sever them. The bows of *'Heart'* began to swing around the Hibernian ship.

One Hibernian warrior, half-naked and with a tattooed chest stood on their gunwale. He hurled himself across the narrowing gap. Arne's arrow seemed to stop him in mid-air. His body fell between the two hulls as his comrades pulled us together. He screamed as the two hulls ground his body to a pulp. His death meant that we were now tied.

Erik shouted, "Arne, take the axe and free us!"

My five men and I ran at the warriors who stood on the gunwale to board us. One, leaping down at me, impaled himself on Wolf's Blood as Beorn Hafþórrsson swung his Danish axe. It was a prodigious blow and Olaf Leather Neck would have envied such a strike. It hacked through two of the legs of one man and the left leg of a second. Arne's axe chopped through one rope as Benni, Ráðgeir and Haaken slew the two men who had managed to reach our deck. I glanced down the ship and saw that Sámr and the younger warriors had made a shield wall and were slaughtering the ones who had boarded us in the middle. Haraldr led the men of Cyninges-tūn to attack their flank.

"Dragonheart, the other two ships are closing."

"Sever the grappling hooks!" The men who had boarded were fighting for their lives. We outnumbered them and I heard the sound of axes hacking through ropes. There was a twang as the last one was cut. We suddenly leapt forward and we were free. The Hibernian ship drifted for her crew had abandoned the oars to fight us. Six men still remained aboard our drekar and one had a helmet. I took him to be the leader. They were facing Sámr and the men at the mast. Sámr showed no fear as he blocked the blow from the wickedly curved sword. Sámr still had some growing to do and he was not as tall as the Hibernian. He hacked with his sword into the thigh of the leader. Blood spurted. The rest of the Hibernians were slaughtered but Baldr and the others allowed Sámr to end the fight he had begun. It was another milestone on his journey to leader. He did not panic when the Hibernian renewed his attacks. He had seen warriors go berserk. He took a second blow on his shield and rammed his sword between the chief's shield and sword. Sámr's sword, like mine, had a point. I saw it come out of the back of the chief. I watched Sámr turn it around and push again. He must have struck something vital or perhaps the chief had lost too much blood from his leg for he fell to the deck.

The crew began banging the deck with their feet. They shouted Sámr's name. This was the first time he had had the accolade. He looked embarrassed more than elated. I looked astern. The two Hibernians were still following but as they were five lengths astern of us it was unlikely that they would catch us. By the time we had taken everything of value from the dead and hurled their bodies overboard then they had given up.

Sámr came to join us. "We were lucky, great grandfather."

"Aye, we were. The Norns weave and they plot. We lost none and that was largely down to you. You used a shield wall and held them." I pointed astern, "They have given up. Clean yourself and then speak with Erik about the course." I smiled, "A leader does not have the luxury of reliving each stroke in the battle." I pointed to his young warriors who were animatedly describing each cut and thrust they had made. "That is for those who follow."

"Aye, I can see that now."

Already the ship's boys were sluicing down the deck with pails of sea water. With luck, there would be no stain. Erik was as proud of his ship as any wife was of her home.

Sámr threw himself into the navigation of the ship. We were now in the widest part of the sea between Hibernia and Gwynedd. As dusk approached, we saw the island of Ynys Enlli, called Bardsey by Norse sailors. The smoke coming from the monastery told us that the hardy monks still lived there. We did not bother them. They were poor monks who had neither gold nor silver. They spent their lives meditating and speaking of their god. I thought it pointless but it was their way.

We managed to tie to the land before darkness fell. We lit fires and began to cook shellfish collected by the ship's boys. I found a quiet part of the beach, behind a rock. I could not empty my bowels on the ship. The older I grew the harder it was to hang over the stern. Perhaps this was Odin's way of telling me to stay at home. When I had finished, I saw the puffins who lived on the island diving beneath the water for fish. We would take some of the birds to eat and some of their eggs. We never took too many. This was a larder for us. Once we left it then we would not strike land again for many days. We would sail south into waters where there would be neither ship nor land. We made the most of our fire, hot food and ale that was still fresh. By the time we reached the land of the Moor and the Arab, we would have no ale left and we would be reduced to drinking rainwater. The shelter over the prow doubled as a reservoir for water.

I saw that Sámr looked weary. He wandered over to me with his wooden bowl filled with stew as though he was a man asleep. He had had little sleep in the night and he had fought a battle. I waved him closer to me, "Come, Sámr, you have done well. A good leader knows when to rest. This is the time to let others work. We are safe here and you can sleep all night. There will be ship's boys to watch. Tomorrow begins the real lesson in navigation. We are going to a part of the ocean that even Erik Short Toe and I have rarely seen. Neither your father nor my son has done what you shall do. Be guided by Erik and, if you need to, then ask questions. When he learned from Josephus he was like a chattering magpie."

He looked relieved, "I do not want to let you down."

"And you will not. Your men did well."

He nodded as he ate, "Some told me that it was harder fighting on a ship than they had expected.

"And there is no way that you can practise that skill on land. Your men will learn or they will die." He had filled his mouth again. "You will need oathsworn. I was lucky I was Ulfheonar and they became my hearth weru. You will need to find those who would be oathsworn."

He finished chewing. Some of the limpets had been more than a little tough. "Baldr already swore an oath. As for the others? I think that I will wait until we have returned from this voyage. Some may not meet my standards and, for others, I may not meet theirs. The promise that we make each other is for life as Olaf and Rolf showed."

I nodded but said nothing. My great-grandson was showing more wisdom than either of my sons or my grandson. They had been too eager to have oathsworn warriors. I saw now that it had been my fault. I had made them think that hearth weru were easy to find and they were not. After he had eaten Sámr left me to lie amongst those like Baldr with whom he had fought. Already they were reliving each blow from the battle. Sámr just sat by the fire and listened. He was the first to cover himself with his cloak and to sleep. He was showing wisdom. I sat and watched for a while and then I too lay down to sleep. We were still within the shadow of Wyddfa and I dreamed.

I was in my hall and I watched the fire as it slowly died. I looked at my hands and they were wrinkled and veined. Suddenly the fire which had been dying began to grow. The flames licked the walls of my hall and it became shrouded in smoke. The smoke was so thick that I could not see the fire. Blindly I ran for the door, or where I thought the door should have been. The smoke was like dragon smoke. It shocked and it blinded. When I burst out of the door, I saw that Cyninges-tūn was on fire. People lay dying and I heard screams. Then I saw them. They were Danes and they were led by Sven the Boneless. Even as I watched I saw Karl Word Master slain and Cnut Cnutson tumble from my walls and then they came for me. I was surrounded and all that I had was Ragnar's Spirit. Then a hawk swooped down as Sven the

Boneless swashed his sword at my head. I fell and I fell into darkness.

Chapter 5

When I woke, I found that I was bathed in sweat. Dawn had yet to break but I saw a lightness in the sky. The dream had been a warning. Aiden had taught me that much about dreams but he had always interpreted them for me. He was in the spirit world now. Perhaps he had sent the message and hoped that I would decipher it. I could not while I was not at home, I needed Kara and Ylva. As I had been the subject of the attacks then so long as I was at sea my home was safe. The dream had stirred the memories of the Danes I had fought. I had slain too many of them both in the Land of the East Angles and in Dyflin. They would neither forgive nor forget. They were Vikings. They saw me as old and every enemy wanted my sword. I had often thought about throwing it into the ocean as we sailed but I knew that would anger the gods and make the Norns vengeful. The sword was both a blessing and a curse.

I made water and then went to the ship. Erik, one of the ship's boys, was standing at the gangplank. "Is there aught amiss, Jarl?"

"No, Erik. I woke and at my age, that means I cannot return to sleep. I will sharpen my sword."

He nodded and then said, hesitantly, in a quiet voice that expected a negative reply, "Jarl, could I touch the sword, please, Jarl Dragonheart?"

I smiled, "What for? Would you have some of its strength?"

He shook his head, "I am a scrawny, Jarl. At home, they called me a runt. My father was not a big man. I am not meant to wield such a sword. But I would like to touch it so that a little of its magic may come into my life."

I took it from its scabbard and let him hold it, "When I was younger than you, I was also someone who was so small that a good wind would blow me away. Work at your arms. I hewed trees in Norway for Old Ragnar and that gave me strength." He was holding the sword and he nodded, barely able to speak. The sword had that effect. Even after all these years I still felt the power of the gods race up my arms when I wielded it.

Erik Short Toe awoke and shouted, "Dawn is almost upon us, rise!"

Erik, the ship's boy, looked up at me. The moment of magic was gone. He reverently handed me the sword, "Thank you, Dragonheart. I was afraid to ask you."

"Never be afraid to ask for anything, Erik, the worst that could happen would be that someone might say no. If that happens then you are no worse off and they may say yes. Just because I am jarl does not mean that I do not know what it is like to be a ship's boy. Remember, I began my life as a slave. The way we end our lives is in our own hands."

I went to the whetstone and began to sharpen the blade. Erik Short Toe came over to me, "Did Erik Galmrsson bother you?"

"No, he wanted to hold the sword. What is his story?"

"His father was Raibeart ap Pasgen's wife's brother. The family came from Orkneyjar. Galmr Hrolfsson was his name. He was almost a dwarf and that is strange for his sister, Gefneir, who married Raibeart, was a beauty and tall."

I nodded, "I remember her now. I did not know she had a brother."

"They kept to themselves and lived up the river from the shipyard. He fished. They only had one child. The two died last winter. It was some disease. There was no talk of violence. Erik came to me to ask for help because he had woken and found them dead. Poor bairn did not know what to do. We buried them and took him in. He had no other family."

"Raibeart?"

He shook his head, "Gefneir was embarrassed about her brother. I like Raibeart but his wife?" He shook his head. "How could you abandon someone of your own blood? I do not think Raibeart knew of it. He was raiding the men of Walhaz when this happened. Erik now shares a sleeping chamber with Arne."

I nodded, "I spoke to him and I think he would be a warrior rather than a sailor."

"He will be too small."

"That is in the hands of the gods. When we return home, if he will, I will take him to my home. Kara and Ylva may be able to help him grow."

"That is kind and we will miss him for, despite his misfortune, he is a cheerful lad. My wife dotes on him but that, I think, is because she feels sorry for him. And she said it was a sign that he had the same name as me. He is like the lame animals she finds and tries to bring back to life." He shook his head, "She always fails but I love the fact that she tries. I married a good woman." Erik Short Toe and his wife were well-suited. This would be Erik's last voyage for when *'Heart'* retired so would he. The couple would enjoy a happy life with grandchildren. He had deserved it. They both had for she had brought up the family while he was away at sea.

We headed south and for the first three days, the sun shone enough to help Sámr and Erik Short Toe navigate. Then, on the fourth night, the skies began to pour forth a deluge of rain. The winds and the seas were no worse but the decks swam with water. I covered myself in my sealskin cape and my cloak but even the old sail did not stop all the rain.

The good news was that we were able to fill the empty ale barrels with rainwater. That way the water would have the vague taste of ale.

It rained, intermittently, for two days and by the end of the storm, all of us were soaked through. The lack of sun and stars meant that although we knew we were heading, south, our exact position was unclear. Erik Short Toe asked for Sámr and me to join him at the steering board. He looked from me to my great-grandson, "We have a choice. We continue south or we head east." He pointed to the pennant flying from the masthead, "Now might be a good time to head east as the wind will aid us. It may change soon, we do not know. The trouble is we do not know where we will make landfall."

I said nothing for I wanted Sámr to make the decision. He looked from me to Erik and then to the pennant. He nodded, "The Norns have spun. They sent the rain so that we would be unclear about our position and they need me to make a decision. Head south and east, Erik."

Erik Short Toe shook his head, "No, Sámr Ship Killer, you are ready to take the steering board. You take us south and east."

It was one of those moments which decide a warrior's future. He nodded and took the steering board, "Prepare to come about. Ship's boys to the sheets." He pushed the steering board over and we headed towards the land of the Moors and Arabs. If we had miscalculated then we would hit Africa. That would not be a disaster but Sámr would fret about it. I hoped we would make landfall in the land taken over by the followers of Islam. The Franks had lost it and the fanatics from the east had begun to eat into the land of the west.

We noticed, as we headed on our new course, that the air was warmer and there was less rain. We had no idea when we would hit land but all of us hoped that we had missed Syllingar. Of course, the witch could still entrap us but that possibility seemed remote out here in the empty ocean where the only sea birds we saw were solitary and high in the sky. The odd bird overhead and the fish in the sea were different from those we were used to. We saw more dolphins and there were sharks. The ones we saw were bigger than we had seen before. This was new to us all and the sides of the drekar were lined as the crew watched the water become slightly less grey and a little bluer.

The exceptions were Erik Short Toe and Sámr. They worked more hours than anyone. Erik was devolving more and more responsibility to Sámr as the voyage progressed. Here, I could not help my great-grandson. He had done nothing wrong but if he was to make a mistake then it should be one he made rather than one I advised.

I spent time contemplating the threads the Norns had spun. The blue stones had saved me from the witch and yet there were none on the blade. As I fingered the pommel, I realised that when he had touched the blade Odin had chosen me. His stones around my neck had saved me. They were on the sword which now slept with Aiden and were a link to the past, my past. What was Odin's purpose for me? It was Baldr who gave me the answer. I saw him practising with Bergil. Baldr was not of our people for he had come from a land far from the sea in the hot plains. Aiden had come from Hibernia. I had come from the Dunum. Brigid, my deceased wife, came from Dyfed. Aethelflaed came from the land of the East Angles. Germund was from Miklagård. Atticus was a Greek, as had been Josephus. Raibeart was from the old people and Ebrel and Bronnen, from the land of Om Walum. My task was to be the blacksmith who forged those disparate people into one blade. I needed to make my people a clan that would survive. We had to become an island against the Danes, the Mercians, the Picts and the Hibernians.

The winds eased after a day or two and our progress was slower. Erik, however, became more hopeful of landfall. "Dragonheart, I can smell the land. That is something I cannot teach Sámr. He will learn it, perhaps." He turned to Stig, one of the elder ship's boys, "Tell the ship's boys there will be a silver penny for the first to truly sight land!"

That was all the incentive the boys needed. They eagerly peered towards the horizon, their young eyes seeking the smudge which would tell them of land. I joined Erik Short Toe and Sámr by the steering board. "You have almost successfully passed the first part of this test. Thus far you have learned to navigate. The voyage home will be the last test."

He nodded and I studied the man who would lead my clan when I had gone. He was a man but he still had growing to do. He had not spent much time at the oars and was not as broad as some of the others his age. He and Baldr looked different. They were leaner. Sámr reminded me of me when I had been his age. I had not spent as long at the oars as others. I had to learn to fight differently. I used my head and Sámr would have to do the same.

Haaken joined us. He was becoming bored. He had no Olaf Leather Neck to tease. He had no one with whom to banter. The warriors on the drekar were in awe of one of the last of the Ulfheonar and Dragonheart's shadow. He was eager to get to land and to use his skills, "Well, Sámr Ship Killer, where do we land?"

I sighed. Haaken was blunt. I had not wanted pressure on Sámr. My great-grandson, however just smiled, "Let us look at the charts and see eh, Haaken One Eye?" The chest with the maps was between my chest and Erik Short Toes'. He opened it and took out one tied with a piece of blue cord. Erik had made Sámr copy all of the maps from Whale Island before we had left. It had taken him many hours but the act of replicating them had seared them in his mind. Our maps were simple things. They showed rivers, landmarks and settlements. Their names were not the names the locals used they were ours. Josephus had used the proper names and so Erik's maps had an occasional word like, 'Al-buhera', but most were words like, 'broad river', 'strong walls', 'rocks are here' and the like. Citadels were marked with a tower.

I watched Sámr run his fingers over the runes and the lines he had drawn a month ago. He jabbed a finger at a river with a citadel symbol. I recognised it. Atticus, when he had looked at the maps after Sámr had copied them had told me it was Portus Cale. Atticus' voice had been filled with fear. "Jarl, it is full of Moors and Berbers. They are a fierce people and very cruel. They are not Christian!" Portus Cale had a tower drawn upon it.

I said nothing. Haaken pointed at a river some fifty miles north. "What about this one? It is closer to home and there is no tower drawn there."

Erik Short Toe shook his head, "Sámr is right, Haaken One Eye. That river has a narrow entrance. It can be easily blocked. Besides it is many years since we travelled this far and they may have built a tower there now."

Haaken nodded, "Then how will we take a citadel?"

Sámr smiled, "We do not. We step the mast and sail, at night, up past the fortress. We will raid beyond their defences. There will be halls filled with goods waiting to be traded. The Moors are like us, Haaken, they trade."

"How do you know?"

Sámr was not put out by the aggressive tone of Haaken. He said, patiently, "Because I have spoken, during the watches, with Erik Short Toe who was trained by Josephus. Before we left, I spoke at length to Atticus of Syracuse. I ask and I listen. Perhaps those skills might be something you might acquire."

I laughed and put my arm around Haaken, "I have been saying that for years. You are right, Sámr. Although it will be hard for you, Haaken, keep your thoughts to yourself until Sámr has had a chance to explain what we will do or have you forgotten the purpose of this voyage?"

He grinned, "You are right and that is a rarity! I will listen. Speak on Sámr Ship Killer!"

"We wait off the coast until dusk and then row up the river. You are right the citadel will be well guarded and they will have horsemen, for the Moors are known for their horses, but we will raid south of the river. The people who are there, the native people, are kept as almost slaves. Atticus told me that. The Moors keep a tight rein on the land. We will

41

only have to fight the Moors for the other people will see us as saviours. We do not take slaves from those people and we just take from the Moors."

I looked with new eyes at Sámr. He had thought this out well. "You learned this from Erik?"

He shook his head, "When I played chess with Atticus, he spoke to me of how the Moors had taken over much of the land which had been ruled by the Romans and the Byzantines. The Moors are passionate about their religion and they try to convert the Christians. The ones they do not convert they either kill or enslave. We often use nature as an ally. Let us try to use these people."

Haaken spoke, "But we do not speak their language."

He smiled, "Baldr knows some of the words! There were other slaves with him amongst the Franks and they came from this land. It is worth a try. Baldr has skills with languages and the Norns sent him to the clan for a purpose."

It was the optimism of youth and I realised that I had lost it many years ago. I was far more pessimistic and cynical these days. Despite that, I added a word of caution, "It is one thing to sneak in and quite another to sneak out. The sheepdog and the shepherd may be asleep when we enter the sheepfold but they will be alert when we try to leave."

"I know. I have ideas on how to extricate ourselves but first I would look at this stronghold." He saw the doubt on our faces, "If I am to learn how to lead then I need to take chances do I not, Dragonheart?"

"You are right but first we need to find Portus Cale."

Erik Short Toe nodded, "The river there is wider than any save the one much further south. The trick will be to work out which river we have found."

The next day we saw land birds amongst the ocean birds. It was Stig who earned the silver penny, "Captain, I see land!" His small hand pointed due east. I could not see it but Stig was sitting astride the mast and yard. I looked at the sun. Arne turned the hourglass. We would have one or possibly two turns before we would lose the light. The wind was still from the north but closer to the northeast. It was not helping us.

Erik looked at Sámr, "We should run out the oars."

Sámr was torn. Part of him knew that we needed the oars and the other part wanted him to continue to steer. Common sense won out, "Take to the oars! Haaken, give us the beat."

"Would you have a song?"

He shook his head as he headed to his bench, "We do not need it yet and I would not alert the Moors to our presence."

Once the oars bit, we began to close with the shore at a faster rate. Before the hourglass was half empty, I saw the line of cliffs. Erik Short Toe frowned, "Arne, up the mast. Let me know if they are high cliffs."

We were closing quickly now and I could see that, by some miracle or an amazing piece of good fortune, we had found a river. Was this Portus Cale?

"They are high cliffs, captain and there looks to be a small settlement. I can see smoke rising in the sky."

I turned to Erik who had a self-satisfied look on his face, "You know where we are?"

"I do. It is an almost deserted part of the coast. The nearest place of any size is Tui which is some way up the river. We are, however, one hundred miles north of where we wish to be." He cupped one hand, "Prepare to come about!" As the ship's boys took their positions he said, "We can, at least, bring in the oars and turn south and east. The wind can aid us once more. We will find somewhere to land. I think we all need the feel of sand and rocks beneath our feet." We made the turn and Erik shouted, "In oars!"

Chapter 6

It was as the sun was setting that Erik Galmrsson spotted the tiny sliver of sand. We edged in under oars, grateful that there were just two huts and they were high on the cliffs. We ground on the sand and the ship's boys secured us to rocks and one solitary tree. Sámr sent Ráðgeir Ráðgeirson with Baldr and five of the younger warriors to investigate the huts while we lit fires and prepared our first hot meal in a long time.

The fires were lit and shellfish were being plunged into the salted water when Ráðgeir Ráðgeirson and the others returned. Ráðgeir put a protective arm around Baldr Witch Saviour as he spoke with us, "Here is a warrior with other skills than just fighting and rowing. Most of the people fled but Baldr found an old man and his wife who did not flee. He has tongues, Dragonheart. He spoke to them and we learned much. More, the others returned. We did not take from them and we did not harm them."

Sámr nodded, "That is good for we try a new approach on this raid. What did you learn?"

Ráðgeir Ráðgeirson spread his arm for Baldr to speak, "They confirmed that Portus Cale lies to the south of us. It is many miles south but they had other news that we could not have expected. The Count of Asturias grows stronger and his men raid regularly into the land captured by the Moors. They are gradually reclaiming it from the Moors. The Moors are reacting aggressively. They execute or maim any they fear is siding with the ones they call the Franks. There is talk of insurrection and rebellion against these followers of Islam. They knew nothing of Portus Cale but told me that the citadel there was a strong garrison."

Sámr said, "You have done well." He and Baldr sat close to Haaken One Eye and me. He looked at me with questions written all over his face.

"Sámr, ask and I shall answer. Who knows how much longer I will be here to answer you?"

He smiled, "I was not going to ask a question for I had an idea how to get by the citadel. My plan was to sneak in and then find a way out. I hoped to use a distraction in their harbour. I would have used a Viking trick."

"And you still can. This garrison is there, not only to hold the citadel secure but also to control the land around. They will use horses. If they have horses then the men will be lightly armoured. That is true, is it not, Baldr?"

"In the east, I have heard of Sarmatians and Byzantines who wear mail all over their bodies and have horses mailed also but they do not ride fast. I believe that these Berber and Moorish horsemen will have helmets, shields and leather armour. They will rely on their horses to make their foes fear them."

"And we do not fear horsemen. Rolf and Olaf may no longer be with us but Beorn and his oar brothers can wield axes and these Moors have yet to face a shield wall. They are not the danger, Sámr."

He looked puzzled, "Then what is?"

"The river! They can use the river against us. I have spoken with Erik Short Toe. The river could be blocked by a barrier of boats. I cannot see a Viking trick to get by those. I can see Viking brawn and muscle but that will cost you warriors."

Einar Long Fingers shouted, "Stew is ready!"

As we stood and made our way over to the cauldron Sámr said, "Then I have a hundred miles to see if Atticus has trained my mind well enough to discover a solution to this problem."

"Aiden spent many hours doing the same with me. No matter how much you are prepared there is always something that you are not expecting. It is how you deal with those problems which mark you as a leader."

The next day we headed south. There was a temptation to sail up one of the two rivers which lay north of Portus Cale but Sámr was determined to stick to his plan. What we did not see was any sign of defences on the cliffs and in the coves. They did not even have watchtowers. That suggested to me that there had been few Viking raids. The wind began to turn as we headed south. It moved around, first to blow from the north and west and then to blow from the west and north. That would help us to sail up the river but not down. We also noticed that the air became warmer and that the wind blew less strongly. I saw some of the more inexperienced warriors begin to redden in the sun. We had no Aiden to provide salve for them and some would suffer.

Haaken and I spent the long, and increasingly warmer days, seated on our chests at the stern. A piece of old sail gave us shade and we talked with Erik for Sámr was now happy to take the steering board. He was more confident using the compass. He had marked our progress on the map. The rivers we had passed had provided markers for him. When we returned home, he would not need Erik's maps and charts for he would have his own.

"You know, Erik Short Toe, that you will have only the ship's boys to guard the drekar when we raid. I will have to be with Sámr and he will need all the men he can get."

45

"If danger comes then I plan on anchoring in the river. We use anchors to hold us against the current. We have enough bows and more ship's boys than I can remember. It will be enough but you, Dragonheart, without insulting you, how will you keep up with these young warriors?"

"You are right, Erik. I have lived longer than any. I thought old Ragnar and Old Olaf were old but Haaken and I have ten years on them. Fear not. I will keep up. I climb up to Old Olaf's lofty top once every seven days. I can no longer run up in mail but I make it to the top and I can speak with Olaf. When I cannot speak at the peak then I know that I cannot go to war."

Haaken One Eye nodded, "Aye, Erik, death in battle holds no fears for Dragonheart. He has seen Valhalla."

Shaking my head, I said, "Do not send me there too quickly, Haaken One Eye. I am not yet ready to go. I would see Sámr and Aethelflaed's children. I may not see them grow but I would see them born and look into their eyes. I would tell them that I will watch over them from the Otherworld."

Haaken shook his head, sadly, "You are lucky, Dragonheart. The sisters have seen to it that I can only sire girls. My daughters all give birth to daughters. It seems that if I am to have a warrior to follow me then it must be one who can suckle the young!"

Erik and I laughed but there were warriors who were women. We had them in our clan although they did not raid. Those who lived at the eastern edges of our land and feared the Dane and the Saxon had women who could wield a sword and sell their lives dearly. We had not had an incursion for many years but my dream had told me that we should not relax our vigilance.

Sámr and Erik shortened sail as we neared the mouth of the river which passed by Portus Cale. I looked to the west and saw that the sun was beginning to set. The further south we went the shorter became the sunsets. It had surprised Sámr that there should be such a difference. Erik had told him that in Orkneyjar sometimes the setting sun took an hour to disappear while closer to Africa it could be as brief as a blink.

As soon as Stig spied the bubbling mouth of the estuary the sail was lowered. Once again there was no sign of a tower or citadel and we were able to drive south and east while we took down the mast. We would row up the river in the dark but we would have to do so silently. We would be reliant on the ship's boys and their eyes. Sámr would not be steering. We would need every man at an oar and Haaken and I would need to be two extra lookouts. There would be other opportunities for Sámr to steer up a strange river.

The sun set as quickly as a hall door closing and plunging the world into darkness. Once Haaken had set the beat with the haft of a spear we went to the prow. Once he stopped banging the only sounds which could be heard were the creak of the oars and the hiss of the wood sliding through the water. The river was wide enough to appear like the Water at home. We were shallow draughted and Erik Short Toe was confident that we would not ground. His fear was striking hidden mudbanks. That was why I watched, with Erik Galmrsson, at the steerboard side of the dragon prow and Haaken and Stig were on the larboard side.

I sniffed. The air smelled differently here. It was not just the warmth of the air it was as though the air was heavy and filled with exotic scents and aromas. I did not know the land well enough to identify them but I stored them in my mind. I had no idea how much time elapsed but I smelled men. It was the smell of woodsmoke and dung, both human and animal. The banks also drew closer to us. Erik Galmrsson's bare arm signalled when we were too close to the bank on our side and Stig did the same on the other. I heard horses neighing in the fields above us. Horses suggested Moors. There was no moon and we would just be a shadow moving on the river but the horses would smell us. The river twisted and turned but they were long bends and gentle sweeps.

Haaken spotted the citadel. Even in the dark of night, the white walls rising above the river could be clearly seen. I would have to be Sámr's eyes for he was rowing and I switched my view from one bank to the other as we passed Portus Cale. The smell of the town was both exotic and pungent. It was a large town and the river was filled with the waste that the inhabitants produced. I saw many ships in the river. Some were Frankish by their rigging but there were also the lateen-rigged ships of the Blue Sea. They were on both sides of the river. There was little noise for this was the middle of the night. Odin was watching over us for he hid us from any sentries on the walls. Without our mast and sail, we were almost invisible.

What worried me was that the river was narrower here than I had expected. Had there been a deck watch on the ships we would have been seen as we ghosted up the middle of the river. When we came back down there could be a barrier of boats filled with armed men. The Norns had spun for we passed the last house and turned in to darkness.

There were no signs or smells of houses. The land by this section of the river was without people. We were now watching for a place to land. Arne whistled and pointed to the steerboard shore. There was a small beach and it was surrounded by trees. We would be hidden. I waved my arm to signify to Erik Short Toe that we should land. By my reckoning, we had less than two hours until the first hint of dawn. We had much to do in that short time. We had to make a camp and turn the ship around.

Erik shouted, "Steerboard oars in!" We ground onto the sand. We would not be stuck for as soon as we unloaded, we would float.

Sámr showed his increasing maturity when he took eight of his younger warriors and the Hafþórrsson brothers. He left Erik Short Toe to see to the ship for he had to ensure that there was no danger nearby. I saw that he took Baldr with him. The young warrior's knowledge of languages might be the difference between success and failure. Once again, I thought of the threads which had tied us together. He had been shipwrecked in the middle of the Blue Sea when we found him. Had we not then he would have been dead, my granddaughter Ylva might have come to harm and we might be in even more danger than we were. *Wyrd*.

When half of the crew had disembarked Erik halted the rest and, as the drekar floated off the mud, he turned her around using the oarsmen to scull around. Dawn was already breaking as *'Heart of the Dragon'* edged her way back to the south bank of the river we later learned was called the Douro. Haaken and I had stayed ashore and we acted as ship's boys, catching the ropes and securing them to trees. It was more than fifty years since I had last done that. We made a camp in the woods as the ship's boys disguised the drekar with branches, vines, leaves and twigs. In time it would appear dead but by then we should have gone.

It was almost noon when Sámr and his scouts appeared. I had not been worried but the length of time had made me a little concerned. He looked a little anxious and weary as he sat with Haaken, Erik and me and shared a horn of ale.

"There is a small stronghold five miles to the south of us. There were armed men on the walls. We passed many farms. The Moors look to be using the locals as slaves to work the fields."

"And what of warehouses?"

Sámr shook his head, "We saw none but we did not have time to head downstream."

I stood, "Then Haaken and I will take a couple of men and we will stretch our legs."

Haaken stood, "Aye we have done little save create blisters on our arses. I am ready for a walk!"

"But you cannot go alone!"

"Sámr, we are Ulfheonar but if it makes you feel any better then we will take Haraldr Leifsson and Snorri Cnutson." I already had my cloak and seal-skin boots. With my sword and dagger that would be all that I needed. The two warriors I had chosen I knew well. Siggi was the grandson of Cnut who had been with me when Odin had touched my

48

blade and Haraldr's father had been my standard bearer. I was comfortable with both warriors. As soon as my three companions were ready, I set off through the woods. No words were needed. I led.

I wondered why there was no riverside path and I discovered the reason just four hundred paces from the drekar. There was a cliff of rock which stabbed up from the forest floor. It meant we had to wade through the shallow water at the edge of the river. As we did so I saw ships on the river. They were heading downstream on the rising tide. Now that daylight was here, they might spot our drekar. We had done a good job of disguising it but we would be seen eventually. They would not notice us.

Our cloaks had been brown once but they had faded to a dull colour which helped us to blend in with the trees. I led and I listened for the sound of people and animals. I heard neither but as the wind was coming up from the west, I smelled smoke. It grew stronger and so I moved more slowly. I heard voices and I held up my hand. I went on all fours and moved across the ground which rose slightly. The wood ended and there were tilled fields. I saw pigs snuffling in them. There were men and women clearing the last of the vegetables which had been in the field. Atop a horse was a Moor. He was as black as night with a small buckler and curved sword. In his hand, he had a whip. Even as I watched I saw the end flick out and catch a girl on the buttocks. She squealed in pain. The others worked even more frantically. I could see the house. It was two hundred paces away and I spied another Moor there. I slid backwards and joined the others. Without saying a word, I gestured for us to continue along the river.

We were now getting closer to the port. I saw that there were warehouses on the opposite bank. There were not many but they were targets. We would have to use the drekar to raid but we could do that. We had covered five miles when the river took a sharp turn and I saw the city. There were ferries and small boats crisscrossing the river. We had avoided being seen by any for we had found the river track. As it had passed through trees, we had been able to hide when we heard any noise which suggested danger. I could see the stronghold but not the buildings on our side. There was a road ahead. It passed through a small settlement. It looked to me as though there were quays ahead and, perhaps, buildings which might contain cargo. I was debating heading towards the road when I heard, from my left, the sound of horses coming down the road. I waved my arm and we all headed back into the cover of the woods. We had seen enough and we could return to Sámr.

Haaken and I were Ulfheonar. As soon as we were away from the road, we threw ourselves beneath the nearest bush and covered ourselves

49

with our cloaks. Haraldr and Siggi tried the same after they had seen us disappear. They were not as experienced as we and Siggi took too long to find cover. I heard a shout and the horsemen began to gallop through the woods. I guessed that they had marked Siggi's position for the shout had come just as he lay down, twenty paces from me. I had laid down facing the road. The hood of my cloak covered my head and I could see clearly. There were five riders. They were Moors or Arabs. I say Arabs for three had lighter coloured skin. They had swords.

It was obvious that they had not seen me or Haaken when the first four galloped passed me. As the last man drew near, I rose, drawing my sword as I did so. His horse's head reared and it neighed when my head appeared next to it. I swung my sword at the horseman's side. He was not holding a shield and my blade came away bloody. He fell from the horse's back.

I was moving, next to the horse, even as the dying man was falling from his horse. Haaken had risen with me and as the Arab just ahead turned his horse Haaken pulled the horse's bridle with his left hand as he lunged with his right. His sword sank into his unprotected stomach. The remaining three men ahead turned their horses' heads around and that allowed Haraldr and Siggi to stand. The three came for Haaken and me. I drew Wolf's Blood. The horses were not moving quickly and that gave us a chance. A Moor swung his curved sword at my head. It was a long sword. I blocked it with Wolf's Blood. Bagsecg Bagsecgson had made a strong weapon. Sparks flew but the dagger did not bend. I brought over Ragnar's Spirit and hacked through the Moor's arm. His left arm was holding the reins and as he fell backwards, he pulled his own horse with him. He landed on the ground and the horse fell on top of him. Haraldr and Siggi attacked the fifth horseman as Haaken calmly held his sword in two hands and as the last surviving Moor rode at him, he hacked sideways biting into the horse's neck. Lifeblood spurted and the horse crashed to the ground. Haaken, with a speed which belied his age, ran at the Moor and stabbed him through the throat. Haraldr slew the fifth one.

"Siggi, Haraldr, get the horses." Haaken and I began to collect the weapons. I searched the bodies for coins. They had jewels on their fingers. The other two returned with the horses. "Tie them to a tree. We will dispose of these bodies. I know that they will be found but any delay helps us."

We carried them to the river. Trees had been swept downstream in a storm. Logs had made a natural dam and we lodged the bloody bodies beneath them. If someone searched, they might find them but as we had been the only ones down by the river for some time, I was confident that they would lie undiscovered until we had left the river. We put the weapons on the four surviving horses and led them back along the river.

"What about the dead horse?"

"It is too big to move. We will have set them a puzzle. While they decipher the clues, it will give us time but my great-grandson no longer has the luxury of time to scout. We will have to raid on the morrow!"

Chapter 7

When we led the horses into the camp there were looks of amazement from the younger warriors. They had not raided with us before. Sámr looked concerned. I shook my head, "Fear not, there were five warriors and they are dead. Their bodies are hidden but we need to raid sooner rather than later." My more experienced warriors came to stand close to us as we spoke. "There are warehouses on the other side of the river. We would have to use the drekar to raid them. On this side, there may be warehouses but we did not see any. We walked five miles before we found the road and saw the outskirts of the settlement on the southern side of the river. We spied two large houses. They are guarded."

Haaken brought me over a horn of ale. We would soon run out. We were on the last barrel. I drank to give Sámr time to think. He looked up at the sky. The afternoon was wearing on and soon it would be dark. "What is the road like along the river bank?"

"There is no road. In fact, for much of the way, there is no path either. We had to wade through the river."

Lars Long Legs said, "That is better for it means that no one will be there."

Baldr nodded, "And the gods have sent us four horses. I can ride and I know some others can. You say, Jarl Dragonheart, that there is a road ahead?"

"Aye. It is five miles or so from here."

"Then we can pick up the road to the east of us. We saw it earlier today. We can ride to meet you and act as mounted scouts."

Haraldr, still smarting from his earlier mistake, shook his head, "It will alert the Moors to our presence. Better we stay hidden."

Sámr's voice was commanding, "We can do both. A horse can travel faster than a man. We leave before dawn and Baldr and his riders an hour or so later. The Moors will not think anything untoward about men riding horses. If you wear cloaks and do not wear helmets then you might fool anyone who gives just a cursory glance." And in that moment the plan was hatched. I had not had to say anything. Sámr had weighed up opinions and chosen his course. That was the mark of a leader.

Erik Short Toe had set the sentries and the ship's boys guarded the drekar. We did not risk a fire. That would come when they knew that we were there. Haaken and I had campaigned so often together that we both chose the same place for our beds. We gathered leaves and grass to lay beneath our cloaks. Here, the air was so warm that a Viking needed nothing to cover him. We were just finishing when Haraldr and Siggi came over, "We are sorry we let you down, Jarl Dragonheart! You could have been killed!"

Haaken laughed, "Haraldr the gods have a better end for Dragonheart than to be ridden down by five black savages. Besides, they did not see us."

"Haaken is right. You are not Ulfheonar. We have spent our whole lives doing this. Cnut, your father and grandfather spent every moment of every day honing skills to be able to hide in plain view. I am just sorry that you had to guard two old men who should be sitting watching the sun set over Old Olaf."

Siggi shook his head, "Jarl, I watched you today. Your movements were faster than mine and had I not known that you fought alongside my grandfather I would have taken you for a young warrior. The gods truly favour you." They left us having made their apology.

I did not bother Sámr. All would be well. If he made mistakes then he would learn from them. I ate well and Haaken and I had the last two horns of ale from the barrel. They were almost like a stew. I slept a dreamless sleep. I was far from my homeland and far from the spirits who watched over me. This was as much a test for me as it was for Sámr.

I woke early. I needed to make water. Erik Short Toe was up already. "Will you warp the drekar into the middle of the river?"

He shook his head, "If Baldr rides east and you attack west then, as there is a rock between us and our enemies, we should be safe. Besides, putting the ship in the river will attract more attention." He nodded towards Sámr who lay sleeping between Baldr and Bergil Sharp Blade. "He has done well."

"He has my blood, Wolf Killer's and Ragnar's. If you add Erika to that then it should be no surprise."

"And yet Mordaf and Ulla War Cry are not the same warriors."

"Mordaf has none of Erika's blood. He has Welsh blood in his veins and Ulla? The witch almost did for him. When he was taken at Syllingar it sowed the seed of fear. He will be a warrior but not a leader. The gods, not I, have chosen Sámr."

I left Erik and went to wake Sámr. He smiled. In those few moments, before he rose, he was like the small boy I had shown around the Water. I suspect, in his eyes, I had not changed but he had. I missed that small boy who followed me around and was so eager to emulate me. He was still copying me but in a different way.

"It is time to rise. We need to strike and strike quickly."

"Aye, great grandfather. I am ready."

I went aboard the drekar for I would be wearing mail and my helmet. I would carry my shield. Our best defence was to be prepared to face

anything. With my helmet, mail and shield I was an Ulfheonar ready to
go to war, I would hold Ragnar's Spirit. Once I was armed, I went ashore
and ate. I was not hungry but I knew that I would need something in my
belly. I saw Baldr talking to the three young warriors he would take with
him. I waved him over.

"Aye, Dragonheart?"

"Take no chances today. At best you are a diversion. Sámr will need
you when he leads the clan."

"I know but riding a horse is what I was born for. We will not let
Sámr down. I will be cautious but I will be there should the clan need
us."

"Good."

Haraldr and Siggi led the warriors off. Haaken and I were behind
Sámr and the men of Cyninges-tūn. Ráðgeirson, Benni and his brothers
were with them. Our most experienced warriors were around Sámr. The
sun was up when we reached the road. The farms and houses which we
had passed could be raided on the way back. The hall which we had seen
by the river and the road was a better target. We waited in the woods
while Ráðgeir Ráðgeirson and Sámr scouted it out. They returned after a
short time.

"There are eight Moors and Arabs with weapons. They have a granary
with sacks of grain. There is a fountain!" Sámr pointed out the
architectural feature only because it told us that this was a rich home.
"Great grandfather, I would have you and the men of Cyninges-tūn head
along the river and cut off the escape route to Portus Cale."

His eyes pleaded with me and I nodded, "Of course. Will you signal
when you need us?"

Relieved he said. "Aye!"

I let Ráðgeir lead us off. I had Ragnar's Spirit in my hand and I had
slipped my shield around to my front. We did not use the road. We went
along the edge of the river. There was no path and, sometimes, we had to
step into the water. Ráðgeir then led us through scrubby growth to the
road. We had barely reached the position when we heard the clash of
steel on steel. There were shouts and screams. Sámr had launched his
attack.

"Ráðgeir, divide the men in two. Half watch Portus Cale, the rest
form a shield wall with Haaken and me."

Haaken and I stood in the centre and men formed along each side of
us. There were only ten of us. The bulk of the men were with Sámr. We
had barely locked shields when I heard the thunder of horses. Four
Arabs, wearing conical spiked helmets and with spears and small shields,
appeared ahead of us. They had obviously fled Sámr's attack and that

54

boded well for it meant we had divided the warriors who would face Sámr and the others. These four were going for help. We must have looked like a pathetically thin line. They could not see Ráðgeir and the rest of the warriors for they were twenty paces down the road. The Moors came for us and I watched them pull back their spears. They had not fought Vikings before. They thought we would flee. We would not.

Haaken and I were in the centre and the two spears came for our heads. Considering he had but one eye Haaken had amazing reactions. His shield flicked up almost contemptuously to fend off the shield as he swung his sword at the horse's head. When the horse was hacked in the neck its body crashed into Haaken, knocking him to the ground. There was a gap. The spear which came for me was aimed at my eye. I watched it come towards me. I did not flick my shield I punched it at the head. The spear shattered and splintered. The Moor lowered his shield to block the sweep from my sword. I swung it around. My blade followed his horse which headed for the gap between me and the prostrate Haaken. The edge of Ragnar's Spirit slid over the cantle and then tore through the mail-covered tunic of the warrior and into his back. I felt the blade jar on his spine. He threw his arms in the air as his back was broken. Even though he was prostrate Haaken rolled away from the hooves of the riderless horse. Beorn and Benni both swung their axes at the two riders who followed. Even as they were hacked from their horses, the warrior whose horse had knocked over Haaken was being butchered by my warriors. No news would reach Portus Cale.

Leaving Ráðgeir to watch the road I led my men to the hall. By the time we reached it, I saw that all of the guards and the lord lay dead. The locals were cowering in fear. As I approached, I heard Sámr say, "Baldr, speak to them. Tell them that if they tell us where their lord keeps the treasure then they will come to no harm." I smiled to myself. My great-grandson would not harm these ordinary folk in any case.

"The rest of you find wagons and begin to load the sacks of food." He sheathed his sword and I sheathed mine. I took off my helmet and let my coif slip over my shoulders. The day was hot and I was sweating. I saw why the local warriors did not wear mail. "Did Baldr find anything?"

"On the road leading here, he spied a large hall. It was in the hills about a mile from the road. He and the others were not seen for they sheltered in woods. It is much larger than this place."

"Word will soon spread that there are raiders."

He nodded, "I thought to head there when we have recovered the booty. We have more horses. Baldr can take men and wait at the road which leads from the hall."

"The men will be weary." I was not complaining. I was stating a fact.

"I know but, as you say, if we do not try to take it now then we may not have another opportunity." He shook his head, "These decisions which you made look easy are hard!"

"Aye, but you are choosing the right paths."

Baldr came over to join us. "These people have been badly used. They beg us to tie them so that when they are discovered, they will not be punished."

I nodded, "Make it so. Haraldr, fetch Ráðgeir and the rest of the men. We will be moving sooner rather than later!"

It was noon when we reached the drekar. Baldr led seven others to watch the road. One of those who had been with him when he had discovered the hall waited with us. We had sacks of wheat, salted meat, wine and some ale. Baldr had discovered two chests of coins. I nodded, "That will be tax money. From what I have been told the Caliph demands much gold from his subjects. Perhaps that is why the workers are so ill-treated."

Sámr said, "You need not come. You have both done more than many others."

Haaken shook his head, "Do not let the odd strand of white hair on my pate fool you, Sámr Ship Killer. The Dragonheart and I may not be as fast as we once were but we can march all day and fight all night if we have to!"

In truth, I was weary and aching. The wound in my leg had healed but I had felt twinges as we had marched. The wine we had drunk and the slices of salted pig meat helped revive me and we set off through the woods. The ship's boys and Erik Short Toe would load the drekar.

The wood became thinner and more open as we approached the road. We passed an abandoned charcoal burner's hut. Then we reached the road and Baldr's guide led us along it, west. I was pleased when Sámr ordered us all off the road and into the scrubland which lay to the south of the road. We could still be seen but our numbers were harder to determine. I still had my helmet hanging from my sword hilt and my coif was around my shoulders. Like the other veterans, we carried our shields upon our backs. Some of the younger warriors carried them on their left arms. They would learn.

We did not see Baldr and his men when we reached the stone track which led up into the hills. He and his young warriors had hidden their horses. They ghosted up to us. Baldr pointed towards Portus Cale, "A carriage and many riders headed that way not long before we spied you. We let them go but I fear that they are heading to Portus Cale. They will pass the house we raided."

Sámr's face fell. Haaken said, "It is the Norns, Sámr, that is all."

56

I was still hopeful, "Aye, Sámr, your plan still works in fact if riders accompanied the carriage then there will be fewer guarding the hall but daylight burns and each moment we dally places us in greater jeopardy."

"Baldr, have two men stay here with the horses. They can give us a warning. The rest of you spread out and let us approach this hall."

We let the younger ones spread out before us. This was part of Sámr's training. I noticed that Ráðgeir and the men of Cyninges-tūn were close behind Sámr. Haaken and I were at the rear. I slid up my coif and donned my helmet. I drew Ragnar's Spirit.

They had cleared the land on the hillside and terraced it. There were olive trees and some vines. It meant we had no cover for the last five hundred paces and there were men on the low wall. There were not many of them. The afternoon sunlight glinted off their helmets and I counted only three but, as we dodged and ran between the trees and vines, we were seen. There was the sound of a bell and the gates slammed shut. The younger warriors were keen, too keen. Sven Einarsson paid the price for not holding his shield before him and he was struck by an arrow. He was two hundred paces from the walls. These Africans had bows which were as powerful as a Saami bow. I saw that more men now manned the walls. There were at least twelve and they all had bows. The others heeded Sven's death. Beorn and Benni ran to flank Sámr and they held their shields before them. I heard arrows thud into their shields. The walls would not present a problem. They were barely three paces high. As I stepped over Sven's body an arrow thudded into my shield.

"Haaken, make for the gate! I do not relish climbing a wall!"

"Aye, Dragonheart. Let these young wolves make the leap! We have leapt enough ere now."

I saw Sámr organizing the men to climb the walls. We had made a mistake. We had not brought any bows. If we had then we could have kept down the archers. I saw another young warrior, Lars Eriksson, struck by two arrows. He was another who would not return to Cyninges-tūn. There were men on the gate. Siggi and Haraldr were with us and we held our shields above us as stones were dropped from the fighting platform. If the stones could be lifted then they would not damage our shields. Only part of the stone wall would damage them. Einar Long Fingers had an axe and he ran up to the gate. I could hear the sound of battle above us. Einar swung at the tiny gap between the two gates. His blade bit into the bar which held it. He was very accurate and, through the tiny gap, I saw four men begin to brace it. Einar's fourth blow shattered the bar and I shouted, "On three we push! One, two, three!" There were five heavy mailed men pushing and just four Moors holding the gate. It was no contest. The gates burst asunder. Two of the Moors

57

kept their feet and they ran at Haraldr and me. The curved sword had a good edge and that worked to my advantage. It bit through the leather covering of my shield and stuck in the wood. I swung my arm left and his half-naked body was exposed as his shield was drawn aside. Ragnar's Spirit gave him a quick death as I scythed into his side.

I looked up as the others were dispatched. They had a tower. The gate was halfway up its stone face and the only access was along the fighting platform, "Follow me!"

I led my handful of warriors towards the ladder which led to the fighting platform. There were two archers on the top of the tower. They began loosing at us as we ran along the platform. Arrows smacked into my shield. One clanked off my helmet but we came to no harm. This time there was no gap for Einar to use. He would have to hack at the places where the planks were joined. Haraldr, Haaken and I held our shields above Einar as he methodically began to hew large slivers of wood from the gate. I looked down into the courtyard. Sámr and the others had cleared the walls and were heading to the hall. That was the right thing to do but there would be Moors and Arabs within the tower. Benni Hafþórrsson and Beorn Hafþórrsson raced up the ladder to join us. Beorn also had an axe. He helped Einar to demolish the door.

The door opened outwards and so it took longer for us to break in. As we did so we were confronted by a Moor who wore armour. He was a big man and he filled the stairway. While Benni Hafþórrsson pushed his shield into the warrior's face, his brother, Beorn Hafþórrsson swung his axe beneath the Moor's shield to hack through his legs. The two of them scrambled over the dying man's body and raced up the stairs.

Had they had more defenders within the tower we might have struggled to take the stronghold but the only other warriors were on the top of the tower loosing arrows at Sámr and the rest of our men in the courtyard. As we burst into the open, then the four of them turned to send their arrows at us. Benni and Beorn held their shields before them and the arrows thudded into the wood. Haaken and I ran towards the nearest archer. He managed to send an arrow in my direction. It struck my shield as Haaken took his head. The defenders now dead, we were able to survey the scene below us. Sámr and his men were in command.

Benni Hafþórrsson's hand pointed to the west, "Jarl Dragonheart. There are riders approaching from Portus Cale!"

I looked where he pointed. It looked like the ones who had left earlier had discovered our handiwork and were returning to their hall. The battle was not yet over!

Chapter 8

I cupped my hands, "Sámr! Riders are approaching. The fight is not yet done!" I turned to Haraldr, "You and Benni stay here. Use the bows and keep us informed of the movements of the enemy."

As we raced down the stairs Haaken asked, "How many were there?"

"It was hard to tell but it looked more than an escort for a carriage. I am guessing that they have brought men from Portus Cale. Sámr may have a real test of his mettle soon enough."

The gates had been shattered by us and were no barrier to men and horses. As we entered the courtyard, I saw that Sámr had men on the walls. They were using the bows of the dead sentries. They were good bows which were capable of sending an arrow through mail. He was organising a double shield wall. "They have more than forty men, Sámr!"

"We lost five men and I have Baldr watching the servants." He smiled at me, "The Norns have spun well. Where will you fight?"

"Haaken and I will be at the shield end of your wall. We have done this before." I sheathed my sword and picked up a pike. It had a spearhead and a long blade attached to the spear shaft. It was heavy but I would not have to use it for long. Haaken found a spear. We stood next to Snorri Cnutson and Einar Long Legs.

Haraldr shouted, "They are within range!"

Their two bows sent arrows beyond the walls. The eight men on the walls added their arrows to the missile storm. There would be too few to stop the horses but they might thin them and they would, most certainly, distract them. I looked and saw that Sámr was in the centre of the front row and was flanked by Beorn Hafþórrsson and Ráðgeir Ráðgeirson. He was well protected for they were the biggest and the best of my warriors. I could now hear the wild neighs from the horses as they were struck as well as the shouts of men as they were hit. Sámr had positioned the shield wall so that we were just ten paces from the gate. Only two men at a time could ride through the gate. Therein lay hope.

I could see the horsemen as they approached. There were some encased in mail. These were the warriors of which Baldr had spoken. They would take some killing. We had just forty-two men in our three ranks. Horses added to the weight of our enemies. It would be a close-fought battle.

The first two men through were carrying spears and they rode at Sámr and Ráðgeir. One of the riders had a body encased in mail. Only his eyes could be seen. The other had a mail vest. Behind them, another five horsemen burst through and they spread out. The Norns had spun and a

59

second fully mailed rider came directly towards me. I held my pike in two hands with my shield hanging over my arm. My pike was much longer than the curved sword he held. His horse had a mail hood over its head. The rest of its body was without armour. I heard the clash of spears on shields as the first Moors and Arabs struck our line. I kept my attention on the mailed man coming for me. There were two other men close behind him. They were coming for me so that they could roll up our line from the left. I swung the bladed part of the pike not at the horse's head which was encased in mail but at its throat and chest. As soon as the razor-sharp blade bit the horse reared and tried to pull away. As it did so it turned the rider so that his left side was exposed. Haaken needed no urging. Two-handed, he rammed the spear into the horsemen's side. The head tore through the mail and into the lower part of his stomach. The wheeling horse aggravated the wound and it tore a hole in him. He fell to the side and the next two riders had no choice but to veer away.

Neither of the next two men was encased in mail. They had voluminous layers of clothes and both wore a helmet. They each had a long oval shield. I ran to the one on the right, leaving Haaken One Eye to deal with the other. Ignoring the spear which was rammed towards me I swept the pike across the front of the horseman. The tip of the pike ripped open the layers of cloth and then the blade bit into flesh. It was not a mortal wound but it was a bloody one. As I pulled the head back the blade part scored a line across the horse's mane and it whirled around in terror. It galloped towards the gate. The gate entrance was crowded as more Moors and Arabs tried to enter.

I was about to shout when Sámr seemed to steal the words from my mind, "Charge! We have them!"

We raced to the gate. The four men who had entered already were being butchered and the terrified horse was pressed hard against those at the gate. We had no order but we needed none. A Viking fought well in a shield wall. He fought just as well on his own. I lunged with the pike across the neck of the horse I had wounded. I struck the warrior in the arm. As I pulled it back, towards the ground, I managed to score another line across the leg of the Arab with the voluminous clothes. He began to tumble. Arrows from the tower began to strike the riders in the gateway. With fifteen of us hacking at the three or four men and horses trapped in the gate it soon became clear that they could not get into the enclosure. When Beorn Hafþórrsson swung his axe and hacked into the side of what looked like a leader for he had a red plume, a horn was sounded and the twenty survivors and the riderless horses galloped away. The red-plumed helmet fell from the man's head. The wounded man rode off. He would not last long with that wound. We had won. The eight men on the walls had managed to slay or wound twelve of those outside. We had killed another ten within. We had been willing to die and the Moors had not. I picked up the helmet and carried it under my arm.

"Collect our dead! We will burn them for they will be despoiled otherwise."

Siggi and Einar nodded, "Aye, Jarl Dragonheart."

Sámr turned, "Find wagons! They will return." He looked up at the sky. It was coming on to dusk. "It may not be today but they will come back. Ráðgeir, when the wagons are found fill them." He headed into the hall to find Baldr. I followed leaving Haaken One Eye to watch that all was well done with our dead.

Once inside the hall, I saw that Baldr was talking to one of the servants. He turned and spoke to Sámr rather than me, "We just held them while the battle raged. They say that the man whose hall this is, is the Emir of Astorga."

The man he had been speaking with suddenly became animated and he jabbered away whilst pointing at me. It took some questions from Baldr before he could make sense of what he had said. I suspect the words were spoken too quickly for Baldr.

"He says that the Emir wore that helmet."

"And that makes sense. We have slain an important man. They will not just leave us alone now. They will seek vengeance. How many men are in Portus Cale?"

The man did not know. After half a dozen questions he just told Baldr that there were many. Sámr seemed satisfied, "Let us search this hall for treasure. If he is the Emir then he should have gold and silver."

When we went to the upper chambers, we found a locked room. The helpful servant found the keys for us and we took away four large chests filled with gold, jewels and silver. It was the greatest treasure I could remember finding. We cleared out the food and were about to send the servants on their way when Haraldr, who had descended from the tower said, "Jarl, there is a locked door there."

We had ignored the door for unlike the others it was plain and was on the ground floor. I waved over the servant and pointed to the lock. He took out his keys and opened it. There were steps which went down into darkness.

Sámr said, "Baldr, fetch a torch. Great grandfather let us descend first. You have risked enough today!"

The smell was appalling as we went down the steps. It was a mixture of things that were dead, human dung and sweat. I could not see beyond Baldr's back. Then, as my eyes grew accustomed to the dark, I saw that there were people down there. When they moved, I saw a most pitiful sight. There were nine of them huddled together and four corpses. The four men and five women were all emaciated and dressed in the ragged remains of what must have been fine clothes once. They cowered as we approached for we held swords before us but one man stood before them. He had his fists bunched as though he was willing to fight us.

I said, "Sheathe your weapons. Do not draw them again. These skeletons can do us no hurt. Baldr."

Baldr began to speak. He did so quietly and calmly. The man's fist unclenched. He answered. A dialogue went on for some time. I think they both had trouble communicating with each other. I suspect that Baldr had to use a number of languages. I understood none of them.

He turned and sighed, "This is Sunifred Borrell. He is the nephew of the Count of Barcelona, Wilfred the Hairy. This is his family. They lived close to Tui in the north of the land. A year ago, the Emir of Portus Cale led a force to raid the estates along the river. These are the only survivors. Most of the women and girls were taken to the houses of women which the Moors used. There they are used by the Muslim lords. The four who lie dead died of starvation."

Baldr looked at Sámr who looked at me, "What do we do, great grandfather? I am not prepared for this eventuality."

"This is the Norns. Baldr, do you remember when we found you? You were close to death. These are too. Tell them that we can take them from here and we can leave them at the river which leads to Tui."

He spoke and the man became quite animated. He dropped to one knee and began to kiss my hand. He started chattering away. Baldr said, "He says that if we sail him and the others to Tui then there will be great rewards for you."

I looked at Sámr, "If we take these then we cannot take slaves as well."

He smiled, "We can always get slaves but we cannot annoy the Norns. The Norns wanted us to find these people. We take them!"

When we reached the courtyard, it was already dark. The wagons were loaded and the servants had fled. They did not wish to risk the wrath of their masters. I daresay they had taken treasures from the house. I would not have blamed them. Sámr was already in command, "Baldr, take your horsemen and watch the road from Portus Cale. It will take us time to reach the drekar and we need to discourage them from following us."

"I will." He mounted his horse and shouted to his small band. He had one less to lead as Leif had died in the attack. His body had been burned along with the others by Haaken and my men. All was done well and my

Ulfheonar had sung the saga of Rolf Horse Killer over the pyre. Baldr shouted something to Sunifred. The man nodded. "I told them you would use sign language and that they would be cared for."

Sámr waved his arm, "Haraldr, Benni, get these captives in the wagons. Be gentle with them."

This would be a difficult journey. There were enemies out there who were seeking us. Baldr and his riders were our only method of finding them. We had taken so much food, clothes, treasure, spices and grain, not to mention the rescued captives, that we had been forced to take three wagons. Ráðgeir and the men of Cyninges-tūn marched at the front of the column with Sámr. Haaken and I were at the rear with the younger warriors. It was fortunate that we were travelling along a road or I fear we would have suffered mishaps. It was with some relief that we found the track which led through the woods to the camp. The rough track eventually proved too much for the wagons and when the trees were too close together, we stopped and had to carry our treasure for the last eight hundred paces. We used relays of men. Sámr had reached Erik Short Toe and the ship's boys helped our men to convey the captives and the treasure from the wagons. Haaken and I stayed at the edge of the wood with Haraldr and Beorn. We waited for some time awaiting the return of Baldr. I began to fear the worst. When we heard the sound of horses, we drew our weapons but it was just Baldr. I saw that not all of the men he had taken had returned. Bárekr Ulfsson was not with them.

Baldr dismounted. Shaking his head, he said, "We were about to return here when we were surprised by ten mounted warriors. They were lightly armed and Bárekr thought he was a better rider than he was. He slew one but when he tried to repeat the blow he fell from his horse. They took his head. We led them a merry dance up into the hills and then we doubled back through the woods. They did not follow us but when daylight comes, they will find where we are."

"And by then we should be gone. You have done well, Baldr. Take your heroes to the camp. We four will watch a while longer." I sniffed the air. I could smell smoke and food being cooked. "Tell the cook that he should leave plenty for us!"

Haaken said, as they disappeared through the woods, "This has been expensive for the young warriors. There are eight who followed Sámr from the Land of the Wolf and will not return home."

"And that is the way of the world. Do you think they would change their end?"

Haraldr shook his head, "They are in Valhalla now. They will be talking to my father and telling him of our deeds."

He was right. We waited until we saw the moon rise and then we headed to the camp. The rest had eaten. I saw Baldr speaking with the captives who were still devouring the food as though it was their first meal in a long time. I sat with Erik Short Toe and Sámr. "The drekar is loaded?"

Erik Galmrsson handed me a wooden bowl of stew and a hunk of fresh bread. Erik Short Toe said, "Aye, it is. There has been much traffic down the river. We were seen." He shrugged. "They were small boats and not warships but they will be warned downstream. They know that there is a dragon ship in their river."

"I expected that. It is as I warned you, Sámr, they will block the river." I was not chiding Sámr. This was part of his training. How would he react to this setback?

Sámr smiled. He was chewing but I saw, in his eyes, that he had already thought this out. I ate the stew. It was good. The men had butchered some of the horses from the hall and the meat had made the stew even tastier. Sámr pointed at the river, "Stig and Arne were on watch and they spied some small fishing ships. They are beached just a mile upstream from us. Tonight, we take the ship's boys and four chosen warriors. We steal the boats. We will fill them with kindling. If you are right and there is a barrier of boats then we make fireships and set them loose. The men of Portus Cale then have a choice: they try to put out the fires or they flee. I am gambling that they flee."

Erik Short Toe said, "And even if they do not flee, they can hardly fight the fire and us. I will use *'Heart of the Dragon'* to batter a way through." He looked at me and nodded his approval. "It is a good plan, Jarl Dragonheart."

"It is but make sure you are rested. I will organise a defence of the wagons. It will take time for you to bring the boats. We may be discovered before then." He nodded. "And, Erik Short Toe, we had better load the captives on the boat before they sleep. That will be one less thing for us to worry about."

After we had eaten and I had had a good drink of wine, I chose ten men to come with Haaken and myself. "We will sleep in the wagons. If any follow Baldr's trail or the tracks of the wagons then they will come here. We will bloody their noses. It will allow our men to organise our escape."

Haaken and I shared one of the wagons. I rolled myself in my wolf cloak. I heard him laugh, "What amuses you?"

"It is just that we have another fine saga here. I thought that this would be a dull raid. We would slay some warriors and sail home with treasure. Now I see that the Norns have spun an exceptional spell. Who

64

are these Franks that we rescue? What is their tale? What will we find in their land? Life is never dull with you, Dragonheart, and I can see that your great-grandson takes after you. He has impressed me. He makes good decisions." He hesitated, "Wolf Killer did not. Gruffyd did not."

I knew that Haaken was right. "Perhaps it is down to the place where he lives. Wolf Killer and Gruffyd both moved away from me and had a new home many leagues from the Water. Sámr chose to live close by me. He lives in the heart of the Land of the Wolf and he is surrounded by our spirits."

"Aye, Dragonheart, that makes sense. Perhaps this heralds a time of peace for the Water and our land." The breeze rustled the leaves of the trees but I knew what it was. It was the sound of the Norns and they were spinning.

Haaken and I woke up at the same time. It was not quite dawn but first light was not too far away. We had both had a great deal of wine and nature demanded that we rise. We walked towards the edge of the wood to make water and it was as we lowered our breeks that we heard, in the distance, the sound of hooves. When nature had taken its course, we hurried back to the wagons. I woke Haraldr, "The enemy comes. Go and rouse the camp. We will give them a surprise here."

We had taken the bows from the first hall we had raided. We did not have a large number of arrows but we had enough. We each took a bow and a handful of arrows. The bows were more like the Saami bow than the ones we normally used. I pulled the string. It was hard to pull. These were powerful weapons. I picked up an arrow and nocked it. They were long arrows with tapered arrowheads.

"We wait at the edge of the woods. No one looses an arrow before me. They may pass us by."

Lars Long Nose shook his head, "Jarl, I was one of the last in the column. The wagons made great ruts in the ground. Even at night, they will see them."

I nodded, "Then all the more reason to give them a shock. They will be confident. Send every arrow we have at them and then head back to the drekar. That is my command. Sámr and Erik Short Toe have had warning. They will be ready." I wondered if Sámr had managed to steal the fishing boats. We were all expecting a great deal from him.

The sound of the hooves was drawing closer. Then they began to slow. It was dark but I saw the shadows moving along the road. A voice shouted something and a second answered it. It was infuriating that we did not know what they were saying. Lars was right. They had seen the tracks. I had an arrow nocked and I drew back the bow. The Arab bow was so close to a Saami bow that it felt familiar. The arrow was a little longer than I was used to and I pulled back further than I might have with my own weapon. I felt the power of the bow. I would not be able to hold this for too long. Then I heard a command. The horses sounded closer as they moved from the road and brushed through the undergrowth. We were forty paces in from the edge and I sheltered behind a large tree. As soon as the shadow appeared before me, I released. The others were waiting for the sound of my arrow hissing through the night and there was a flurry of noise as arrows brushed leaves on their way to their targets. I nocked another. I thought I had hit my first target but the shadow still moved and so I sent my second arrow. This time I saw him fall from the saddle. I sensed a movement behind me and I turned, nocking my last arrow as I did so. A horse's head was less than two paces from me. My arrow hit the horseman in the chest and threw him from the saddle. Another rider followed him. I saw his spear come towards me. I had no time to draw my sword and I had no more arrows. I swung the bow at the horse's head. My hand jarred with the contact as the bow smacked into the horse's head and the animal reared. I was in great danger of being clubbed to death by its hooves. I rolled to one side and, as I stood, I slipped the bow over my back. I saw that Petr Arneson lay dead. A spear protruded from his body. I took out Ragnar's Spirit.

All around me I could hear the sound of men and horses moving through the woods. I had given my men an order and I had to hope that they had obeyed it. I disobeyed my own order and waited. It was an Ulfheonar trick. You remained still even though every particle of your being cried for you to move. I saw a riderless horse. It was close to me. I moved over to it and took its reins in my left hand. I led it towards the river. I hoped that I would be invisible. They would see the horse and not the man hiding in its shadow. I passed the bodies of some of the dead horsemen and, ahead of me, I could hear the sound of battle. I walked. My years of experience had honed my senses. I could see, by dawn's early light, that Ráðgeir had a shield wall before the drekar and arrows were thinning the riders who had found us. A voice in my head shouted a warning. I let go of the horse and, holding Ragnar's Spirit in two hands, whirled around. I was just in time to see a rider with a plumed helmet lunge at me with his spear. I stepped to my right and swung my sword. I hit his oval shield. It was not as well made as mine and I heard him cry as first the shield and then a bone in his arm broke. I did not wait. I ran after the horse and the distracted rider.

I heard Erik Short Toe shout, "Back aboard the drekar!"

A flurry of stones and arrows smashed into the Moorish and Arab horsemen who raised their shields for protection. In that moment Ráðgeir shouted, "Second rank, board. Front rank, one step back!" I saw that Haaken and Haraldr were in the front rank.

I could not see Sámr. Where was he? I had no time for speculation. If I did not break through their ranks then I would be marooned amongst my enemies. I was under no illusions as to my fate. The rider I had wounded could not control his horse and I ran after it. The horse ran through the enemy horsemen. They did not look behind them and I made for the gap.

Ráðgeir shouted, "Back aboard!"

As my men threw themselves into the drekar Ráðgeir stepped forward and, swinging his sword hacked through the head of the horse with the wounded rider. It was at that moment that one of the Arab horsemen turned. He saw me. I must have shocked him into immobility for he did not move. Running at him I hacked across his back and his scream alerted the others. I was twenty paces from the drekar.

I heard a voice shout, "It is the Dragonheart! He lives!" Ráðgeir stood his ground. I would not die alone. I heard hooves behind me. The worst thing to do would be to turn around and I braced myself for the blow. I spied hope. There, standing on the gunwale, I saw Erik Galmrsson. He was whirling his sling. He let it go and I watched its flight. I was sure that the stone would hit me but it did not. I heard a crack and a neigh from behind me. The sound of the hooves stopped.

Reaching Ráðgeir I turned and saw that the stone had hit a Moor in the middle of his head. He had been killed instantly and his body had pulled the horse over. Eager hands pulled the two of us aboard. I crashed to the deck and then the larboard oars pushed us away from the bank.

I looked up and saw Haaken One Eye. He shook his head, "The only one not to obey Dragonheart's orders was Dragonheart himself! I cannot take my eyes off you for a heartbeat can I?" He reached down and pulled me up. "And now you had better come and watch your great-grandson and the other young fools. They have four fishing boats and they are ready to fire the enemy fleet!"

Chapter 9

I ran with Haaken to the prow. I saw that the captives were huddled at the prow beneath the canvas. For them, this must be their worst nightmare. They were being saved from those who would have killed them by those who normally raided them! The Norns had been busy and their threads stretched as far as from one world to another.

We turned and walked back through the rowers to the steering board. We now had fewer men at the oars. Not every chest was manned. Some had died on this raid and some were in the fishing boats which raced ahead of us. I saw that there were two men in each fishing boat and they just wore breeks. They had no mail and no weapons. I guessed that they had a flint or a pot with lighted coals. Haaken was right, they were fools but I was proud of Sámr for he was doing what I would have done when I was younger. Erik Galmrsson brought me a horn of ale. We had found some in the hall. It was for the servants but we would drink it.

"Thank you, Erik Galmrsson. I owe you a life."

His face lit up into a broad smile, "I have the honour of being the one who stopped a warrior from hurting you."

"Nonetheless it shall be repaid, now climb the prow and tell me what you see when we turn the last bend of the river before Portus Cale."

He ran and I emptied the horn of ale. The mast was still on the mast fish. The crew were rowing. Our losses and the fact that eight of the crew were in the fishing boats meant that we were just single-oared. The current helped us but the wind did not. Nor would the wind help Sámr's fireships.

I walked to the steering board. Erik Short Toe shook his head, "When Haaken One Eye came back alone we were sure that you had finally fallen. Sámr had left to fetch the fishing boats and I was just wondering how I would explain your death to him."

"I was never in danger but I am grateful that Erik Galmrsson has such a good eye and a strong arm." We turned one bend and I knew that there was just one to go. "I have sent him to the prow to see what awaits us."

"It may be nothing. They might not be as clever as you or Sámr." Erik Short Toe was a sailor. He was not someone who thought of strategy. The men of Portus Cale were such men.

"We have hurt them. We raided the Emir's hall. He was wounded. The Franks who live north of here are flexing their muscles and he cannot afford to have the people he controls rebel. He wants his captives back and he wants our heads on pikes along his walls."

"And we sail to Tui?"

"If we can pass the mouth of this river then aye, we do. I gave my word and we have been promised a reward."

"I do not trust Franks."

"Nor do I, Erik Short Toe, but if there is treachery then we will be in the heart of their land and vengeance will be sweet. The Norns sent the captives to us. We have to follow the thread. We have upset the Sisters enough of late."

"Aye, you are right there." He nodded, "Here is Erik and the last bend is there."

Erik was breathless from his run down the drekar, "Jarl, they have boats strung across the river. They have hawsers binding them together. There are armed men on both banks and on the ships."

Erik Short Toe asked, "How big are the ships?"

"One is as big as we are and the rest are smaller. Sámr Ship Killer and his boats are sailing towards the largest ship."

I nodded, "Then let us help. Haaken, fetch your sword. We may have work to do."

Ráðgeir, who rowed the nearest oar, shouted, "Aye and let us sing. We will tell these Moors that Vikings are in their river and they are not afraid!" He began to sing.

It was a simple song but one we used when we wanted speed and that was what we would need. We would follow the four fire ships into the hole that they made and we would smash a hole in the barrage.

Push your arms
Row the boat
Use your back
The Wolf will fly

Ulfheonar
Are real men
Teeth like iron
Arms like trees

Push your arms
Row the boat
Use your back
The Heart will fly

Ragnar's Spirit

69

Guides us still
Dragon Heart
Wields it well

Push your arms
Row the boat
Use your back
The Heart will fly

Erik Short Toe shouted, "Ship's boys. Have ropes ready for the swimmers!"

As we passed the cowering captives, I gave them a smile. They had no idea what was going on for Baldr was in the fishing boat with Sámr. The hurried plan I had concocted with Erik was to sail between the large ship and the smaller ship to her steerboard side. Sámr and his fire ships would be, hopefully, setting fire to the larger ship. Haaken and I would try to sever the rope which bound them. That was the plan. It was flimsy but Sámr had set us on this course when he had decided to raid beyond Portus Cale. The raid had brought more success than we could have dreamed of but there was a price. We were entrapped in a Norn's web. I glanced across at the furled sail. Perhaps when we raised the mast and the sail then Ylva and Kara's spell might negate the Norns.

Ahead, I saw that the fishing boats were having to tack against the wind. Arrows flew from the ships. A bobbing boat was a hard target and the sail and the mast got in the way of their missiles. Even so, Ketil Ingarsson was struck in the arm by an arrow. He would struggle to swim. We were gaining rapidly on the fishing boats and that helped for the archers switched to us. As the fishing boats neared the line of ships so the effect of the wind was lessened and the powerful current drove them forward. It was then that Sámr and the other boys lit their fires. Their boats were close enough now so that they would be bound to foul the larger ship. I watched as Sámr and Baldr waited until their mast and sail were on fire before they jumped overboard. They were just five paces from the moored ship when they did so and their boat struck first. As the fire burned through a rope so the oil-covered sail flew into the air and attached itself to the bow of the ship. Flames licked around the ship's prow. In this climate, the wood dried and would burn quickly. The hull of the fishing boat was filled with kindling and as the fire took hold a wall of fire leapt up the strakes of the large ship. I saw that Ketil was being aided in the water by Arne and Sven but I could not see Sámr nor Baldr. Where were they?

70

Erik Short Toe moved the steering board a little towards the swimmers and shouted, "Stop rowing!"

The delay in our reaching the ships would allow the fires to grow. All of our fire ships had struck. The ship's boys hurled their ropes as far as they could throw them. Six young warriors held the ropes but where were Baldr and my great-grandson?

"Row!"

And then I saw them. They had swum to the next ship along from the one which was burning and using their knives they were sawing through the hawser between the burning ship and the smaller dhow next to it. I saw men on the dhow aiming bows. I ran to the larboard side and, grabbing a spear which lay there, hurled it the thirty paces to the dhow. I was aided by my height and the fact that the wind kept the tip up. It plunged down and struck an archer in the shoulder. As he fell the others turned and their attention was diverted. Sámr and Baldr swam away from the converging prows.

Then our bow hit the rope. Baldr and Sámr must have weakened it enough for *'Heart of the Dragon'* to break it as Erik shouted, "In oars!" We did not want oars shattering on the dhow. There was a sickening crunch as our hulls came together and the dhow's strakes splintered. Men fell overboard as the small dhow was destroyed by the sheer weight of our ship. I heard screams in the water and hoped that they were not the screams of Baldr and Sámr. I turned and ran down the centre of the drekar. Haaken hurried to the young warriors who had been hauled aboard. Ketil would need help. Erik shouted, "Out oars! Row!" My men glanced up at me as I ran. They had not seen Sámr and Baldr hauled on board like the rest. They knew why I ran.

I saw the burning ship begin to settle lower in the water. The Arab longphort was shattered. The ropes still held them to the banks and there was none of them big enough to tackle a drekar filled with Vikings. As I neared the stern, I saw that Arne, Stig and Erik had ropes out and were peering over the stern rail. What had they seen?

As I neared them, I heard Arne shout, "Pull!" and they began to haul on the ropes. Reaching the gunwale, I saw that they had caught two human fish. Sámr and Baldr climbed up the stern. They had survived.

Erik Short Toe shouted, "They live!" The crew cheered.

I helped Sámr over the side and hugged him, "You had me worried!"

"I am sorry, great grandfather, but I knew that the rope would stop you. How is Ketil?"

I laughed, "He lives and you are a leader now for your first thought is for your men." I swept an arm behind us. "The Emir will remember the Vikings who came. I do not think that others will find this as easy a target as we did. He will build more towers and have ships capable of fighting drekar."

Baldr, who was draped in a cloak given to him by Arne, shivered as he shook his head, "Easy?"

Erik Short Toe nodded, "Aye, Baldr, we have had to extricate ourselves from more difficult places. Had they had bigger ships then we might not have succeeded. I know you lost warriors but, as the Dragonheart will tell you, they were fewer in numbers than we might have expected. We have a hold filled, almost to overflowing, and a drekar which is still sound."

I nodded, "And when you are dressed and warmed you had better go to our guests and explain what has happened. They were terrified during the escape."

We had all day to reach the sea and we slowed down the rate at which we rowed. By the time we reached the mouth of the river noon had passed and we stopped where the current and the wind kept us in one place. We raised the mast and then the sail. I heard gasps from the women captives as they saw the wolf. It was incredibly lifelike. Erik turned the steering board and we headed north towards Tui. With the wind from the west, we would not have to row although the voyage to the north would not be as swift as we might have liked. We would sail up the coast at a gentle pace.

Another of the captured barrels of ale was broached and the last of the bread we had taken was eaten along with cheese and ham. I went with Sámr to join Baldr and the captives. We took food with us. The women still viewed us with suspicion but I saw respect in the eyes of the men. I said, "Baldr, ask him how far up their river we will have to travel."

I noticed that there was less confusion and explanation when they spoke. Their understanding was growing. Baldr said, "He said that it will take two days to row up the river."

"And ask him how we stop his countrymen from attacking us."

This time the conversation went on longer. Eventually, Baldr nodded, "He says that he and his son will stand by the dragon. They will wave to let the people know that they are safe."

Sámr seemed satisfied but I was not so certain. The Norns had spun and we would have to live with whatever they threw our way. Even if we received no more treasure the raid had achieved all that we might have hoped. Sámr had shown that he could lead. Already he had done better than my son, Gruffyd, who had tried a similar raid in Om Walum and been captured. We had grain, spices and treasure. True, we had no slaves but we could always find slaves. Sámr's men had been blooded. The ones who survived, all fifteen of them, would form the core of his crew when he led alone. As I sat with Haaken at the steering board and watched the sun set over the Unending Sea I wondered if this would be my last raid. If I was to truly hand over the reins of power to Sámr then it ought to be. I was too far from Wyddfa, Úlfarrberg and the spirits of home to make a good decision. We had many days yet to travel to reach the Land of the Wolf. This raid was not yet over.

We reached the mouth of the river after many hours of sailing. While we had sailed north along the coast, I had spoken, through Baldr, with the captives. From Sunifred Borrell I learned much. He was an important lord. The Count of Barcelona had arranged a marriage for him with an Asturian heiress. She was the beauty who clung to her son's arm. I was surprised that her relatives had not tried to rescue her. Using Baldr to translate I bluntly asked the question. He had smiled sadly as he had answered. Baldr said, "Sancho of Pamplona is a rival of Wilfred the Hairy. This marriage was to end the enmity between the clans. The Count must have delayed in paying the ransom for them which was demanded by the Emir. When they return to Tui, he will be forced to give Sunifred that which is owed; an estate and the ransom which was promised."

I had seen then why the Moors had not been driven from this land. I had seen nothing in their weaponry to suggest that they were invincible but the divisions between the followers of the White Christ were helping the followers of Islam. I was glad that we had no such divisions in my clan. Ragnar and Gruffyd accepted Sámr's position and that was good. The only danger we faced was the Danish threat and that was on the other side of the land.

I also learned much about the geography of the land. The river upon which Tui lay was called the Minho. Sámr and I had amended our maps for he volunteered much information. We were rescuing him and his family but who knew if we might raid again in this land?

The entrance to the river was narrow but then it widened so wide that we could barely see the other banks. The wind helped us and the estimate of two days to progress up the river proved to be totally inaccurate. We had waited outside the estuary until dawn and we reached Tui by sunset. Our fears were proved groundless. There were few places along the river with enough people to threaten us. There were terraces of vines and olive trees and animals grazing but no towers. Tui was different. It had a citadel high on a hill and I would not have liked to assault it. The gates were barred and the walls manned as we tied up at the quay.

The captives looked much healthier than they had when we first rescued them. Sunifred and his son had even made an attempt to speak our language. As we were tying up, he spoke to Baldr and Baldr turned

73

to me, "Lord, Sunifred says that he hopes he can continue this friendship with us. He likes the way we fight and he sees honour amongst us even though he thought we were barbarians."

I was not insulted. I knew from Atticus how those from ancient cultures viewed us, "Tell him that the men of the Land of the Wolf never forget a friend but we live many leagues to the north and I do not think that our paths will cross again."

He had nodded and I wondered if I had roused the Norns once more.

We did not dress for war. None wore mail. Baldr and Sámr wore their finest clothes. I did not bother for I had brought only plain tunics. Haaken and I went with the captives along with Sámr and Baldr, to the citadel. Our men were less than happy that we were placing ourselves in danger but I doubted that they would try to harm us. Although we wore no mail, we kept our swords

I let Sámr walk with Baldr and Sunifred at the head of the small column. I stayed behind the women. We passed through the streets of Tui. One wide avenue led to the gates of the stronghold. We saw no faces for the people hid behind their doors. I saw a square and guessed that there would be a market. When we reached the gate Sunifred spoke to those on the wall. The conversation took longer than I expected. Was there trouble? Sunifred had implied that he would be welcomed with open arms and that appeared not to be the case. Eventually, the doors creaked open and we were admitted.

Inside the walls, the stronghold looked like the ones we had seen in Frankia. This one had stairs leading to an entrance halfway up a wall. The guards were well-armed and they viewed us suspiciously. I observed them. Who knew if we might have to fight our way out? They had pot helmets, short swords, small round shields and each of them held a spear. They wore no mail at all. Only two had leather jerkins studded with metal. They would not cause us much trouble if we had to fight our way out. When we reached the main hall, the captives were admitted but the four of us were forced to wait outside. Two guards watched us.

"What is wrong, Baldr Witch Saviour?"

"I do not know. I did not pick up all of the words but I gathered that Sancho of Pamplona is away in the east fighting Moors and the town is ruled by his nephew Pedro Theon. I got the impression that he was not pleased to see Sunifred."

Haaken smiled, "Then we may get to raid this town of Tui. The citadel may be well protected but the town is open. Without ships, we could raid all along the river."

Sámr shook his head, "Before we go to war let us see what Sunifred can do. We gave our word and I would not like to go back on it without good cause."

I had said nothing but I was proud of Sámr. It was why he would lead the clan whereas Haaken would have been a disastrous leader.

We heard raised voices from within. The arguments seemed to rage for quite a while. Eventually, the door opened and a servant gestured for us to go in. Without being told I guessed which of the men was Pedro Theon. He was little older than Sámr and wore very expensive clothes. His fingers were bedecked with jewels. His hands looked as soft as a woman's. He was no warrior.

Sunifred spoke to Baldr. The conversation went on for some time. The occasional glances thrown in the direction of Pedro Theon told me that he was being referenced. Baldr nodded and turned to us, "It seems that the temporary ruler of Tui did not expect Sunifred and the others to return. They thought them dead. It will take time to sort matters out. Sunifred begs our indulgence and asks us to be patient and wait on the river. He will let us know when matters are resolved."

Haaken made to speak but Sámr interrupted, "Tell Sunifred that we are happy to wait but we will need to buy provisions at the market."

Baldr translated and Sunifred nodded and spoke. "He says of course and he will have ale, wine and food sent to us. He says he knows how to be a civilised host even if his nephew does not." The lord we had rescued was embarrassed by the actions of his countrymen.

As we headed back to the ship Baldr elaborated, "There is more to this than Sunifred spoke. Count Ordoño of Asturias is related to Sunifred's wife and when the Count's name was mentioned I saw fear in the eyes of Pedro. I fear there is treachery afoot."

I nodded, "I could smell it in the air. It will do no harm to spend a few days here. After the collision, Erik Short Toe will wish to examine the drekar and it might be interesting to buy in their market. We have coin enough and it will save us having to call at Bruggas or Lundenwic."

Sámr nodded, "Is this another lesson about being a leader, great grandfather?"

"It is, this one is called patience. Haaken here has none! Let us wait and see what the Sisters have spun for us."

Chapter 10

Although darkness had fallen, we made ourselves comfortable on the quay. It must have been built by the Romans for it was made of stone. We lit a fire there and men laid their blankets and cloaks on the stones for beds. Erik Short Toe had the old sail brought out and made into a shelter. It would be for the sun rather than the rain. Ketil was still recovering from his wound as were three others. This would help them to recover. The ship's boys ran lines from the ship into the river so that we could fish and have fresh food.

As Erik Galmrsson tied his line close to the steering board, I approached the two Eriks. "Erik Short Toe, you told me that Erik Galmrsson, here, would be a warrior."

"Aye, I did but I also said that he was too small." Vikings spoke their mind and a true Viking never took offence at the truth.

I looked at the boy who was not the youngest of the crew but was the smallest. "Erik Galmrsson, I owe you a life and that life, if you will have it, is to live with me at Cyninges-tūn and be my shield bearer while I train you to be a warrior. You have no father and I would be as a foster father to you."

His eyes lit up and he nodded, "Aye, Jarl Dragonheart. That would be an honour!" He looked at Erik Short Toe, "Would that be agreeable to you, Captain?"

Erik Short Toe grinned, "Aye! You are a good enough ship's boy but you do not love the sea. A sailor has to love the sea or he will come to hate her. Go with my blessing. If we need you on the voyage home then you will still be a ship's boy."

"Aye, Captain."

I put my hand on the boy's shoulder. "Then, Erik Shield Bearer, your first task is to take my fur ashore and make me a comfortable bed."

"Aye, Jarl!"

Erik Short Toe said, "That was kindly done but I fear you will have much work ahead of you."

"And with Sámr well on the way to being trained then I will have the time. Our threads are entwined and I can do nothing about that besides, I like the lad. I was left alone with Old Ragnar. I will try to do for Erik what Ragnar did for me."

The next morning, we were rewarded with fish taken from the river. We ate well. I went with Erik Shield Bearer, Baldr, Sámr and Haaken to the market. We had silver in our purses. We might be viewed with suspicion but the burghers of Tui would happily take our money. We needed food but also some of the items they produced that we could not get at home. Both Nanna and Aethelflaed had complained about the poorly made cracked pots they had to use. We found some good clay pots. I had feared that we might be charged exorbitant prices but, perhaps, the sight of our beards and swords deterred them. We spent the morning spending coin. When I found a carved spice box which, despite the high price I paid, was worth it, I bought it. The other lay beneath the ground with Uhtric. Sámr used much of the coin to buy wine and food for the crew. It was another lesson in leadership; a good leader looked after his men. I was pleased when he found a local fletcher and bought a hundred arrows to use with the Moorish bows we had captured. The fletcher had them sent to the drekar and we sought refreshment.

We found a place with tables outside where they served ale, wine and food. We sat for I was keen to observe the town. Sunifred's words were a warning. We might have to fight to get that which we were owed. We had finished our food and the jug of ale and, having paid, were about to leave when we saw a Frank riding a horse. He was followed by an armed retainer and leading four pack horses were two slaves. I recognised, by their dress, that they were Norse. They still wore sealskin boots. Their beards and moustaches, although untrimmed were still the mark of a Viking. The confirmation came as they stopped by the square. One of the horses was limping and I saw one of the two thralls bend down to examine the hoof of the horse he was leading. I saw his hammer of Thor dangling. The Frank spoke the same language as Sunifred. He came from this area. One of the Vikings said something and pointed to the horse. In reply, he was given a tirade of what sounded like abuse and was then smacked about the head. The armed guard took out a whip and began to beat the man.

I turned to Baldr, "What did the man say?"

"I did not pick up all the words, Lord, but I gather that the horse has a stone in its shoe and has become lame. The Asturian blames the slave."

"Asturian?"

"He has the same accent as the Lord of Tui."

The Norns were spinning, "Come, Baldr. Sámr and Haaken, watch our backs! Erik, stand clear." The two of them stood and moved to the side. I strode up to the guard with the whip and as he lifted it, I grabbed it and tore it from his hand. The Asturian shouted something and the guard went to draw out his sword. I might have seen more than sixty summers but I had been fighting for my life for long enough to react quicker than he did. As his sword came halfway out of its scabbard, I grabbed his hand and arm and brought my knee up to snap his right wrist. The blade rattled to the cobbles. The Asturian lord looked shocked.

"Tell him, Baldr, that I do not like to see slaves ill-treated and I do not suffer men to draw weapons on me."

Baldr spoke and the man spat out a vitriolic reply. The guard held his arm and glared daggers at me. I was not worried. Baldr smiled, "He says he will have you whipped and then your head placed upon the walls of the town."

I turned to the Vikings, "Do you wish your freedom?"

"Aye, lord, but this is Lord Aloitez and he is a powerful man. He knows the Count of Tui."

"And I am Dragonheart. I care not who he knows. I bow the knee to no man. Baldr, tell the man I will buy these slaves from him." After Baldr had spoken the Asturian shook his head. "Then tell him I will take them from him and he will be out of pocket."

Behind him, I saw men approaching from the stronghold. They were dressed in the livery of the nephew of Sunifred. Erik Shield Bearer said, "Should I fetch more men, lord?"

Haaken One Eye laughed, "For these overdressed apologies for warriors? I think not."

The four men arrived and Lord Aloitez began to shout what sounded like orders. To his surprise, the leader of the guards shook his head and then spoke. I saw the two Viking slaves smile as he did. I looked at Baldr. "He said, Lord, that you are not to be harmed. This is by order of the Lord of Tui."

The Asturian was obviously not happy and he mounted his horse and shouted to his guard. The two Vikings began to move. I said, "You two stay here."

They looked from me to the Asturian and then, letting go of the reins of the horses, walked over to us. The Asturian shouted at them and they answered. He shouted something else and the guards from the stronghold led the animals away.

Haaken rubbed his hands, "More ale. Baldr, order it if you would. We have guests!" He turned to the Vikings, "I am Haaken One Eye. If you have heard of the Dragonheart then you have heard of me."

The elder of the two nodded, "We have heard of you both. I am Aðalsteinn of Orkneyjar and this is my sister son, Dagfinnr. We are grateful to you but you know not whom you anger. This lord knows the Count of this land. He has power. As he left, he said he would have our left legs hamstrung as a punishment."

I nodded, "Sit and tell me your tale. Let me worry about upsetting Franks!"

They nodded and, nervously, sat. Haaken poured them some ale and after they had swallowed what must have been their first decent ale in a long time, Aðalsteinn of Orkneyjar wiped his untrimmed moustache and began, "We sailed and raided with Jarl Thorfinn Eysteinsson. We had a bad winter and my wife and sister died. Dagfinnr's father had been slain in a battle with the Picts and so we decided that Orkneyjar held little for us save sad memories. We signed on with the Jarl. We raided the Hibernians. It was hard fighting with little reward and then we heard of the Clan of the Horse. Hrolf the Horseman and his son, Ragnvald, were having success against the Franks and we joined them for a season."

Dagfinnr shook his head, "It was a good life there for the winters were kind and the Franks could not withstand the ships and horses of the Clan. We would have been there yet except that the Jarl fell out with Thorir Thorsten. He was a Hersir and close to Hrolf the Horseman. It was our Jarl's fault but we suffered for it. We left the Haugr and sailed south. We raided the rivers of the Franks for a season. We survived but that was all. Many of the men believed that the Jarl had been cursed. None turned against him but ..."

I nodded, "I know. When a leader makes bad decisions then it sucks the heart out of the men." I did not look at him but Sámr knew the comments were meant for him. I now knew why the Norns had sent these Vikings into our lives. They were another lesson and it was not one which I could teach to Sámr. He had to hear their tale.

Aðalsteinn of Orkneyjar continued the story, "We met a drekar which was heading north. It was a Dane and they had raided this land. Their hold was filled with treasure and they had many dark-skinned slaves. They said raiding was easy in the land conquered by the Moors and we believed them. The Jarl led us south. We all agreed that it was better than raiding the Franks. We sailed until we found a wide river. There were few settlements for the first twenty miles but then we found unguarded farms and monasteries. The mistake we made was raiding a house of women." He looked at me, "You know, the ones who cover their bodies and heads in layers of clothes?"

I nodded, "They are called nuns." We had captured two, Deidra and Macha. They became part of our clan. The followers of the White Christ held such women in high regard.

"Aye well, it brought the wrath of the Franks upon us. We had not seen any warriors and the Jarl thought that there were none. He was wrong. Dagfinnr and I were lucky. We had been tasked with loading the treasure from the holy place in the hold. There were six of us and the rest of the crew had left with the Jarl to raid again. We watched as horsemen swept in from every direction. The Jarl and the crew made a shield wall but it merely delayed the end. The ones who did not die in the battle were butchered after and their bodies were dismembered. I think that saved us for they had satiated their anger. They came to the ship and surrounded it. Ulf was the jarl's uncle. He was like a foster father to the Jarl and he told us to surrender. Our deaths would not bring glory. We did so and were enslaved. They burned our drekar and took us far to the north. The Lord you angered bought us. He is a cruel man. Ulf died soon after we arrived. He was beaten to death by Lucidiol, the man whose arm you broke. The others died in the last few years. I think the fact that we were related was the only reason we survived. We had each other to hold on to. We would not blame you if you left us for we are cursed. We have had no luck."

Sámr said, "Then your luck has changed now." He turned to me, "Dragonheart, let them touch Ragnar's Spirit."

Sámr was clever. I did not believe that the men were cursed but they did. Touching my talisman might be the act that they needed to break what they saw as a curse. I took out the sword and gave it hilt first to Aðalsteinn. His eyes widened as he touched the blade and he felt its power. He handed it to his nephew. Dagfinnr almost recoiled when he touched it. "Is this magic?"

"It is the Allfather's work."

Erik Shield Bearer said, "Lord, I think that they return." He pointed and I saw Lord Aloitez, Lord Sunifred, his son and ten guards marching down towards us. There was no sign of Lucidiol.

Baldr rose and greeted Lord Sunifred when they reached us. Lord Aloitez glared at us. After a short conversation, Baldr said, "Lord Sunifred wonders why we attacked Lord Aloitez and his man and why we stole his property."

I smiled and laid my purse on the table. "Explain to him what happened, exactly what happened!"

Baldr grinned, "Aye, lord." He began to speak. Dagfinnr interrupted at one point to clarify some word which Baldr had said wrongly. Then Lord Sunifred spoke to Lord Aloitez. When the lord replied he almost spat out the words. It was obvious to me that Lord Sunifred was of a higher rank. The Asturian nodded and hung his head. Lord Sunifred spoke to Baldr. "He says you can have the slaves. They are worthless anyway."

I emptied the purse onto the table, "Tell him to take what he thinks they are worth."

Baldr translated and I saw the look of incredulity on the faces of the two men. Lord Aloitez took half of the coins. Lord Sunifred said something and Baldr said, "He said that is too much!"

I shook my head and gave him half of the remaining coins, "Tell him now it is enough for I know the value of real warriors!"

Lord Aloitez grabbed his money and left with the guards who had been unnecessary. Lord Sunifred said something to Baldr. "Lord Sunifred would like to speak with you and me in private."

I was not happy about leaving Sámr and the others out of this but I guessed that whatever he had to say was not for the ears of our two new men. I nodded and said, "Haaken, spend the rest of the money and then take the new men back to the drekar. I think we may need to keep watch tonight."

"Aye, Jarl Dragonheart.

I rose and followed the lord and his son to a quiet corner of the square. He spoke quietly and urgently to Baldr. Baldr nodded and then conveyed the message to me, "He fears that you may not receive the reward you should. His nephew is the reason they were taken in the raids. He colluded with the Moors. He lied to Sancho of Pamplona and Count Ordoño of Asturias. He believes that their lives are in danger."

When he had finished, I asked, "How does he know this and what does he intend to do about it?"

I could see that Lord Sunifred expected a different reaction from me. He spoke again and this time it was a longer conversation. Baldr had to interrupt him a few times to clarify words. "He says he knows for there are women of the house who were loyal to his wife. They fear for their lives but they told the Lady the truth. As to what he wishes to do he says he can do nothing. He has no men here and he believes that his nephew let you have the slaves for he thinks that you will leave when there is no chance of a reward."

"Then he does not know me. Ask him does he want us to deal with his nephew?"

When Baldr translated he was asked a question. "He says, what do you mean, deal with?"

"Tell him that I can take Pedro Theon prisoner and Lord Sunifred can hold him until Count Ordoño returns. I am guessing that not all of the men are loyal to his nephew?"

After an exchange, Baldr said, "No. He says there are those who are still loyal to him."

"Good. Then tell Lord Sunifred that this is what we will do." I explained my plan. Both father and son nodded for I needed his son to help make the plan succeed. I knew that Sámr would not be happy about it for it was a risky plan. It relied on the men I led being better than the ones we faced in the stronghold. We parted after clasping arms and I headed back to the drekar with Baldr.

"You will only need six men to go with you, Jarl Dragonheart?"

81

"Let us just say that I would like more than six but the plan will not succeed with any more. We have to be invisible and we have to get into the citadel quickly." I stopped, "This is risky, Baldr. If you think you cannot do it then I will take Aðalsteinn or Dagfinnr. They have the words."

"I am happy to be coming." He laughed, "I do not think that Sámr will be though!"

Chapter 11

Baldr was right, Sámr was not happy. I finally got him to calm down when I pointed out that if anything happened to me it would be up to him to get the rest of the crew home. He accepted it albeit reluctantly. I chose the two Hafþórrsson brothers, Haraldr Leifsson and Ráðgeir Ráðgeirson to come with me. They were all big men and could think on their feet. We just took swords and daggers. Helmets, mail and a coif would be unnecessary. We left once it was dark. We headed up the river and then cut back across country to approach the town from the north side, the side away from the river. A great deal depended upon Sunifred's son, Guiterre. He was younger than Sámr. He had been a captive for some time. If he failed then we might be captured and that would be a disaster. We went to the north side for there was no gate there. The rocks upon which the wall was built were like a cliff. We would need help to ascend. Guiterre would throw down a rope and we would climb into the citadel.

We reached the far side of the walls. We knew how to scout and we peered into the dark to identify where the sentries watched and patrolled. The sentries on the wall had a brazier at each corner. We waited in the shadows and watched as the solitary guard on our wall patrolled up and down. It soon became quite clear that there was just one. When he reached the tower, he seemed to spend some time at the brazier. There he spoke to the sentry from the east wall. Guiterre would have to wait until the sentry took a rest or relieved himself. We were just fifty paces from the walls and we would have to react quickly. This was why I had only brought six men with me. Even the seven of us might be seen.

We did not see the youth but sharp-eyed Baldr spotted the rope as it snaked down the wall. "There!"

We ran. I was the slowest but not by much. Haaken struggled too. Baldr reached it first and he held the rope tight to enable the others, who were much stronger, to ascend first. The four of them did it so quickly that by the time Haaken and I reached the wall two were on the fighting platform and two were almost at the top. I held the rope to allow the other two to climb and when Baldr reached the top I started to climb. Suddenly I found myself rising through the air as the two Hafþórrsson brothers hauled me up.

When I reached the fighting platform Ráðgeir was walking towards us. "I have laid out the guard and tied him up." He shrugged, "He was an old man."

"Baldr!"

Baldr spoke urgently to Guiterre and then pointed to the left. We let them lead the way. I did not like it for I was reliant upon someone I did not know but we had no choice. When we reached the bottom of the steps Guiterre held up his hand. He peered around and then gestured for us to follow. The corridors were lit by torches in sconces. It made for areas of shadows between them. Although it was nighttime, it sounded as though people were still awake. I heard laughter. I doubted that the laughter emanated from Guiterre's father. I worked out that we were on the floor above the great hall in which we had been received. That meant we were on the floor where people slept. It was an enormous citadel. We passed through two doors. We had not seen any sentries. I suppose that made sense. They had the walls protected. Why should they guard the inside?

I saw Guiterre stop at a door and listen. He frowned and hurried back to Baldr. He whispered in his ear. Baldr came to me and spoke quietly, "He said that Lord Theon is not in his chamber. He thought there was something odd when the guard was not at the door. They must be downstairs in the hall."

This was a complication. I whispered, "Tell Guiterre to fetch his father and as many men as he can trust to the Great Hall. We shall have to confront them there."

He nodded and while he told Guiterre what to do I drew my sword and the others copied me. From now on I would lead. Guiterre hurried off back down the corridor. We walked ahead. We opened the door and the noise became much louder. The light was brighter and we could feel the heat from the room. We had no idea how many people were there. It could be four or five. Equally, there could be twenty. I had six men with me and one was a youth. This would not be easy. I saw the top of the stairs ahead. They followed the west wall. I gestured for the others to remain where they were and I slipped along the shadows to the head of the stairs. The top corner was also in shadow. If any looked up then they might see me but I had to have an idea of what lay before us. I did not run. I moved along the back wall as slowly as I could. There was a balustrade which overlooked the hall. As I moved, I saw a table through the pillars and there were twelve men seated around it. Two servants stood by the fire but their attention was on the table. I recognised Pedro Theon and Lord Aloitez. The others were unknown. They were drinking and at least half were drunk. I saw two with their faces in their platters. There was no time to delay. As I started to move down the stairs, I waved for the others to follow. Baldr would be the last, Ráðgeir would see to that. He was not experienced enough to be at the fore.

I made it halfway down the staircase, which was both long and wide before I was seen. It was a servant who spied me. I saw his eyes widen and, as his mouth opened, I hurried down the last few steps. He shouted something and pointed. All eyes turned to me. Only Benni and Beorn were with Ráðgeir and in sight. The other three were still at the top of the stairs. With the exception of the servants, the two drunks and Pedro Theon, every hand went to a weapon. They rose and lurched towards me. I drew Wolf's Blood and as the first sword came down towards my head, I blocked it with my sword and used Wolf's Blood to rip through the tendons of the man's right hand. The blade fell to the ground and I pushed him from me. The sound of cries, the clash of steel and the shouts of the Lord of Tui would bring others. We had to have him in our hands by the time help arrived.

"Baldr, take the Lord of Tui!"

"Aye, lord."

Two men came at me. They had seen how I had dealt with the first one and they came at me from two sides. They had had a great deal to drink and they saw my grey hairs. Even with odds of two to one I had an advantage. They would be overconfident. As they both lunged, I held out Wolf's Blood and I slashed with Ragnar's Spirit. While I did so I stepped forward. I was rewarded by both my blades striking theirs. My step forward allowed me to pass them and spin around and I swung Ragnar's Spirit at the lord to my right. He was confused by my movement and his sword struck the air while mine scored a long line through his upper arm. As the second lord tried to take advantage and slash at me, I blocked the strike with my dagger and, bringing my weapon down point first, stabbed him in the thigh.

Lord Aloitez tried to make use of what he thought was my distraction. I sensed his movement and I whirled to fend off his sword with my own. He saw I had a dagger and he drew his. It looked like good Spanish steel. I did not worry. Mine had been made by the finest blacksmith in the Land of the Wolf. He tried a sweep at my head while stabbing with his dagger. I parried his sword with my own but I did not try to block his stabbing blow. Instead, I turned my body and the blade slid into my tunic merely grazing my side. In my left hand, I held Wolf's Blood. I flicked the razor-sharp blade up and ripped through the muscles of his left hand. The dagger dropped. He was shouting at me. I had no doubt they were curses. All around us, the lords were losing to warriors who were fitter, better trained and sober. It was an uneven contest. My fear was that more warriors would be summoned and we would be outnumbered. I did not wish for any deaths. Already my plans had gone awry. A death would only complicate matters. I would incapacitate the lord and end the battle.

Lord Aloitez had fear in his eyes. He began to flail rather than strike at me with his sword. If I had been able to speak his language, I would have told him to surrender. I could not and we fought on. I blocked his sword with mine. He made the mistake of trying to turn and force my sword hand down. My left hand, holding Wolf's Blood, was held out for balance and, as he turned, he stepped into the end of the dagger. His eyes widened when the tip touched his flesh. He compounded his error for he tried to move away and merely succeeded in enlarging the wound as it tore a long line across his belly. He staggered away and sat on a chair at the table. He tried to stem the flow of blood with his right hand. I saw entrails mixed with the blood. I had, accidentally, gutted him. I had not meant to do so. *Wyrd.*

Six men were down as Lord Sunifred entered. He had with him his son and the other two men who had been rescued by us. Along with them were a bishop and two warriors. He shouted something. As he held up his hands, I saw that Baldr had his sword at the throat of Pedro Theon. The other lords laid down their swords. The bishop raised his crozier and began to speak. He pointed at Pedro Theon who seemed to shrink before the cleric's gaze. When he had finished speaking Sunifred pointed at Pedro Theon and the two warriors went to him and carted him away. Two priests came in to see to the four wounded lords. Lord Aloitez was beyond salvation. He was dead.

I looked and saw that my men were all intact. We had not suffered wounds. The Bishop and Sunifred spoke and then they waved Baldr over.

Ráðgeir came to me, "That was easier than we might have hoped, Jarl Dragonheart."

I shook my head, "I am not sure about that. The Norns were spinning, Ráðgeir. I had planned on capturing the Lord of Tui without recourse to killing. I have slain an important man. He may have deserved death but, I fear, it has put us in danger."

Beorn snorted, "Jarl Dragonheart, a Viking who is not in danger sits in Valhalla, drinking."

After wiping the blade on my bloody tunic, I sheathed my sword and did the same with my dagger. Erik Shield Bearer would soon have his first lesson in cleaning and sharpening a blade. The others sheathed their weapons. While they waited, they went to the table and began to eat some of the food and drink the wine. They were warriors. Fighting gave them an appetite. I saw the priests look around to watch them. Distaste was written all over their faces.

Haaken came to me. He handed me a goblet of wine, "I watched the man die, Dragonheart. You could have done nothing about it. You did not try to kill him. It was as though some force pushed him onto your dagger." He sipped the wine and nodded approvingly. "Could it be the spirits? Was it Aiden?"

I shook my head, "I did not sense his presence. The man was foresworn and perhaps it was his panic or, more likely, the Norns. When we rescued the captives, I thought it was good fortune but now I see it was a lure from the Sisters to entrap us. This voyage is not over yet. We have eighteen miles to get to the sea. Until we see its waters I will be armed and ready."

Baldr came over. He sighed, "Lord Sunifred thanks you. The death of Lord Aloitez has made things more complicated, lord. He asks us to return to our ship, board it and await his men. He will send that which he owes at dawn and then you must leave."

Beorn had heard the last part, "We run away? Why? I have seen nothing here to make me fearful. We could take this town with the ship's boys."

I shook my head, "Peace, Beorn. We came here not to raid but to honour an oath we made at Portus Cale." He nodded and I turned to Baldr, "What was the purpose of the Bishop's presence?"

"He was an important part of Lord Aloitez's plans, lord. He arrived this afternoon and heard what Lord Theon had done. He had been told that Lord Sunifred was dead. It was Lord Theon who told him. He is foresworn. The Count may be angry with us but not Lord Sunifred." He shook his head, "I think that they will blame us for this. The death of Lord Aloitez will be laid at the door of Vikings. The family of Lord Sunifred and the Bishop will know different but these are dangerous times. If word got out that Lord Theon had conspired with Moors to have Christians kidnapped then it might make the Count's position untenable. He is planning an invasion of the land to the south. He is away, at the moment, gathering men. They will compromise and Lord Sunifred will regain the power that was lost."

I nodded. It was *wyrd*. We had done nothing wrong and yet we would be blamed. Perhaps it was for the best. Beorn was right. We could easily take this town. Perhaps, one day, Sámr could return with ships and take all of the treasure of this town. "Come, let us return to the drekar. This night's work is done."

As we left, I saw that my men had taken the larger pieces of meat and a jug of wine. None tried to stop them. My men deserved it. We left the castle and walked through an empty town to the drekar. Lights burned at the quay and I saw guards. Sámr had heeded my words. He must have been watching from the drekar for he joined us. He looked happy to see us.

"I feared the worst. All went well?"

I shrugged, "The Norns were spinning. Baldr will tell you. I need to speak to Erik Short Toe." Nearing my captain who lay asleep at the steering board, Erik Shield Bearer jumped up. "Find me a clean tunic from my chest. This one is bloody."

"Aye, lord."

I shook my captain awake. "Aye, Dragonheart?"

"We will be leaving this morning. We have outstayed our welcome. We await some chests and then we go."

"We are ready. I will tell the boys. All went well?"

"It went the way the sisters determined it would." Erik returned and I took off my sword belt. "Clean the sword and the dagger and then sharpen them." He nodded. "Be gentle with them. They are older than you are." I took off my tunic, my boots and my breeks. Naked, I dropped a bucket into the river and then sluiced away the blood and sweat of the battle. It was not my steam hut nor was it my water but I needed to be cleansed. Turning the soiled tunic inside out I dried myself and then donned the fresh tunic. By the time I was dressed dawn was breaking. Sámr and the crew were aboard and the ship's boys were scurrying around.

Haaken came over to me as Arne and Erik Short Toe prepared for sea, "The barrels of water and ale are secured?"

"Aye, Captain.

"We have more cargo to come aboard, remove the decking at the prow. There is space there." He turned to me. "How many chests will there be, Dragonheart?"

"I know not but however many there are that will be enough. It is an unexpected treasure. We should not worry about the quantity."

The fires ashore had been dampened and I had had my weapons returned when Guiterre and six men carrying three chests made their way through a town which was just waking up. I went to the gangplank with Baldr and Sámr. Guiterre spoke to the men who carried the chests aboard. I noticed that the chests were the same size as the ones we used to row.

He spoke to Baldr. Baldr replied and then spoke to me. "He says that his father is grateful for what you have done but his position now, as Lord of Tui, means that he cannot be associated with the men who attacked the Count's stronghold." I nodded. "He sent the chests to make any prying eyes think that these belonged to you. They contain silver and spices. They are not filled with coins." I smiled. That would have been too much to ask. "Guiterre says that he is sad that we will not meet again for he admires us and you especially. You are older than his grandfather who walks with a stick and cannot see his own feet. You are a great warrior. He hopes to be as great as you are one day. He wishes to drive the Moors from his land."

I stepped forward and held out my arm, "Farewell, Guiterre, and good luck."

He could not have understood my words, save, perhaps, his name but he smiled and clasped my arm. He said something. Baldr said, "He wished you good luck and God speed."

I laughed, "Aye, Baldr, but whose god?"

He then spoke to Baldr and took out a leather bag. He handed it to Baldr. They clasped hands and he stepped from the drekar.

The six men had returned ashore. Sámr shouted, "Ship's boys, prepare to cast off!" We had no one on the shore to untie us and so the boys would untie and then leap back aboard. The three of us walked up the gangplank and then Sámr and Baldr pulled it aboard. The four ship's boys untied the ropes and then leapt to the side. They clambered over the gunwale.

Erik Short Toe shouted. "Out oars!" The steerboard oars pushed us off from the quay and the current took us. Once we were clear of the bank Erik shouted, "Row! Haaken, a steady beat."

Sámr and Baldr each had an oar. The two new members of the crew also had an oar. This would seal them into the clan better than any initiation ceremony. They shared an oar and were next to Baldr and Sámr. My great-grandson had learned the subtleties of command.

I turned to Erik Shield Bearer, "Fetch me a couple of the bows we took from the Moors and a dozen or so of the arrows we bought. Have the ship's boys keep a good watch on the steerboard side. Until we reach the sea then we are in danger."

Haaken came over to me. "You think there will be trouble?"

"Let us just say that I have an uneasy feeling. There are ten lords who will wake this morning and they will have wounds, cuts and bruises. They will have hurt pride. They will want vengeance. I hope that their wounds and thick heads will keep them in Tui but until we reach the sea then I will be vigilant."

Erik brought us the bows and the arrows. Haaken said, "The two of us defend the drekar?"

I laughed, "We have done so before. Besides, I just hope to discourage any who try to attack us. We saw no ships on the way up. An attack has to come from the land."

Haaken nodded, "The current is strong and the men are rowing well. How will they catch us?"

"We waited for dawn before we left. They may not have. They have good horses. They could be ahead of us already."

We saw no sign of any enemy as we slowly sculled down the river. The current was sluggish. We would raise the mast and sail once we reached the wide, open expanse of water close to the narrow entrance. As we neared the lake-like mouth, I began to believe that my fears had been groundless. Then I saw them. The horsemen had ridden to the low cliff which overlooked the mouth of the river. There the river was less than a hundred paces wide. They could hurt us.

I went to Erik Short Toe. "We need to stop. If we raise the mast and yard we can use just half of the crew to row through the gap."

"Half the crew?"

"Aye, the other half will need to use shields. Remember these people know how to use bows and they can rain death upon us."

"Aye! In oars. Raise the mast."

We would continue to drift towards the mouth and the water was wide enough that we were in no danger of grounding. Sámr came towards me, "Can they stop us?"

I nodded, "The entrance to this river is so narrow that they could send rocks down the cliff. If we grounded or were struck then they would fall upon us. I intend to have half of the crew protecting the other half. It will mean we travel through slowly but we might be able to escape unscathed if Haaken and I can deter them with arrows. I will issue the Moorish bows to the ship's boys. We have enough arrows for them and we can hope that we have luck on our side."

"I did not think they would follow."

"I hoped they would not but, all the way down the river, I have dreaded the worst. You should know that the Norns are mischievous and vindictive. Rescuing Ylva, Gruffyd and Mordaf from their clutches has not enamoured me to them. I am lucky that Odin favours me. Now organise the men with the shields. You choose the ones to row and the ones to be the protectors."

The mast was locked into position and, with reefed sail, the yard was hauled into position. As soon as we cleared the river mouth, we would release the sail and head north and west. Once we had sea room we could turn north and east and take advantage of the southwest wind which blew.

I shouted, "To your oars. Ship's boys, take a bow, nock an arrow." As the boys grabbed the powerful bows we had captured I watched Sámr organise the rowers. He was using just eight oars on each side. It made it easier for our men to protect them with shields. We had no such luxury. We would have to stand on the steerboard side, towards the prow, and endure whatever they sent at us. A helmet would merely have restricted our view. Added to this the ship's boys had no helmets. It was unfair for us to be protected and the boys not.

Erik Short Toe saw that the oars were ready and he shouted, "Row!"

This time we did need a chant and Haaken, as he strung his bow, began it. It was the song of Haaken and me and our rescue of Ylva. It was one of the two sagas he particularly liked. The other was Rolf's End.

The Dragonheart sailed with warriors brave
To find the child he was meant to save
With Haaken and Ragnar's Spirit
They dared to delve with true warrior's grit
Beneath the earth they bravely went
With the sword by Odin sent
The Jarl and Haaken will bravely roar
The Jarl and Haaken and the Ulfheonar
In the dark the witch grew strong
Even though her deeds were wrong
A dragon's form she took to kill
Dragonheart faced her still
He drew the sword touched by the god
Made by Odin and staunched in blood
The Jarl and Haaken will bravely roar
The Jarl and Haaken and the Ulfheonar
With a mighty blow he struck the beast
On Dragonheart's flesh he would not feast
The blade struck true and the witch she fled
Ylva lay as though she were dead
The witch's power could not match the blade
The Ulfheonar are not afraid
The Jarl and Haaken will bravely roar
The Jarl and Haaken and the Ulfheonar
And now the sword will strike once more
Using all the Allfather's power
Fear the wrath you Danish lost
You fight the wolf and pay the cost
The Jarl and Haaken will bravely roar
The Jarl and Haaken and the Ulfheonar

The drekar began to surge forward. The current aided us and the men had a song to sing. I saw the two new men as they rowed and struggled to hear the words and sing them. I concentrated on the horsemen on the low cliff. They had dismounted and I saw them moving large stones into position. Others took out bows. By shading my eyes, I was able to see them better as we neared them. There were at least four lords with them. They had the plume on their helmets. I guessed they were four of the ones we had bested the night before. I also thought I could see a warrior with a sling. I was not sure but it looked like Lucidiol. I had hurt him twice. I had broken his arm and taken away his paymaster.

I nocked an arrow for we were approaching the tiny gap quickly. The closer we came to the mouth the faster was the current. It made Erik's job harder. It was fortunate that we had no sail to obscure his view. He would aim for the middle of the narrow channel and he would not have the luxury of the ship's boys to guide him. They were defending the drekar.

The warriors on the cliff top, just thirty paces above us, had the advantage of height and arrows began to rain down on us. Stig was guarding Erik Short Toe with a shield for if he fell, then we were doomed. We were fortunate that there was no order to the enemy. They did not concentrate on one place. The arrows fell at the prow, where the rowers rowed and at the steering board. They had but fifteen archers and it was not enough for we could see the arrows coming down. The ship's boys were agile enough to evade them and Haaken and I seemed to bear charmed lives. I heard arrows thud into shields, the deck, the hull and the mast but there were no cries from our men. We were still too far away to be effective. I also wanted to do the most damage to their most dangerous of weapons, the rocks. Some of the ship's boys could not wait and they sent their arrows into the air. Most fell woefully short and I think that encouraged the Asturians. Arne, Haaken and I waited. We were less than a hundred paces from the shore. I could see the enemy clearly for the cliff was a low one. I saw two men pushing a huge rock towards the top of the cliff. They were pushing up a slight slope. Once it reached the top then its weight would send it crashing down the cliffside slope towards us. Other rocks were being moved as well. At best the rocks would send a wall of water towards us and that might swamp us but at worst they could strike the oars or the hull and that would be a disaster.

I pulled back and aimed at the rock. I had not used one of the bows before. The rock was a bigger target than the men behind and if I hit the rock then the arrow might be deflected and do some damage. I released. Haaken and Arne must have had the same thought for we all sent our

92

arrows at the nearest rock. I followed the flight of mine and saw it hit the top of the rock. It was close enough to one of the men pushing it for splinters to strike him. My arrow then flew up and into the side of one of the lords. It made all of them duck. I was not sure which one but either Arne or Haaken hit one of the men pushing the rock. He fell backwards and the rock rolled back, crushing the leg of the other warrior. The ship's boys were now in range. Their arrows still fell a little short but I saw one hit one of the rocks and it deflected sideways to strike another warrior.

I sent another arrow at the next rock and, as I watched it arc, I saw that one rock had been pushed over the top. It careered down the slope. It hit a patch of rocks at the bottom and threw them in the air. They landed ten paces from the drekar's prow. Water fountained in the air and the distraction cost Stig his life as an arrow struck him in the chest and pinned him to the larboard strakes.

We were now level with the warriors and they managed to send more stones over. We were closer now and I had the measure of the bow. I could not see the rock pushers but I could see the plumes of the lords. One of my arrows must have hit one for he staggered forward clutching the arrow in his neck and then plunged over the cliff. Erik had managed to put the steerboard over to take us away from the rocks but, even so, one rock struck the oars, shattering three of them and sending splinters of wood into two oarsmen. The rest sent a wall of water to us. It was like a small tidal wave and it flooded over the stern of the ship.

"Raise the sail!"

Haaken and I ran, with Arne, Erik Shield Bearer and the other ship's boys to release the sail. The arrows still fell but we were beyond the rocks. I heard a cry as the wolf sail was released. Haaken One Eye had an arrow sticking through his leg. He was a warrior and he continued to pull until the sail was billowing.

I ran to him. "Lie down and let me get this arrow out."

He lay down and smiled up at me. "It makes a change for me to be the one with the wound. Be gentle eh, Dragonheart, I am an old man!" he laughed, "Like you!"

I joined in his laughter. We were warriors and we were alive. I snapped off the arrowhead and then pulled the arrow back. I saw Haaken wince and grit his teeth. The blood spurted, "Erik Shield Bearer, fetch me vinegar, honey and a bandage."

While I tended to his wound Haaken said, "Now we just have to venture far to the west, avoid Syllingar, the men of Wessex, Om Walum, Hibernia and Walhaz and then we will be home!"

I laughed, "Is that all?" We were alive and life felt good.

Then I saw that the ship's boys were looking at Stig's body. I had forgotten the death which had been the price of our escape. I walked to Erik Short Toe. "Let us bury this hero and send him to the Otherworld. Has he family?"

"A mother."

"Then she will have Stig's share and more."

We buried Stig in the blue seas off the coast of Asturia. I saw Erik Shield Bearer. He had tears on his cheeks. When we resumed our course, I called him over. "Sometimes, Erik, a price must be paid. Stig was that price. It is sad but inevitable. The Norns spin and cut threads."

"Aye, I know."

He was upset and I wondered how I could rouse his spirits. Baldr and Sámr had replaced their oar on the mast fish. They had finished tending the wounds of those injured in the attack. I was just happy that they had not been injured by the splinters when the rock had struck us. Sámr came over to us and Baldr followed.

"You were right great grandfather, they came for us."

"Always expect the worst, Sámr, and you will rarely be disappointed."

Baldr handed Sámr the leather bag that Guiterre had given him. "What is this?"

"Guiterre paid attention to the drekar, Sámr Ship Killer. He knew you wanted one. It was his gift to you."

Sámr opened the leather bag and took out an hourglass. We had not found one on our travels. Now the gods had sent us one. *Wyrd*!

Part Two
Danish Vengeance

Chapter 12

The journey home was a long one. We had to fight winds from the south and west. We had to endure storms and rain. We had buried Stig and the memory of his loss made us all determined to get the other boys home safely. Haaken's leg did not begin to heal until we had passed Ynys Môn. Both of us knew this was a sign of our age. When we were younger, we would have laughed off an arrow in the leg. Now we knew that Haaken would have a wound which would make him limp and ache in the cold.

It was on the last part of the voyage that I spoke to Erik Shield Bearer. He had been quiet since we had left Asturias. I took him to the steerboard side of the prow so that I could see Wyddfa while we spoke. I found it a comforting presence. "So, Erik Shield Bearer, you have been silent for some time. Are you having second thoughts about living with me and being my shield bearer, if so, then I release you from any obligations? I do not want to force this upon you."

He shook his head vigorously, "No, Jarl. I want this more than anything. It is just that I wonder why Stig had to die. He was my friend. He was excited for me when I became your shield bearer. And now he is dead. He was the only one to die. Why was he chosen and not me?"

I was relieved that this was the issue. It was common in young warriors after a battle. Death seemed remote when others were dying but when those close to you fell then you recognised your own mortality. "He was unlucky or, perhaps, the Norns decided that his thread was to be cut. Any of us could die. The arrow which struck Haaken could have hit his chest or neck and then he might be dead. As I said when we buried him, the Norns always wish a price to be paid."

"But you have lived a long time. Why are you not dead?" He suddenly realised what he had said. "I am sorry, Jarl Dragonheart! Forgive me! I did not…"

I held up my hand, "I am not offended. Know that when you carry my shield and tend to me that I like honesty as I will be honest with you. I have died. When I went to Miklagård I died and saw Valhalla but Odin decided it was not my time. Your time or any of those on this ship's time could be today, tomorrow, or next year. We do not know. That is why we live for the moment. We know that life is precious. Do not grieve for

Stig, that cannot help either of you, instead rejoice in the times you had and remember those. Aiden, the galdramenn, died not long ago and not a day has gone by that I do not think of him but it is not with sadness. It is with the joy of what we did together and the belief that one day I shall see him again. I have lived a long time but that does not make it any easier to lose those that I cherish." I pointed northeast. We could just see the land of Mercia beyond Caestir. "The sight of those lands means that within a day we shall be home. You will fetch your goods from Erik Short Toes and we will ride north to Cyninges-tūn."

He took a step back, "Ride? But I have never ridden!"

"Then that is something to look forward to and when you sleep at night you can tell Stig for he will be in the spirit world and he will envy you that you learned to ride and he did not."

"But if I fall off?"

"Then you will mount again and hold on tighter. You learned to scale the mast. You will learn to ride a horse. You will learn to use a sword and spear. You will make a shield. In short, Erik Shield Bearer, you shall become a warrior and I hope that I live long enough to see the transformation."

We had been away for a long time. The voyage out and the voyage back had each taken many days. We had spent longer in the land of the Moors than we had planned. It was more than a moon since we had left. I saw my son's and grandson's drekar were both tied up at the quay. That meant they were only recently returned and their ships had not been sent to the shipyard to be maintained. My son and grandson were at home. It was not long after noon as we approached Whale Island and I knew we would be seen. Those families who had crew on board would come to the quay to meet us. The days of Astrid, Elfrida and Bronnen coming to greet me had long since passed. I did not mind. They had their own lives and an old warrior coming home safely was not something to be celebrated. The wind was with us and the crewmen were able to prepare themselves. Those with wives and mothers washed themselves down and combed their hair. It would take up to two hours for us to actually land. We had time aplenty. Others sorted out their chests. The treasure would be taken to Cyninges-tūn. I would divide it up and the crew would come for their share when they were ready. The exception would be Erik Short Toe and his ship's boys. They would get their share first. Stig's mother would receive his payment. It was no compensation for the loss of a son but it was better than nothing and I would see that she was given extra. As we had arrived back so early in the day the majority of the crew would travel to Cyninges-tūn with me. Only two warriors lived close to Whale Island. Most of them came from my town or the land to the south of it. I knew

96

that Ragnar and Gruffyd would be unhappy but I had much to tell Kara and Ylva. I needed to know if they had dreamed.

Aðalsteinn of Orkneyjar and Dagfinnr came over to speak with me after Erik had gone to secure my chest. "Jarl, we owe you our lives and we thank you for bringing us here to the Land of the Wolf but we have nothing save the clothes your men gave us. We have no home and we have no coin. We have not a sword between us!"

"Not true, my friends. You have your share of the treasure from Tui."

"But we did nothing!"

"Who knows? Perhaps if we had had two fewer men rowing then the horsemen with the bows might have caught us. I am Jarl Dragonheart and it is my decision. I know that Sámr, my great-grandson, will not object. As for the other things. My great-grandson and I both have large halls. There will be room for you. We have a warrior hall in Cyninges-tūn and as for swords, helmets and weapons? I have enough to equip a shield wall. You are now in the Land of the Wolf. You are of the Wolf Clan and we look after our own. That is our way."

They smiled their gratitude. "Thank you, Jarl. It is good to be in a clan once more. We have seen how your men fight for one another. It is good."

We were now less than a mile from the tricky entrance to the harbour. This was not the time to make mistakes and Erik Short Toe reefed the sails so that we barely edged in. We nudged in gently to the quay and the ship's boys scurried ashore to tie us to the shore. Sámr stood aside so that I could be the first down the gangplank. I shook my head, "You were the leader. To you goes the honour."

He walked down the gangplank and was greeted by his father and brother. Gruffyd and Mordaf were not there. Their hall now lay some way out of Whale Island. I was not surprised. I was disappointed but not surprised. After Ragnar had greeted his son and when I had stepped ashore with Haaken he said, "When we saw the drekar we sent word to Kara, Ylva and Atticus. The raid went well?"

I nodded, "I daresay Sámr will tell you all. For myself, I need to get back to Cyninges-tūn quickly. I need to have conference with my daughter and granddaughter. I will give Erik and his boys their share and then we will leave. I beg your understanding."

I saw that he was disappointed. Sámr showed his new maturity. Despite the fact that he wished to get back to Aethelflaed he said, "Baldr and I will spend the night here and we will tell you all although I fear we will not do it justice. For that, we would need Haaken One Eye."

"You are too kind" Haaken loved praise. It was like pouring pig fat onto a fire! It made it burn fiercer.

I returned to the drekar. Erik Short Toe had gathered all of our treasure, grain, wine, ale and chests on the quay. Ráðgeir and my men had brought horses and wagons from Ragnar's hall. They began to move the cargo from the quay. I opened one of the larger chests we had been given at Tui. We had two identical ones and then another three chests we had taken from the hall of the Emir. "Is this enough, Erik?"

"It is too much."

"No, it is not for you were a teacher as well as a captain. And besides, you will need coin for *'Heart'*. She took some damage on this trip."

"Aye, like all of us she is getting tired."

I clasped his arm, "Farewell, my friend. Erik has gone to say farewell to your wife."

"Aye, she will miss him, I will miss him. I know that you will care for him."

I smiled, "I cannot thank you enough for what you did for Sámr."

"Jarl, it is no more than you did for me and when he has a son then I will be honoured to train him too… if I am spared." A breeze came from the south. The Norns were spinning.

By the time Erik Shield Bearer returned with his bag of belongings we were ready to move. Erik and I did not ride, we sat on a wagon and had a leisurely journey home. We were fortunate for we reached the Water just as the sun began to dip behind Old Olaf and we saw the Water bathed in a golden light. It was a magical moment. I took it as a good sign. The land welcomed back the warriors of the clan and all was in harmony. Erik looked ecstatic. He had never been this far north before. His family had farmed north of Úlfarrston.

The ones who lived south of my home left us as we passed their homes. By the time we reached the walls of Cyninges-tūn, we had lost a third of our number. Karl Word Master and Cnut Cnutson greeted us. Haaken had left us to go to his home and I saw the worry on their faces as Karl asked, "All went well, Jarl?"

I knew what they meant. "Aye, Karl, we have lost no more Ulfheonar. Haaken took an arrow in his leg and I daresay that will become a saga which we will all endure at Samhain!"

They laughed for we all knew Haaken. We liked him for despite his bombast there was no truer warrior.

"Your daughter said that you would be tired and would need your rest. She will see you on the morrow."

I nodded. That was good for it meant that she had not dreamed of some disaster to greet me. "Have some men unload the grain and food into the granaries and the rest into my hall. Atticus can make his scratchings on the parchment. Come, Erik, let me show you your new home."

Atticus and Germund awaited us at the door. Both looked pleased to see me but I saw them looking curiously at Erik. I was used to his diminutive stature but they were not. "This is Erik Shield Bearer. He will live with us." I nodded to Germund, "This is Germund and he was a Varangian Guard. He will help to train you. Erik here would be a warrior."

Germund was a Viking and he was blunt. He nodded, "Good, I like a challenge!"

"And this is Atticus. He will teach you to read, play chess and use your mind. He was Sámr Ship Killer's teacher."

Atticus gave a mock bow, "And you look young enough for me to mould. Come, we have food waiting."

"Germund, there will be treasure, spices, weapons and pots. Put them somewhere safe until Atticus can make an inventory of them. We have a short time to divide them up."

We entered my hall. Had Erik not been with me then I might have gone across the Water to visit the grave of Erika and to speak with Aethelflaed but I remembered when I had been a little younger than Erik and sent to Old Ragnar's house. I would not have liked to be alone with strangers. He knew me and I had to stay with him. We sat at the table in the middle of my hall and I saw him looking around. This was both grand and new to him. It would take some time for him to become accustomed to it. I would need patience.

As we waited for the food he asked, "Do you live with just Atticus and Germund?"

I nodded, "I had a wife but she died and I had a servant who lived here from the day we first raised this hall but he is dead. I seem to outlive most people."

"The crew said you are the greatest Viking to have walked the earth. Is that true?"

I shook my head, "I am just a warrior who does the best he can for the clan."

"And I am of your clan now?"

"You are. All who choose to live in the Land of the Wolf are in the Clan of the Wolf."

He beamed, "That is good!"

Atticus brought in the food and the ale. I saw that he had watered it for Erik. This was not the food of Uhtric but I liked it. I watched Erik frown as he tasted it. I smiled, "One rule here is that you have to clear your platter. I remember when I was a slave and had little to eat. I remember those days."

"But what if I don't like it?"

"It is good training for when you are a man. A man has to endure many things he does not like. A real man gets on with it and the others complain."

Atticus sniffed, "It is called free will! If the boy does not like my food, I will cook him something else."

"No, you will not."

There was steel in my voice and Atticus nodded. "Do not worry, Erik, you will get used to it. It is good food."

"I am sorry, Atticus, I should not be so ungrateful."

That moment bonded the boy and the old Greek. Germund asked me about the raid. His lame leg prevented him from raiding but he still enjoyed the tales of heroics. Atticus was also interested in the land for the land of his birth and the followers of Islam had been enemies for many years. He did not seem to mind our paganism but the fact that the Moors, Seljuk Turks and Berbers either converted or killed Christians somehow appalled him. I said nothing although I suspected Christians might have done the same. My people did not mind another's beliefs. A belief was personal to a man.

Germund said, "I would be interested in seeing one of these bows, lord. Are they like the Saami bow?"

I nodded, "We brought a number back with us."

Atticus smiled, "They are called a composite bow and they use different woods and horn to give strength to the bow. That is why they are shorter than the bows the clan makes and uses."

"All I know is that they are powerful. So, Germund, I task you with helping Erik Shield Bearer become stronger and then training him to use the sword and shield."

Erik looked crestfallen, "You will not be teaching me, lord?"

"No, Germund would be the better teacher. He learned properly. The tricks I use are self-taught. Besides, I have much to do. My work to prepare Sámr to be the leader of the clan is only just begun. We have made a good start."

Atticus asked me about Sámr's progress. After I told him he added, "We have kept an eye on Aethelflaed and Nanna. They seem happy enough. Your daughter and granddaughter visited every day." He shrugged, "Of course that might have been to visit the grave of Aiden."

"No, Atticus. They need not visit his grave to speak to him. Kara will speak with him each night."

I saw the scepticism on Atticus' face. He believed in heaven but not in the communication between the Otherworld and ours. To me, it seemed obvious. Christian dead would wish to speak with those they loved. Perhaps Christians had lost that connection. That was sad.

"And so, we have more spices. How will you divide them, lord?"

"We will keep a quarter and I want you to divide the rest up. We let those who wish the spices take them. Whatever is left will go to Kara. I have a new cedar wood spice chest. It has a key and you shall have it."

Germund laughed, "I fear, old friend, that you will be working long hours for the next few days. I have never seen so much treasure and coin."

Erik Shield Bearer bobbed his head, "I will help you, Atticus, for I think that the jarl will not need his shield bearer for a few days."

Atticus laughed, "I can see that you have wit and wisdom. I will be glad of your help and you are right. The jarl will speak with his people for that is his way. They will wish to see and speak with him. He is a talisman. He is the clan. This hand over of power to Sámr will not be as easy as you expect, Jarl Dragonheart."

"I know. I now have to temper the steel that will become the sword tip of the clan. Sámr must become as strong as Ragnar's Spirit."

That night, as I lay in my old and familiar bed, I did not sleep as well as I might for I dreamed. That was not a surprise. I had been away from my home for some time. The last dream had been Wyddfa.

I saw Úlfarr the wolf. He padded down from the top of Úlfarrberg. His long legs ate up the ground and he ran towards Grize's Dale. I saw him sniff the ground around the remains of the hall in which Wolf Killer and Elfrida had first lived. His ears pricked and he looked around. I saw his hackles rise and his teeth bared. Suddenly he leapt at a figure who was hiding in the undergrowth. His teeth fastened on to a Dane. The Dane had the skulls of small animals hung from his neck. Úlfarr's teeth sank into the throat of the Dane and blood spurted. An axe came from nowhere. It took Úlfarr's head and the head of the Danish skull taker. I could not see the Dane's face. A hand reached down and picked up the wolf's head. He held it up and turned around. It was Sven the Boneless. Around him, Danes rose in numbers beyond count. They began to bang their shields rhythmically. In an instant, I was a hawk in the sky and I saw them flooding across the Land of the Wolf. Flames preceded them. An arrow soared from their midst and I could not avoid it. I began to fall towards the earth. It grew closer and closer. Then all became black.

I sat upright and I was sweating. I looked around. Had I screamed? There had been no sound in my dream. I rose and went to the jug and horn which stood on the table. I poured myself some ale and drank it. Úlfarr had been the wolf which protected Sámr when he had been young and he had died ensuring that he lived. I would see Kara for I had no doubt that she had seen my dream. Aiden had given me an insight into the reading of dreams and I saw that Úlfarr connected my great-grandson and my son but how did Sven the Boneless fit into this nightmare? I went back to bed and slept fitfully. I did not dare enter the dream world again for I feared what I might see.

Chapter 13

Atticus gave me a strange look as he served Erik and me the bread and cheese. "You dreamed last night, Jarl Dragonheart."

"I shouted?"

He shook his head, "I was not disturbed but your bed looked as though a battle had been fought and the jug of ale was empty. I recognise the signs."

I ate. Atticus was becoming more like a galdramenn each day. Had Aiden become a ghostly shapeshifter and taken over the Greek's body?

Erik asked, "Dreamed?"

I looked at Erik. I would dream again and I did not want the young boy to be afraid. "I sometimes enter the dream world and I see things which are more terrifying than battle."

"What can be more terrifying than battle, lord?"

Atticus asked, "How old are you, Erik Shield Bearer?"

"I have seen eleven summers."

He nodded, "You look younger. The Jarl is right. you need building up. I will serve you food to make you twice your size." He waved a hand as though to focus himself. "When you have seen a little more you will learn that there are terrors beyond battle. I have never been in battles but I know of terrors which still make me wake and shiver. I do not believe in the dreamworld of the Dragonheart but I do believe in the evil of man. If Jarl Dragonheart has dreamed then it means he is troubled and he will seek the advice of his daughter. And you and I will go with my tally stick and begin to count."

"Tally stick?"

Atticus rose, sighed deeply and shook his head, "I have much to teach you. Come let us make a start. Germund we shall need your brawn to go with my brain."

I finished my food and looked at Ragnar's Spirit hanging on the wall. I wondered if I should keep it in my bedchamber in the future. Odin had touched it and that might help me fight off the daemons of the night. I would ask Kara.

Getting to Kara's hall took longer than I hoped. My people were keen to speak with me. Bagsecg Bagsecgson had been my blacksmith. He had died some time ago but one of his sons, Haaken Bagsecgson, was still the weaponsmith for Cyninges-tūn. As I passed his workshop, he waved me over, "Jarl Dragonheart, did you bring any metal which might be reused?"

"The Moors and Asturians have good swords. I fear not. When Atticus has organised the booty, I will bring a sword so that you can see the quality."

"Good. My father taught me that a good weaponsmith is always learning. He improves his skill with each sword he makes."

"And I will need a helmet and a leather jerkin making. I have a shield bearer. He is small as yet but he will grow."

"Good. It is good that you have a shield bearer although your people worry about you, Jarl, you go abroad too much."

"You and I know, Haaken Bagsecgson, that I never choose to go from this valley. The Norns..."

He clutched his hammer of Thor, "Aye, Jarl."

I had four similar stops as I walked the five hundred paces to Kara's hall. I did not mind for all spoke with concern in their voices. It reinforced my determination to make the clan as strong as I could before I left it to Sámr.

Deidra and Macha had also died the previous winter. It felt strange to enter the hall and not recognise the women who served Kara and Ylva. Two of the women of the hall took me to the heart of the hall, the room where they ate. The fire was burning; it burned all year. They brought me ale and some cheese. My daughter's women made the finest cheese in the Land of the Wolf.

"You dreamed." Ylva's voice came from behind me and her hand was on my shoulder.

I was not surprised that she knew. She and her mother knew all that went on along the Water. "Aye. You dreamed too?"

"I saw the wolf die and the Danes."

"Where is your mother?"

"She went to visit Aethelflaed. She was summoned there last night."

A sudden fear gripped my heart. Had something happened to Aethelflaed? Was the dream to do with her?

Ylva smiled, "All is well, grandfather. She will return with Aethelflaed and Nanna. Their husbands will be here before noon. So, tell me all that happened in the hot lands. We had glimpses from the spirit world and we know of the deaths but they were young that died and only you saw all."

I told her everything and left nothing out. My granddaughter had even more power than her mother. Each year that power increased. She was descended from a volva and a galdramenn. While Sámr would lead the clan, Ylva would guard the land!

"I will not try to interpret your dream until my mother returns." She smiled, "Is Sámr ready to lead yet?"

104

I laughed, "You know that he is not but he has made huge strides. Most importantly my men trust him Beorn, Benni, Haraldr and Ráðgeir all follow him and know he will make good judgements. He still has much to learn but I know that when I am gone you will have your eye upon him."

"Is this your way of asking if we have dreamed your death?" I shook my head. "Well, we have not. As far as we know you still have many years to rule this land. But it is good that Sámr has made such strides." She poured me more ale, "Are you disappointed in Ragnar and Gruffyd?"

I gave her a sharp look. Had she been reading my mind? "A man can never be disappointed in his offspring. Wolf Killer did not turn out the way I hoped but I was never disappointed in him. The same is true of Ragnar and Gruffyd. I may have made Sámr my successor but I still love all of my children and that love is without limits. Perhaps the disappointment is in me."

"That you are not perfect? That is arrogant, grandfather. You are not a god, you are a man with all of man's foibles. You are better than any other man and that is why the clan is so strong. I fear that we have storms ahead and the clan will need that strength!" She held up her hand as I opened my mouth. "I have said too much and we wait on my mother."

We did not have long to wait. The three women arrived. I did not know why my daughter had been rushed across the Water for the two young women looked in the best of health. "You are both well?"

Both blushed and said, together, "We are."

Kara came over to kiss me on the cheek, "Do not worry, father. This is not warrior work." She turned to the two women, "If you would go with Ylva you can prepare the chambers you will use this night when your husbands return."

I said, "They will not return to their hall?"

Kara shook her head, "Father! Do you not think we wish to celebrate with Sámr and Aethelflaed? Is it just you who gets to enjoy Sámr's company?"

"I…" In the world of a shield wall and men, I always knew what to do and say but amongst women… it was as though they spoke a different language.

My daughter said, "Go. My father and I have much to speak on."

When we were alone, I was going to ask about Aethelflaed but Kara divined my thoughts, "Aethelflaed is fine and she is healthy. Your story is more important. You dreamed?"

"Twice. Once at Wyddfa and again last night."

"I know but I need to know exactly what you dreamed. I glimpsed only part of the dreams. They were sent to you for they concern you directly." I nodded. "And then tell me of the raid for that is important too. "

I told her all, I had learned with Aiden, that even the smallest detail was important. When I had finished, she nodded and went to fetch ale for us.

"Tell me about this Sven the Boneless. You saw him in the dream?"

"Aye, and he led Danes. When we went to Dyflin to avenge Erika and her family he was one of those who fought against us. I let him and his crew go but I told them that if I saw them again, they would die."

She sipped her ale, "You should have killed them all and burned their drekar. You are Dragonheart but sometimes I see a Christian heart instead and that may well be the undoing of you and, perhaps the clan."

"It is good that you are not a warrior for you are a hard woman."

"But I am a warrior. I am just a different warrior from a man. What is done is done. If it is Danes and if you saw them at Wolf Killer's old home then we know they are coming from the south and east. They will not be coming by sea. Asbjorn and the men of Windar's Mere gave up being Vikings long ago. The only time they raid and fight is when you command them. You must visit with them and warn them of the danger from the Danes." She smiled. "The spirits must want you to survive."

"How so?"

"They warned you that the attack will come when the Water is covered in fog."

"That happens often!"

"Not as often as you think and it is mainly in the winter or early mornings in summer. If the Danes risk the High Divide in winter then they are more foolish than I give them credit for. We warn Karl and Cnut and the rest of the watch to warn us when they see a fog. Better a disturbed night than a slit throat."

We heard laughter from the cooking area and the three women re-entered, "How is my husband? Is he well?" Aethelflaed paused, "Was he wounded?"

"They are both without wounds and both did well. Baldr's skill with tongues helped us and Sámr learned to lead. Both have come back rich. He has and I have much to divide."

Nanna said, "And the two of them stay at home now?"

I looked at Kara. Her face was impassive. "That is their choice. Sámr needed me to guide him on a raid. I have done that. Now what I need to teach him can be done here along the Water. I will not take him away but I know not what the Norns have in mind."

106

Each time I mentioned the Norns in the presence of a Christian they clutched their crosses.

Cnut Cnutson sent a messenger to tell us that Sámr and Baldr had been spied riding up the road next to the Water. "I will go and greet them."

There were fewer people to greet the two young warriors. Yesterday had been the celebration of our success. I felt sorry for Sámr but it was another lesson learned. He was the future leader. He was learning to balance the needs of the clan with the needs of his family. His mother, father and grandmother had needed to speak with him. He would have other days when he would ride in glory at the head of his victorious warriors.

Karl Word Master joined us, "It seems a lifetime ago since we marched up that road, Dragonheart. With Cnut's father at your side, we brought back riches and stories of great honour. I am pleased that I have had a life which is useful; watching your walls."

"Aye, and most of those warriors now sit in Valhalla where they tell those tales." I gave Karl a sideways look. "You wish that it had not been a wound but a glorious death?"

"I did when first I was wounded and then I married. My son now has three young bairns and I get to see them grow. Had I died then I would have missed that. I know I may not see them grow up but they have met me and when my son talks of his father, the Ulfheonar, then they will know what I look like."

Cnut nodded, "And Snorri's wife gave birth three months since. He does not know me yet but I will tell him of his grandfather when he is big enough. I will sing the song written by Haaken One Eye of when his grandfather was there when the god touched Ragnar's Spirit."

We spied the two men leading laden horses. There were four of Ragnar's men with them. They would return to Whale Island with the wagons and the horses. Sámr was doing as I always did when I returned. He was taking in the grandeur of the Water and the mountain. He was leading his horse for the last few hundred paces. When he neared me, I turned to walk between them.

"How are Ragnar and Gruffyd?"

"Envious of our success. Gruffyd had been proud of what he had taken but when he heard from my father how many chests of treasure were taken, he became silent."

"It is good that you did not bring up the matter. It would sound like boasting. Sometimes we are favoured when we raid and sometimes not. The two men we rescued told us that."

"Where are Aethelflaed and Nanna?"

"They are with Kara and Ylva. They are holding a feast for us and you are to stay in Cyninges-tūn tonight." I saw his face fall and I spread my arms. "I know but my daughter is a volva and one does not argue with a volva. It is for one night and Aethelflaed and Nanna seem happy about it." He seemed mollified. "Besides, I need your help to tally the treasure. Atticus and Erik Shield Bearer have been working all morning and they will continue for the rest of the day. Dividing treasure is a skill which all leaders need."

"You gave Erik Short Toe and his boys theirs?"

"Aye, as you know they always have the first of any treasure even before the jarl."

We had reached the hall of women and a slave waited to take the horses. Sámr turned to the men who had come from Whale Island. "If you spend the night in the warrior hall, we can send grain and coin back to my father." I looked at him. He shrugged, "We took plenty."

"I was not criticising. It is a good decision, but do not expect those who receive your bounty to be grateful. It does not work that way."

We entered the hall and I could see that Sámr was curious about the lack of a welcome from his wife. He did not know that Kara and Ylva were the mistresses of surprise. When we entered both Nanna and Aethelflaed were seated on a fur-covered bench and they were covered in flowers. Around their heads were garlands of flowers.

Sámr said, "But…"

Aethelflaed held out her hand, "Come, husband, and sit by me. You are to be a father."

Nanna held her hand out, "And, Baldr, so are you."

I looked at Ylva who shrugged. The late journey across the Water was now explained. While the two couples embraced, I moved closer to my daughter and granddaughter. "You have dreamed? This is good?"

Kara nodded, "Birth is always good. How a child turns out is up to the parents. What do you think, father? Is Sámr a bad man? Will Aethelflaed turn out to be evil?"

"You are right but I wondered if you had dreamed."

"We always dream. If you mean have we dreamed a bad ending then the answer is no. The children are not yet born and the Norns have yet to spin their threads. Ylva and I will weave a spell to protect them while they are in the womb and then another when they are born. The children will be as protected as any but once the Norns have spun then it is beyond our control."

"That is all that I ask."

While the six of them spoke, I drank ale and worried about Sven the Boneless. As a warrior I did not fear him I had beaten both him and his

108

master Garðketill the Sly. He had left with just one crew of men and they did not worry me. It was the Danes he might bring with him. I had put the noses of the Danes out of joint when I had gone to the aid of the King of the East Angles. They had been beaten by me there and when we led them a merry dance past Wihtwara. I had killed their witches and I had killed Egill Skulltaker. I had fought and defeated Sigeberht the champion of Lundenwic. They had reason enough for vengeance. I would not have worried save that I had dreamed and Kara confirmed my dream. The Danes were coming. It was just a matter of when. I took my leave of the six of them for it was late afternoon and I wished to speak with Erik and Atticus.

When I reached my hall, I saw that the chests had been emptied and the table sagged under the weight of coins, "I fear, lord, that our meal will be late this night. I have yet to make my tally and we have the table to clear."

I shook my head, "I came to tell you that Erik and I will not be eating here in my hall this night. Kara is holding a feast."

I had thought that the old Greek might be upset but he looked relieved. "Good for I can finish the tally of the coins and tomorrow, with your help, Jarl, we can divide it up. I can count it but I would not share it."

"Erik, we need to bathe. Both of us stink of sea, oil and sweat. Have you any decent clothes with you?"

He shook his head.

Germund said, "There are clothes, lord, in a chest in one of the storerooms. I am guessing they belonged to Lord Sámr or Lord Gruffyd."

"Excellent. Germund, take Erik and try on the clothes. Fit him with the best that there are. Then bring him to the bathhouse. Have the slaves heat the water."

As they left Atticus said, "He needs his head shaving. I am sure there is wildlife there."

"There may be but let us take one step at a time. The others will not notice. Do not put that thought in his head. He will be embarrassed enough about eating with so many strangers."

He nodded, "He is a good boy, lord, and willing to learn. He has a quick mind and picked up what he had to do in a heartbeat. It is why we have almost finished."

"Then finish for the night now. You and Germund need food and the wagons do not need to return to Whale Island until noon. There is time."

"No, lord, for I will rest easier if the task is complete. It is my way."

"As you will."

Germund was aware of Erik's nervousness and he came to the bathhouse to help my shield bearer. He made it seem easy and I was grateful. Germund had lived in Miklagård and understood grooming. He showed Erik how to bathe himself. When we emerged, he helped us both to comb and oil our hair. I did my beard and moustache myself. The tunic which Germund had found had been one which Wolf Killer had worn. It was silk and came from Miklagård. Germund had a good eye. Erik could not get over the softness of the fabric. Atticus wagged a finger, "Do not spill food on it! It is the devil's own job to clean it!"

As Erik did not know who the devil was the point was wasted. Walking through Cyninges-tūn, passing the homes of my people, Erik drew close to me. "Lord, I have not eaten at the same table as fine folk. Erik Short Toe and his wife ate simply." He swept a hand down his tunic. "I fear that I will do or say something wrong and I do not want to let you down."

I put my hand on his shoulder, "This is my family and they will do nothing but make you welcome. Listen and you will learn much. My daughter and her daughter are the two most powerful witches you will ever meet and yet they are the most gentle of ladies. You will enjoy this night."

As I had expected the night was joyous. Erik ate all that was put before him. He was polite and courteous and he listened. He was like one of those sponges we had seen in Miklagård. He soaked everything up. Ylva and Kara, as well as Sámr, were aware that Aethelflaed and Nanna did not need a warning of war. We kept to other matters. Baldr and Sámr spoke of the sons they would have and Ylva teased them by asking what was wrong with girls. She knew how to toy with them. As Baldr was called Witch Saviour because he had saved her life, she was gentler with him than Sámr. Sámr was a blood relative and she teased him until he waved his hands and shouted, "I surrender!" It was the sort of evening I wished I could have enjoyed with Brigid, Gruffyd, my son, and my daughters, Erika and Myfanwy. It was not meant to be. Brigid was always too concerned with the way the children ate and what they said. Erika and Brigid had fought all the time and Gruffyd had seemed sulky. Perhaps I was being rewarded for the patience I had shown and given, at the end of my life some pleasure.

I did not drink too much and, aware that Baldr and Sámr had not seen their wives for a month I left early. I did not retire when I reached my hall. We had brought back a barrel of the powerful red wine for which Portus Cale was renowned and Atticus had opened it. I sat with him and drank. Erik stayed awake for a while talking about all that he had heard until he fell asleep. Atticus and I played chess for a while. Out of the three games, I beat him once. I was improving.

Chapter 14

I woke early and walked along the water as dawn broke over the eastern shore. It was a beautiful time of day. Ducks swam amongst the reeds and grasses at the margins of the Water. Fishes rose to take the insects on the Water and my fishermen were already sailing for the best places to fish. In Cyninges-tūn, the people were rising. Those with animals to tend headed for the pastures early. This was what I missed whilst I was at sea or raiding. The order and easy life in my valley were special. This was why I protected my people.

I returned to my hall. Germund and Atticus had heard me rise and food was waiting. A dishevelled Erik appeared when I had almost finished, "Sorry, lord."

"Don't be. When you have eaten then help Atticus finish the tally. We need to divide the treasure. He nodded, "Germund, have the grain destined for Whale Island loaded onto the wagons. There are plenty of men in the warrior hall. And this afternoon I need you to prepare horses for Erik and I. We will be riding to Windar's Mere, Ketil's Stad and Stad on the Eden tomorrow. We have work to do."

Atticus looked at me nervously, "Will there be war, lord?"

"Perhaps. Now finish your work. I will go and fetch Sámr; if he has risen!"

Kara and Ylva were with their women making a new batch of cheese. I put my head into the cheese making chamber, "Is Sámr arisen yet?"

Ylva said, cheekily, "He may be arisen but he is not yet up!"

Kara looked shocked at the impropriety, "Ylva!"

She laughed, "They deserve their pleasure."

I changed the subject, "I intend to ride to my three jarls and apprise them of the situation. If we are all correct then the Danes will come and come in force. I would have them build signal towers in their land. They have not gone to war for a while. They can build towers. This time we know that they will come for me."

Kara nodded her agreement, "This stronghold is where they will come. They see you as the head of the clan. If they destroy you then the clan is theirs as is the Land of the Wolf. They do not know that there is an heir."

Ylva said, "An heir who is not ready. I know my cuz. He will be ready in the fullness of time but not yet. He has a family to raise first. He has to find who Sámr Ship Killer really is."

"I did not have that luxury!"

Ylva squeezed my arm, "You are Dragonheart; you were chosen by the gods. You cannot compare Sámr to you. If you do then he will be doomed to failure."

Kara said, quietly, "Remember Wolf Killer."

I nodded. They were right. "You are right to chastise me. When he wakes send him to me. I would divide the treasure."

It was almost noon when Sámr and Baldr arrived. They looked at me sheepishly. I tactfully avoided any comment. I had already laid out the treasure in piles. "You led this raid with me, Sámr, this is how I would divide it." I went to one pile. "This portion is for the men who raided. It includes those who did not come back. This next is for you and this one for me. The last pile is for the people of Cyninges-tūn. You may make any changes you wish."

"They have as much as you."

"And that is right. They are the clan and without the clan I am nothing. If you disagree then take whatever you wish from their share and I will make it up from mine."

I saw him debate and then he shook his head.

"I have put the spices in three piles. One is for me. One is for Kara and the rest for whoever wants it."

"I could take it all?"

"Of course." He said nothing. "The grain, pots and other goods are in five piles. One for you and one for me. One for the crew. One for Cyninges-tūn and one for Whale Island."

Baldr said, "Lord, you give much to those who did not risk anything."

"Because they are the clan. There are women, children and the old. They cannot raid. Should they have a life which is without pleasure?" He shook his head. "Sámr, all of this is part of your training. These are the choices a leader makes. I hope I am a good leader for this is the way I have always done it."

"And I am learning."

"Tomorrow I ride with Erik Shield Bearer. There may be danger coming." I told them both what I had learned. I saw Atticus pale. Sámr and Baldr did not. They were made of sterner stuff.

"You need some men to go with you."

I shook my head, "The men I could take have just been away from their families for long enough already. I will not take them."

Baldr said, "You could take Aðalsteinn and Dagfinnr? I know from speaking with them that they are grateful to you and it would not hurt to show them the Land of the Wolf."

"Perhaps you are right. I will ask them."

113

Sámr looked relieved. "If war is coming then we need to prepare our defences." He was looking at Baldr.

"You could bring your families within this hall."

"No, great grandfather; there may come a time when I live here but I believe that it is part of my preparation to make my hall stronger. Besides, I have hearth weru now. I chose them on the voyage back and they would live by my hall. We need to make them a hall and put a strong palisade around it. You chose a good site when you first lived there. The steepness of the slopes to the north and the east allow nature to defend."

Sámr chose his share and Baldr arranged for the hearth weru to ferry them across to their home. Word had spread and the men of Cyninges-tūn who had been on the raid came to the hall for their share. Atticus had all of their names noted down and he and Erik made certain that they all had their due and their names were crossed off the tally tablet.

Aethelflaed and Nanna came to my hall in the middle of the afternoon. They were ready to return home with Sámr and Baldr. As we parted at the wooden quay, Sámr said, "Be careful, great grandfather. You are no longer as young as you once were and your dreams have warned you of the dangers that lie close by. The Danes may not wait for vengeance. I remember the assassins. If it was not for Úlfarr I would be dead. They came in the night and we saw them not. That was many years ago and people are not as vigilant."

He was right, of course, people did forget and no sentry, save an Ulfheonar, would be as good as a wolf watcher. Our borders had not been crossed for some time. We had bested our enemies beyond them. "I will watch out for myself and I will be careful. I may have grey hairs but I am still Ulfheonar."

I bade them farewell and watched the boats take them across the Water. The hall to which they sailed rose above the flower covered graves of Erika and Aiden and it was good. The spirits would watch over the heir to the Clan of the Wolf.

Aðalsteinn and Dagfinnr were more than happy to accompany me. They were real warriors and had wanted an opportunity to repay me for their rescue. They had said, many times, that they would pay me back the money I had given for them. I had dismissed it out of hand. I had done no more than I would have done for any of our people enslaved far from their homes. They had clothes now, there were the clothes of dead warriors in the warrior hall. They had no seal skin boots yet. They had leather boots they had found in the hall. I had helmets, swords and scabbards. They were all good ones. The poorer ones had been melted down and reused. I had two good metal studded leather jerkins and they took those. I also had many shields. Some belonged to warriors who had perished at sea and were not buried with them. They chose two good ones. They would repaint them before they used them. It did not do to use another warrior's mark in battle. In my stables, I had sturdy horses and we went to choose four. One had to be a small one for Erik and, after we had chosen one for him, Aðalsteinn, Dagfinnr and I gave him his first lesson in riding. When he did not fall off, he was delighted. We chose a steady horse. Maelgwn was an older mare. We had bred many small horses from her. We used them for the boys who rode between Cyninges-tūn and Whale Island.

As Erik and I headed back to my hall, I felt weary, I had not travelled far and I had not fought yet my body felt as though it had. "Germund, light the fire in the steam hut."

Atticus looked pleased, "That is the right thing to do, lord. It will be good for you and I can prepare the food." He looked at Erik. "And it might be good for your young shield bearer to experience the steam hut." He stroked his hair as he spoke. I knew what he meant. The steam would help eradicate the infestation in the young man's hair.

"Aye, a good idea, Erik, fetch a good tunic and your comb. I shall induct you into the pleasures of the steam hut."

He was nervous but having braved the beast that was a horse then the steam hut seemed harmless. Leaving our clean clothes outside we entered. The heat was fierce and it took Erik's breath away, "Lord! It is too hot! It is dragon fire!"

"Aye and when you have endured this you can face a dragon. Trust me." There were four wooden stools and I placed him on one and then sat opposite. "Your body will rid itself of all impurities. Do not speak, there is no need. I find it helps to close my eyes. Sometimes the spirits come and I enter the dream world." I did not think that would happen for it only occurred when I was alone or in danger.

I waited until the sweat was pouring from me. Atticus had carved two bone sticks he called strigils and I used one to scrape my body clean of dirt. When Atticus was with me, he did my back. That done I ran my comb through my hair and beard. I crossed to the other side and picked up Erik's comb. It was well made but not as fine as mine. "I am going to comb your hair. I fear there are beasts living there."

He nodded, "Aye, lord, I have felt them. I tried to comb them out but I failed."

"If your mother had been alive then she would have done this. I will do it for you." A mixture of my comb and Erik's yielded results. I threw the insects onto the hot stones where they sizzled. "Now we go and plunge into the Water. Then we return. It will harden your body."

It was dark as we headed back to my hall. Erik beamed, "I feel clean, lord. That steam hut is like a miracle. When I felt the dragon's breath, I thought I would die, but having endured it I would go in again tomorrow!"

I laughed, "Once every seven days is enough but I am pleased you enjoyed it. I will let Atticus go with you next time. He is a Greek and he knows how to cleanse a body far better than I."

The next morning, we left Cyninges-tūn not long after dawn. Three of us were mailed although our helmets hung from our saddles. We were warriors and we would heed the warning I had been sent. If Danes were a danger then we would be prepared. We rode north towards the bridge of Skelwith. I had three who were new to the Land of the Wolf and, as we rode through my land, I pointed out features and gave them their names. I pointed towards the dale of Lang where Aðils Shape Shifter lived. I pointed to the mountain which dominated the east, Úlfarrberg, and I told them the story of the wolf, Úlfarr, which had saved my kin. When we crested the col, which led to Windar's Mere, they were in awe of that piece of water, "Jarl Dragonheart, it is like a sea!"

"Aye, Dagfinnr, it is and this is the richest farmland in the land of the Wolf. Many people live here. North of this place is the Rye Dale and we grow our cereals there. Asbjorn the Strong is my jarl here and we shall stay the night with him. We have no need to push the animals and besides Maelgwn is no longer a foal!" She whinnied as though she had heard me. Her placid nature had given Erik confidence.

Asbjorn had grown old. That was not a surprise. What was a surprise was that he looked thinner than he used to. Old warriors grew fat. Even Haaken needed a bigger belt. I was the exception for I had had my illness. Asbjorn's son, Eystein, had become a father. A grandfather now, Asbjorn would not go raiding with me. He welcomed me warmly. We were old friends as well as shield brothers. His men had been hunting and we had venison for our feast. I told him of the raid and our success.

His son, Eystein, was envious of what we had done. "I would raid with you, Jarl Dragonheart. Riches such as you speak of would enable me to provide for my wife and son."

Shaking my head, I said, "I doubt that I will raid again." I did not say never for I feared the sisters were listening. "Sámr Ship Killer will lead the clan and he will raid."

"But he is younger than I am!" Eystein was blunt. Other Vikings would be as blunt and this was why Sámr was not quite ready yet to lead the clan. Success in one raid was not enough. He needed to make a name in war too. Perhaps when the Danes came it would be the time.

His father shook his head, "The Dragonheart led this clan when he was of an age with Sámr. This is *wyrd*, Eystein. Forgive my son, Jarl. He tries to run when he has barely learned to walk. He has much to learn."

"There is nothing to forgive. He does not know Sámr and cannot judge." Abashed, Eystein remained silent.

"And I cannot believe that you came all the way to my hall just to tell me that you raided. Interesting though it was, there is something beneath your words, Jarl." Asbjorn might be older and thinner than he had once been but his mind was as sharp as ever.

"You are right. Danger comes. The spirits have spoken to me in a dream and visited Kara and Ylva too. The Danes will come and they will come from the east."

"Across my land."

I nodded, "As they did when Wolf Killer lived here. We had signal towers once and I would have you build them again. Grize's Dale and the farms around those valleys are where they will likely come or perhaps through the valley where Elfrida and Wolf Killer's home lay. Prepare your defences. We both know that they are like fleas on a dog. Man for man we are better warriors but we need to hurt them beyond our homes before we meet them beard to beard."

Asbjorn looked to his son, "Here is a task for you, my son. This might not reap the rewards of a raid but it will make your family safer."

"Aye, father!"

Later that night Asbjorn confessed to me that he had been ill. He had had the coughing sickness. Although he had recovered, he knew it was a warning and he had had to hand over many of his duties to his son. "He is learning, Jarl Dragonheart." He smiled, "We are both training the one to follow us. You are the Dragonheart. I think you will do a better job than I do." A wind flickered the tallow candles in the hall. The Norns were listening.

The next day we headed north for the long ride to Ketil's Stad. We would have to pass Úlfarrberg and travel up the Úlfarr Water. There were fewer farms there but the folk who lived in that valley were hardier. This was, truly, the land of the wolf but not the wolf that was the clan. Real wolves still prowled. When we had had Ulfheonar then we would have come each Þorri to hunt them. It had been some time since we had had a wolf hunt and their numbers had grown. If we had another wolf winter then they would descend and the folk of Úlfarr Water would have to bar their doors and hunker down until the danger had passed.

As we passed the brooding mountain, I sensed fear amongst my three companions. I laughed, "When we come back south, we will have to pass Myrddyn's cave which lies beneath the Lough Rigg. That is a place which makes me fearful That is the true centre of the land for it is inhabited by the spirit of an ancient and powerful wizard who was here before any of our people. This mountain is the heart of the land. One day, Erik, we shall climb it."

"But what about the wolves, Jarl Dragonheart?"

I took out my wolf amulet, "We will have one of these made and then Ylva will put a spell upon it. It will protect you."

Once we had left the valley, we followed the River Eamont north and east. We were now in Ketil's land. Pennryhd had once been a huddle of humble huts before Ketil had established his control over the land. The newly built stronghold now boasted a palisade, ditch and a weaponsmith. One of his sons, Windar Ketilsson, was hersir here. We did not stop for Ketil's Stad was just a few miles further on guarding the crossing of the Eamont. Pennryhd guarded the other. I saw, even though it was more than a thousand paces away, that he had sentries watching from the palisade. We continued along the river to the real heart of this land. Ketil had turned the Roman fort into a formidable fortress which would be hard to take. The village nestled in the loop of the river. They needed no palisade for if danger threatened then they could flee to the fort.

I spied men on the walls and that was unusual. Normally there would be just a couple but there were eight and that did not bode well. Of course, my companions saw nothing amiss in this. They were just impressed by the stone wall made by the Romans and the wooden towers which Ketil had made. The double ditches around the outside had been sharpened and kept clear. They would break the ankles of any who tried to cross them.

I recognised the sentry on the gatehouse, "Is there trouble, Sven Larsson?"

He nodded, "Aye, Jarl Dragonheart, there are raiders from the north. The jarl led his hearth weru to seek their tracks. He has ordered the bondi to be vigilant."

"Then I have come at a good time."

We dismounted to walk through the gates. Being an old Roman fort there were good stables and we took the horses there. Ketil had a warrior hall. I sent my two men to find a bed within and Erik and I went to find Ketil's wife, Seara. She came to the door of the hall to greet me. I remembered her as a young woman. Now she was grey and a grandmother. Age came to us all.

"A welcome surprise Jarl, you are well?"

After I had nearly died that was the first thing which most people said to me. "I am and my family are well too. This is Erik Shield Bearer."

She smiled, "He is a little small to be a shield bearer."

118

He nodded, "Aye, lady but I shall grow. After seven days of my training and eating the food of Atticus I am already the width of a finger taller!"

She laughed, "Come inside, my husband will not be long. The men of Strathclyde are raiding."

We entered the warm hall. "Strathclyde?"

She shrugged, "That was Ketil's first thought but he was riding abroad to discover the truth of the matter. He said he could not trust the reports of those who fled. The men north of the borderlands have been quiet for many years and we did not expect it. Carr normally gives us warning if the raiders come from the east but he saw no one."

I was not surprised that these were not Saxons. The Northumbrians were a beaten force. The Danes now imposed their will through kings they allowed to live. That was my worry, that the Danes might use the Northumbrian weakness to attack us through Ketil's stad. He could withstand raiders but not an invading army. They could sweep down through Úlfarr Water and destroy all of the farms which were north of Windar's Mere and Cyninges-tūn.

Seara's servant poured our ale and another brought in fresh bread and cheese. We spoke of my family and I told her of Aiden's death. Like all of the people in the Land of the Wolf, she knew of Aiden. "Then Kara is alone?"

"She will never be alone. She has Ylva and Aiden speaks to her from the spirit world."

Just at that moment, we heard noises from outside. Seara smiled, "It is my husband. If you will excuse me, I will go and prepare a bed for you and food for this evening."

Ketil had changed little. He was a little greyer and broader but he was not the huge, bloated man that his father, Windar, had been when he was the same age. He clasped my arm, "Jarl, are you galdramenn that you come when we have great danger on our borders?"

I shook my head, "I came to warn you of danger but not from the north, from the south and east. This is *wyrd*."

"Let us talk for we have news to share." We entered his hall and while we drank, I told him my warning first and I told him of the raid on Portus Cale. He supped his ale. It gave him time to think. "Then I think that the two are linked." He put down his horn. "Over the last twenty days or so there have been raids from the north. Isolated farms were attacked. The men were slain and the rest enslaved. They took animals. In all eight families were taken. Because they were isolated it was not until five days ago that we realised we were under attack. Carr came to tell us that he had seen Picts and the men of Strathclyde. They were heading north and driving cattle and captives. By the time we reached the farms the raiders were gone."

"There is an alliance I like not. The Picts and the men of Strathclyde fought each other more than they fought us. What did you discover today?"

"Over the last three days, we went to all the outlying farms. We discovered the extent of the attacks. My son, Windar's, settlement had not been touched nor any to the west of him but the attacks had all been to the north. The land south of the Roman Wall is now lost to my people. We went today, with my son Windar and his men, to the northwest of Pennryhd. I gambled and I was proved right. We came upon a warband about to attack the farm of Arne Svensson. We managed to halt the attack but there were too many of them for us to defeat. The majority escaped us. We killed just four of them. I planted their heads as a warning."

"How many were there?"

"More than a hundred. Had we not been mounted then they might have risked a battle with us but they respect horsemen here. The old people speak of the Roman horsemen who patrolled the border. I do not think they know that we cannot fight from the back of a horse."

"What makes you think that the attacks and the Danish threat are linked?"

"I spied, in their ranks, not just the men of Strathclyde. There were also Picts with their limed hair and half-naked tattooed bodies. In addition, I saw three Danes. They kept to the rear of the warband but I saw them and their Danish axes."

"Then that means that they were either observers or, more likely, paymasters."

"That was my thought, too. If the Danes do intend to attack the Land of the Wolf then they would wish us to fix our eyes here in the north. An attack would draw men here and weaken us."

The Norns had been spinning. I had been sent here for a reason. War had come already and, for once, I was in the right place, at the right time.

Chapter 15

Ketil and his hearth weru sat with me as we decided what we would do. This was Ketil's land. He knew it better than I did. I was Jarl Dragonheart but I would listen to my leaders. Perhaps I should have brought Sámr to see how I worked with my jarls. "What are your plans?"

"Before you came, I intended to take my men and those of my son, north to find this warband and destroy it."

"That is a good plan but we do not want to leave your family and your son's without defence."

"I have sent riders to summon the families of all of my people within these walls. We have arms enough for the women and boys to fight and I will leave ten of the older warriors. This Roman fort will not fall easily."

"And Pennryhd?"

"I will order my son to leave fifteen men there."

"Then it just remains to find them."

"Carr's son, Oswald, and two of Carr's men are already scouting for them. They are hillmen and know the land well."

I turned to Erik, "It looks like you will see your first battle and you will see it soon." His face was a mixture of excitement and apprehension. Stig, his best friend, had died to a random arrow in the heat of battle. He knew how dangerous battle could be.

We spoke of the numbers we would have to defeat the warband. We would have rough parity of numbers. I contemplated sending to the Stad on the Eden for their men but if we were being attacked here then they might also be threatened. We would have to use our superior warriors to win the day. The men from the north were brave but most fought with bare chests and many did not even own a helmet. We both realised that it was unlikely that we could recover the ones who had been taken captive. The lands of the Picts and Strathclyde stretched as far north as Mercia did to the south. The captives and animals would be lost in the remote valleys and villages. We would exact vengeance from all those that we found.

As Ketil had a guest of honour he invited his hersir and hearth weru to the feast. I had fought with most of them but there were some to whom I was a stranger. They were keen to speak to the warrior with the magic sword. Speaking with them gave me an idea of their mettle. All had fought but the ones I did not know had only fought in small-scale encounters. The large battles with hundreds of men on either side were a mystery to them. It gave me much to think on. Ketil and I were the last two to retire.

I knew that we had to find these men and find them quickly. Eight families had already been destroyed. "Much depends upon Carr and his men. We cannot wander the north seeking the raiders."

"I know. And when they are defeated...."

"Do not tempt the sisters, Ketil."

"They will either be defeated or we will be dead and we will not have to worry over much." I nodded. He was right. "As I said, when they are defeated, how do we deal with the threat of the Danes?"

"Have your farmers build a series of watch towers and beacons from here to Úlfarr Water. That way we will know if there is danger here. We can also have them lit if we are attacked."

"You do not wish us to come to your aid?"

"When you hunt the wild boar, you have to be wary of its teeth and tusks. Often the best way is to divert the attention of the boar and then find its vulnerable spot. It seems to me that the Danes have so many men that they could attack us in many places merely to destroy you or Windar's Mere. If you are attacked then let me know. I will send men to investigate but it may be that you have to defend yourselves until I can come. Much will depend upon Ráðulfr Ulfsson at the Stad on the Eden. He will be the furthest from the Danes and so long as he has enough men to defend his walls, he could bring men to aid either you or me."

"Then I am satisfied and I will have my farmers build the towers."

The men of the north gathered north of the Eden. They began arriving at dawn. Aðalsteinn and Dagfinnr would be my bodyguards. They were honoured. As we waited with Ketil for the rest to arrive I turned to Erik. "We may not fight today but whichever day we fight your only task is to carry my shield. When the battle starts then you wait behind the shield wall. If I fall then you get back here. You have had no training yet. Aðalsteinn and Dagfinnr will be there to either die with me or fetch back my body."

"I can fight! I have my bow and my sling."

"Then use them but if an enemy comes for you then run!" I stared into his eyes, "So swear!" I did not want him to die.

He nodded, "I swear."

Most of the men had arrived by noon and Ketil prepared to march towards Pennryhd as north of there was the last place that we had heard of the raiders. Oswald and one of his men arrived just as we began to march west. "Jarl Ketil, my father says that they are at Hautwesel just south of the wall. They are camped there and they have been reinforced by another twenty men."

Ketil turned, "That is thirty miles away. If we leave now, we can be there after dark. Jarl Dragonheart, do you wish a horse?"

I shook my head, "The day that I cannot march with my warriors is the day I sit by the Water and fish with the other old men. Do not wait for me. I will keep up with you!"

We set off using the run and walk technique which we had used for years. We ran for five hundred paces and then walked five hundred. If time was not as important then we would walk for a thousand paces and run for five hundred. Time was vital. If we could get there by dark and remain unseen then the surprise value might swing the odds in our favour. We ran hard.

I was not worried about myself. Despite my age, I could keep going but Erik was another matter. I had him next to me with Dagfinnr on the other side of him. We talked the whole time for that kept Erik's mind off the pain of running and marching so far. We were heading for Halfdenby. It had been one of the first places that the raiders had destroyed. The farm and four huts had been burned. It lay on an exposed ridge where the High Divide began. It made our journey harder but shortened it by five miles. We then descended to the valley of the Tinea. Here we would have cover but, as the afternoon was wearing on and clouds began to gather, then we were more hopeful that we would not be seen. We stopped at the river to fill our water skins and to drink. This was not my warband and so I was not at the fore. Instead, I was in the middle. Ketil had placed eight of his best warriors around me. He did not want me to come to harm before the battle. My sword and my name might make the difference. My red wolf shield was well known.

It was harder to set off after such a stop and I saw Erik gripping his side. It was common when running. You suddenly found a shooting pain in the side. Dagfinnr saw his action and said, "Just run through it, Erik. You need to fight it as you would an enemy. If you wish I can carry the jarl's shield for you."

He gritted his teeth and shook his head, "I am shield bearer. I will run through this pain."

As the valley ran on a north to south alignment the sunset was not gradual. It was sudden as though a candle had been extinguished and we ran in the dark. I hoped that we did not have far to travel but I did not know. We were not on a road. The Roman road which crossed from east to west lay to the north of us. That would have markers. We ran on an ancient greenway. The men in front stopped. One turned, "Jarl Dragonheart, we are here. The jarl would speak with you."

I saw that Erik was doubled over trying to get his breath. I turned to Dagfinnr, "Watch Erik for me. He has done well!"

I made my way through other men many of whom, like Erik, were also doubled over. Those, like me, who wore mail had suffered the most.

Ketil was with Carr and the rest of his scouts. He pointed north. I could see pinpricks of light, "There lies their camp. Two Danes arrived before dark and they have joined them. There are sentries all around. They are wary."

Ketil said, "Do we make a nighttime attack?"

I shook my head, "These men we lead are not Ulfheonar and we have marched a god's distance this day." I turned to Carr. "Is there a way around their camp so that we could attack from the north?"

He nodded, "Aye, Jarl Dragonheart, but it would mean a two-mile walk and your men would have no avenue of escape."

I nodded, "True but we would have the higher ground and the element of surprise would be ours. Our thirty archers would be able to loose over our heads. This way they would be attacking uphill."

Carr looked at Ketil. Ketil was his lord and I was almost a stranger to him. Ketil nodded, "Lead on, Carr, but we will walk this time. I am too weary to run."

Carr knew the land well and he led us, unerringly, around the raiders to a wood which lay between two burns. Neither piece of water was particularly large but they would be an obstacle. More importantly, we were above the village and their camp. The woods in which we camped gave us shelter. We could not speak for fear of giving ourselves away once the raider's camp fell silent but we would eat cold rations, make water and sleep. I had until the morning to come up with a battle plan.

Erik was asleep as soon as he had eaten his last mouthful of food. Carr and his scouts took the first watch. I did not sleep but I lay looking at the cloud-laden sky. I sensed rain and that might help us. We had over a hundred men. Twenty would be used as archers. They also had shields and swords but the bows were the one weapon the enemy did not possess. I planned on a three deep shield wall. With thirty odd men in each line, we would have the front rank made up of mailed men. From what Carr had told me only the Danes and the three chiefs were mailed. We would have to kill those in the first encounter. Arriving in the dark meant I had not had time to choose the best ground from which to attack but I planned on rising before dawn. I had no Ulfheonar with me but I was Ulfheonar and I had my wolf cloak. I would scout out the land myself.

Ketil woke me after a short sleep as I had asked him to. He would have come with me but knew that I would be more silent if I was alone. I did not take my helmet nor wear my mail. As I walked, I counted out the paces. I crossed the narrower burn as the first drops of rain fell. The ground had not been tilled. I smelled cattle dung. The cattle would have been taken north or slaughtered. The land fell gently to the south. It was the kind of ground which, when you climbed it, sapped energy from legs. As I moved closer to the enemy camp the rain started to fall harder. If it rained in the battle then the bow strings would be too wet to be effective. Was this another trick of the Norns? Were they making the ground slippery for the raiders and yet denying us the advantage of bows?

I stopped four hundred or so paces from their sentries. I saw them moving. They were silhouetted against the fires. With cloaks around their heads, they would see little. I was bareheaded but my wolf cloak disguised me. I spied a couple of head sized rocks. They looked to be from the Roman Wall and were a light colour. Picking them up I walked back. Counting the steps going out helped me to place the two rocks close together so that I would be able to see them when the attack began. I was marking the range for our twenty bowmen.

Despite the fact that they were watching for me I still managed to rise, like a wraith, next to Windar Ketilsson and the sentry who were watching for me. They both jumped as I rose up.

"How did you do that, Jarl?"

"Years of practice. I was helped by the rain. It makes it hard to see. Let us hope it stops by the morning or else our bowmen will find it hard." I now regretted not bringing the new bows for Aðalsteinn and Dagfinnr. Hindsight was always perfect! The only new bow we had was Erik's and he was not strong enough to use it effectively. "Keep watch although I do not think that they will come. They do not know we are here."

I went back to the camp. Men had found whatever shelter they could from the rain. Aðalsteinn and Dagfinnr had rigged their cloaks between two trees so that the three of them were dry, I slipped beneath it and took off my wolf cloak. I laid it on the sleeping shield bearer and then sat next to him. The fires I had seen suggested more men than Carr had reported. Perhaps they had had more reinforcements. We would have to hurt them before they closed with us. I wondered at the Danish presence. The numbers did not suggest that they were as allies. I suspected that they were scouts and also to see how the Picts and men of Strathclyde fought. The Danes were ambitious. They had Northumbria as a client. Were their greedy eyes on the land to the north? I doubted that the Danes would fight in the front rank if they fought at all. They wore mail and they would be a threat if they fought. If they stayed at the rear, we would not have to face them in the first attack.

When dawn came it was a grey affair. The division between night and day was almost non-existent. However, as I had sat beneath the cloaks, I was aware that the rain was lessening. It pattered less on the soaked oiled cloak. The Norns were not playing a trick. They had made the ground boggy but our archers would have taut strings. I rose as I saw Ketil and Carr walking towards me. I began to don my mail.

"Well, Jarl, what did you learn?"

"That we can defeat them," I explained my strategy to them and they nodded. "If you gather the men with bows, I will explain my plan to them. Then march a hundred paces down the slope and form our line"

Erik, Aðalsteinn and Dagfinnr had risen and were ready for battle. "Erik, take my shield to the Jarl Ketil's brother, Windar, and place it next to him. Then fetch your bow and join me."

"Aye, Jarl."

As I went, I turned to my two bodyguards. "You two go to Windar. We will be next to him. You two will stand behind me with spears." I saw their faces fall. "You have no mail. You will be needed when we have broken their front rank. Fear not I can fight unaided."

Men were being moved by Ketil, Windar and their hersir. They picked up their weapons and moved from the camp towards the place we would fight. Even though it had been dark I had seen the place where we would hold them. It was where the slope before us would be at its steepest. There might need to be some adjustment when the sun finally broke but not much. By the time I reached the archers, Erik had rejoined us. "I will be in the front rank. When you see me raise my sword then nock your arrows. When I lower it, you begin to loose. Loose into the air and use all the power that you have. I have paced out one hundred and fifty paces to a pair of markers. That will be our killing ground. Keep sending arrows until you have all loosed twenty. Then be ready to pick off any who are close. Today we depend on you twenty men."

"We will not let you down!"

"I know, Sven Haraldsson." I nodded encouragingly at Erik.

I made my way through the ranks of men who were forming our shield wall. Their feet had already churned the ground into a muddy slush. The enemy who would advance towards us would have an even harder time to keep their feet. I would not be using a spear but most of the others held them. They would keep an enemy at bay. The enemy spears were often just fire-hardened sticks. Ketil stood next to me but his son was at the left-hand edge of our line. He would be our anchor. The lightening sky made our line seem pitifully small. I saw the ranging stones and knew that soon we would be seen from the raider's camp. Even sentries huddled beneath sodden cloaks would spy us. I turned to see that all was well behind me and that Aðalsteinn and Dagfinnr were where they should be. Their spears would poke over my shoulders. The archers stood ready behind the third rank. I had just turned my head when a shout went up from the enemy camp. We were seen.

The shock and surprise could be spied from our position just five hundred paces from them. There were frantic gestures and shrieked shouts. We had moved silently and without noise. It would have appeared as though we had materialized from the earth. These were not followers of the White Christ we fought. These were followers of the old ways. I saw men waving hands and shouting orders. Some men formed a ragged line just two hundred paces from us. Behind them, I saw a huddle of warriors conferring. From their helmets at least four of those speaking were Danes. The other two had the trappings of chiefs. They would be the leaders of the Picts and the men of Strathclyde. More men joined the line. It was already fifty men wide and would overlap ours once they began their attack.

Ketil saw their line and said, "I have placed our best men on the flanks in the second rank. We are surrounded by my hearth weru. We will hold them, Jarl Dragonheart."

Had this been my men then they would have sung one of our songs to intimidate the enemy. Ketil's men did not have songs. They had no Haaken One Eye. I began banging my shield with the hilt of my sword. Everyone took it up, banging their shields with their spear hafts. It had an effect on the enemy for I saw them looking at each other. They wondered what it meant. Although I was banging my shield, I was also watching the enemy. The leaders finished their conference and the two chiefs moved to the line. They separated and one went to the middle of the Picts who looked to be facing Windar and the other went to the middle of the men of Strathclyde. I could hear their words as they gave their orders. The Danes stayed at the rear.

I saw that the enemy had a variety of weapons and shields. Some had small round ones. Others had oval ones and a couple had large round ones such as we used. I turned to Ketil. "They are not going to lock shields. Where the Picts meet the men of Strathclyde will be the weak point. If I had been them, I would have used Picts in the front line. We have a chance."

"Aye, Jarl. Lock shields!"

We swung our shields around so that the left edge was tucked behind our neighbour's shield. Spears poked from the top. I felt the spears of Aðalsteinn and Dagfinnr as they slid over my shoulder. I held Ragnar's Spirit ready. The fact that we had stopped banging and presented a wall of shields seemed to spur them. The two chiefs raised their swords and led their men forward. They did not do so at the same time. It was as though two separate warbands were attacking us. I saw that they had three ranks of fifty although within a few paces all order had disappeared and it was a mob of men who negotiated the slippery slope. The Danes remained with about twenty men at the rear. Were they a reserve or did they have another plan?

I concentrated on the attack. I raised my sword. The two bands were now trying to race each other to get to us. It was as though there were two rough wedges. Some without shields had run from the rear rank and were running alongside well-armed men. Some men slipped and fell. They were trampled by those behind. Holes appeared in the lines. We had yet to respond but they were defeating themselves. I saw the first chief reach the stones and I dropped my hand.

Twenty arrows are not a great number but they plunged from the sky and struck the shoulders and, in some cases, the unprotected heads of the warriors. Even as they realised they were under attack a second flight hit them. The first forty arrows had a dramatic effect. Men fell. In their falling, they brought down others and some of those, lying prostrate, were hit by the third and fourth flights of arrows. We had so few bowmen that their arrows were concentrated in the middle of the enemy line. The flanks were almost untouched.

Ketil shouted, as the line was twenty paces from us, "Brace!"

I placed my right foot behind me and turned it at an angle to make it harder for us to be pushed back. Although we had thinned their centre the two chiefs had seen the mail and shields of Ketil and myself. They led their hearth weru for us. It was a Pict who came for me. He had a vest of mail covering his naked chest. His sword was a long curved one and he had an oval shield. On his head, he had a high domed helmet with a pair of wings coming from the side. He had his beard and moustache plaited. He came for me. He screamed as he led his oathsworn towards me. I saw the sweat on his face. Racing through the muddy morass had taken its toll. His legs would be burning with the exertion.

Holding my sword just above my shield and Ketil's I waited for the blow which I knew would come from on high. He would aim for my head. The advantage of a locked shield wall is that you can still raise and lower your shield without damaging the integrity of the whole. I brought it up. My shield had metal studs around the side. The front was studded with metal. It was not light. It was, however, sturdy and when the blow came my arm jarred. The shield took the full force of the blow. The metal rim of my shield would have taken the edge off his blade. I saw that the chief had expected to shatter my shield with the strike.

The spears of Aðalsteinn and Dagfinnr darted forward. Dagfinnr's gouged a line in the chief's cheek while his uncle's spear struck the warrior next to him who was raising his sword to smite Ketil. As the chief screamed, I lunged with Ragnar's Spirit and struck him in his left shoulder. There was no mail there and my tip entered the soft flesh and

128

grated off bone. I twisted and withdrew the blade. Blood spurted and he shouted in anger. He raised his sword again and I saw that it was bent. His strike would not be true. This time, as I raised my shield, I lowered my sword. The blow, when it struck, barely registered for the sword had not hit the shield square. I stabbed forwards. My tip found mail but then slid off the links to strike his thigh. I felt something soft and pushed hard. I felt blood as it poured from the wound to drench my hand. The chief was mortally wounded. He had three wounds but the last one had done for him and I saw the light go from his eyes as his body slumped to the soggy ground.

The men behind me were stabbing with their spears and the ones to my left were hacking and stabbing. When the chief of the Picts fell his oathsworn lost all reason. I had killed him and they wanted vengeance. The six of them who remained tried to get at me. There were bodies before us and a mass of men who had survived the arrows trying to get to grips with us. There were so many that they could not swing their weapons. I did not have to swing mine for it was held below my shield and ready to stab.

The Pictish oathsworn pushed their faces towards me. Their shields were jammed against their bodies as were their weapons. Two men tried to bite me. I pulled back my head and butted one as Dagfinnr's spear went into the eye of the second. The press of men behind began to push us but it was up the slope. The ones behind the front flailed their spears and swords at us but all they struck were helmets. We had good helmets over mail hoods and head protectors. They did no harm. They, in contrast, had helmets only. When our weapons hit them, they dented helmets and heads. Men were hurt. The sheer weight of numbers began to push us back. The man I had headbutted looked stunned and I ripped my blade up into his chest. He fell, dead.

I heard Aðalsteinn shout, "Hold them! Brace!"

Our third rank must have pressed their shields into the backs of our second rank for it felt as though a solid wall had been pressed behind us. The last flight of missiles from the archers broke the enemy. The twenty arrows fell into the men who were at the rear of their line. As our men pushed into our backs so the front rank of the enemy was pushed and they had fewer men to support them. Suddenly the ones before us fell as they were pushed onto the bodies of their dead.

I saw our chance, "Break wall!" I unlocked my shield and, stepping onto the chest of the man who had just been speared in the leg by Dagfinnr, I stabbed him in the throat. There were just a dozen men before us for the rest were fighting on the flanks. Our men who had been in the second rank suddenly joined us and, now more than fifty men wide, we

129

began to butcher the men of Strathclyde and their Pictish allies. We were mailed and they were not. They had struggled up a bloody and muddy slope. We had waited. They were weary and we were not. As I slew a lime haired half-naked Pict who had no shield and just a short curved sword, I saw the Danes. They mounted the horses from the raiders' wagons. They were leaving. They headed south. Had we had horses we might have caught them but they would escape. There was nothing we could do about it and so we concentrated upon winning the battle.

When our archers put down their bows and joined us then the end was not far away. They did not even attempt to surrender. Their chiefs were dead and they were honour bound to follow them. It was like harvesting wheat. By the time the last one had been despatched the muscles in my arms burned. We had won!

Chapter 16

Ketil had lost men. His son had been wounded but the wound was not life-threatening. We first buried our own dead. The soft ground made digging the graves easy. We curved them in their graves and placed their swords in their hands. We laid their shields upon their faces and we buried them. Then we gathered the stripped bodies of the enemy and piled them on top of the graves of our men. We would burn them when we found dry kindling. It would send a message north of the wall that this was the fate of all raiders.

I saw the shock on Erik's face as the bodies were piled up. Some of the raiders had been hard to kill. They had fought on beyond any reason and their butchered bodies bore many wounds. I gave him my shield and helmet. "Go back to the camp and light a fire. We shall have hot food this day."

"Aye, Jarl."

Ketil came over. I pointed south, "The Danes fled?"

He nodded, "I think that you were right. This was mischief to hurt us. I have the men collecting dry kindling to burn their dead. They have wagons at their camp. We will use that to take back their metal. I will send Carr to see where they went."

"It will be a waste of time. They will head over the High Divide. It may take them some time to report to their leaders and that time can be used by us."

The sun had traversed the sky and it was mid-afternoon when we had the wagons loaded and the kindling ready to burn the enemy bodies. Their heads we had placed on broken spears in a line which was parallel to the wall. It would remind those north of the wall of their folly. We lit the kindling and when it caught, we retired to the raider's camp. They had butchered animals and hung them. We cooked and ate the food and then used their camp. We had a long thirty-mile march back to Ketil's home and our horses. We would take a whole day to complete it. We had wagons to pull and wounded men to nurse. We had had a victory but it had been at a cost.

To keep him occupied while the gory work of disposing of the bodies had taken place, I had sent Erik to collect as many arrows from the battlefield as possible. We could reuse the heads and some of the shafts could also be salvaged. There were always arrows which just struck the ground and were undamaged. The result was that he only returned when the pall of smoke from the pyre was rising in the sky and blowing northwards.

Dagfinnr saw him coming, laden with shafts, "Here, young archer, let me help you with those."

The two of them carried the heads and shafts to the wagon. Erik unslung his bow from his back and placed it in the wagon. He rubbed his shoulder, "When I was loosing the bow my arms and shoulder felt as though they were burning, Dagfinnr!"

"That is normal. You are young. As you grow, they will burn less and when you begin to row a drekar you will experience the burning in different places. It is the price you pay to become a man and a warrior but you have made a good start. It is just a pity that their helmets and swords were only fit for melting or else we might have found some for you."

I threw over a purse I had taken from the dead chief. "Here, divide this amongst yourselves and then you can see Haaken Bagsecgson, Erik Shield Bearer, and he will make you a good helmet!"

Dagfinnr said, "Jarl, this is yours by right. It is a full purse and you killed the chief."

I shook my head, "I could not have done it without you. I have more coin than I can ever spend. I need no money, I need no sword. What I need I have; good warriors and a clan."

We spent the night with Ketil. After the long walk, we were ready for a bed and hot food at the old Roman fort. We left the next morning to ride to the Stad on the Eden and its jarl, Ráðulfr Ulfsson. We rode with Windar and his warriors to their home. We were about to leave when Windar said, "I have something in my chest for the young shield bearer. He fought with great courage." He returned a short while later with a helmet. "This belonged to my son. He outgrew it but it will be big enough for Erik." It was a simple helmet with a nasal but, to Erik, it was the most precious thing he owned. Even though we three did not wear our helmets, Erik insisted upon wearing his as we rode west.

We reached the stad before dark. Here we saw that there was no crisis. There were just two sentries on the wall and they were chatting. They smiled and waved as we entered. Ráðulfr Ulfsson was a good jarl. He kept a close watch on the river which bordered the land of Strathclyde. He had a good drekar, *'Sea Eagle'*, and unlike the rest of my jarls, he regularly rowed to sea. His visible presence deterred the Hibernians and the men of Strathclyde from raiding. He often landed in Hibernia where he took animals and slaves. He was a huge broad chested warrior and he let his hair hang loose. Most of us tied it up but Ráðulfr liked the wild look. He and Bergil Hafþórrsson could have been twins! He also used an unusual weapon. He had an axe with a long handle but a short head. It was easier to wield than a Danish war axe and in Ráðulfr's hands, it was deadly.

"Good to see you, Jarl Dragonheart, but I think that your visit does not bring with it news which is good."

I shook my head, "There is danger. We would spend the night with you for there is much to discuss."

He nodded to my two men, "There is room in the warrior hall for your bodyguards and there you will eat well. We captured a trader heading from Strathclyde. She was heavily laden." My two men took the four horses and headed for the stable. "And who is this? One of your great grandchildren?"

I shook my head, "This is Erik Shield Bearer. He is an orphan. I am giving him a home."

We went into his hall. His wife, Agnete, was a buxom and comfortable woman. They had five children, at the last count, and she seemed destined to be a mother far into the future. It suited her. She hurried away with her brood around her ankles to prepare our beds. I sat with Ráðulfr, his eldest son, Ulf, and the leader of his hearth weru, Leif the Silent. Erik stood behind me.

"Erik, sit."

Ale was brought by one of his thralls and we drank. "So, Jarl Dragonheart, tell me of this danger."

I began by telling him of the raid on Portus Cale and my dreams. He clutched his wolf amulet. The Land of the Wolf was a land which had powerful magic and a warrior did not doubt the significance of dreams. I told him of the raid on Ketil's land.

He had supped two horns of ale while I had been telling him and he poured a third. "Now I see why we have had no trouble for a while from the men of Strathclyde. They have been building their forces to raid Ketil but if you say there were less than a hundred men of Strathclyde then where were the rest?"

My jarl was a clever man and I berated myself for not thinking of that earlier. "They could be planning an attack on this coast."

"Then they have made a serious error of judgement. We now have warning. It will soon be high summer and my farmers will have little to do until we harvest the crops. I could summon almost a hundred and fifty warriors."

An idea began to form in my mind. Up to now, we had been reacting to what others did. Perhaps it was time for a bold move. "I think that we should visit their King. Who is the King now?"

"It is still Dumnagual. He has his stronghold at Alt Clut."

"I know the place. I went there with Aiden. Would you be willing to take me to him?"

"That is not a bad idea, Jarl Dragonheart. He is not the man his father was. Riderch would have led all of his warriors to attack Ketil but then he would not have entered into an alliance with the Picts. My drekar is ready and we can go on the morrow."

'Sea Eagle' was a smaller drekar than mine. It had fourteen oars on each side. We were not going for war and we were not double crewed. We hung no shields from our sides but all of the men were armed. Aðalsteinn and Dagfinnr came with Erik and me but they did not have to row. It was a two-hundred-mile voyage. With the normal favourable winds from the south and west and men rowing now and again we could do the voyage in a day. If King Dumnagual proved inhospitable then we would sleep on the drekar. It would not be a hardship.

The waters through which we sailed were familiar to Aðalsteinn and Dagfinnr but Erik saw everything as new. We passed many islands and inlets. We also passed other vessels but when they saw the dragon prow, they all gave us sea room. We were the wolf of the sea and the only ship which might face us would be another drekar. We saw none.

As we sailed, I explained to Ráðulfr my strategy for dealing with an attack by Danes. "This visit, I hope, will make your position less precarious. You are our reserve. You can reach Ketil in one day and me in two. Your walls are the strongest in the land save for Ketil's. You could take many men."

"Aye, I have eighty men whom I could summon and still leave my stronghold well defended." He adjusted the steering board a little. "And I can have men build the watchtowers. We are more fortunate than Ketil. The wall still stands on the east and my men farm to the south of it. We could build wooden towers and send a signal to Pennryhd quickly. It would take less than an hour for a signal to reach him or for one to reach us."

Ketil and Ráðulfr were the better of my jarls. Asbjorn had lost too many friends and fought too many battles. He had grown old and the coughing sickness had taken the fight from him. Ragnar and Gruffyd were too concerned with their own families. Ketil and Ráðulfr always thought of the clan. When I was gone, I feared that Sámr would have to leave Cyninges-tūn and make his home further south. Cyninges-tūn was the hardest part of my land to reach. That was why the people there prospered and were content. It helped that Kara and Ylva were there too. Their presence seemed to act as a spiritual wall for my home. Aiden's death had made me fear for my daughter.

134

When we reached the mouth of the river the sky was darkening ahead. We managed to reach the quay at Alt Clut just before dark. Ráðulfr would not let me go ashore until he had made contact with those in the stronghold. He sent Leif the Silent and two of his hearth weru. They were away so long that darkness had fallen by the time that Leif returned.

"The King is in residence, Jarl, and he is prepared to meet with you but he wants no more than four of you to enter the stronghold."

"Will Jarl Dragonheart be safe?" My jarl was more concerned with me than his own safety.

"He swore that he would."

Ráðulfr turned to me, "I can go if you wish."

"We will both go." I realised this was where Atticus would have been useful. "Erik, you shall come with me. You are clever and can keep your ears open."

Ráðulfr smiled, "And I will take my son, Ulf. If nothing else it will make them wonder what we are about taking such a young warrior as Erik. Leif, you take charge here. If we are not back by noon tomorrow then you had better take the news to Cyninges-tūn that I have lost the jarl!" I could tell, from his voice, that he did not think that was a likely outcome. As we stepped ashore, he said, "Dumnagual is greedy but he is fearful. He knows that we could ravage his lands any time we like. As you discovered at Hautwesel the men of Strathclyde are brave enough but they are poor warriors."

We were greeted at the gate by four warriors. They were in full mail including helmets, shields and spears. I turned and smiled at Ráðulfr. I said loudly and slowly for I knew they would understand my words, "I think they must be really worried about a warrior, an old man, a youth and a child that they send such warriors to greet us."

My words struck home for two of them coloured and one said, "The King awaits. Keep your hands from your weapons"

I turned to Erik, "There, Erik Shield Bearer, you have been warned." Erik smiled and Ráðulfr laughed out loud.

The King was seated on a raised dais. His wife was next to him and he was surrounded by six men who were also armed and mailed like the four who had escorted us in. There was also a man who was dressed more plainly and had no weapons. It was he who greeted us, "I am Teudabur, the King's counsel. I speak your language and I will translate your words for the King."

I nodded, "This is Ráðulfr Ulfsson, the jarl of my lands to the south of you. I am Jarl Dragonheart of the Land of the Wolf."

I saw the surprise on the face of the counsellor and when he translated, I heard the audible gasp from the rest of the room. The King spoke and I detected nervousness in his voice.

"The King says it is an honour to meet such a renowned warrior but he thought you were dead." Teudabur shrugged, "We all heard that you died in the east."

"As you can see, I am alive and still more than capable of wielding a sword or leading an army!" I deliberately used a belligerent tone. His people had attacked mine and I would warn him of his folly in doing so again.

"And what is it that you wish?"

"Some of your men attacked my people close to Pennryhd. We slaughtered them and I am here to discover if the King knew of their intentions." I smiled, "I also give him the chance to tell me if he wishes a war with my clan!"

The words were translated and the King spoke at length. "His majesty is at pains to point out that he wishes to live in peace with his neighbours of the Clan of the Wolf. He would not jeopardise the friendship we enjoy."

He had not answered me. That was patently a lie but I let it go. "There were some Danes present with the men we slew. What does the King know of the Danes?"

This time I watched the King's face as the words were translated. He tried to mask his feelings but I saw the guilt on his face. He answered.

Teudabur said, "The King knows nothing of Danes. They are far to the east and do not concern him."

I smiled, "Good then all is well and the peace can continue but, Teudabur the Counsellor, tell the King that if I discover that there are enemies plotting north of the river then I will take action. I will unleash the Clan of the Wolf. I will unsheathe the sword that was touched by the gods and I will make Strathclyde a wasteland. I will slaughter every man and enslave every woman and child." I put my hand on the sword to make the point, "However, as the King has spoken true then none of this will happen."

I watched as my words were translated. The King had seen my smile and thought I was giving him a polite answer. He visibly shrank back into his throne. When he spoke, his voice was small.

His counsellor translated his response, "The King assures you that there will be no collusion with any enemy of the Dragonheart."

"Good, then we will bid you farewell!"

As we walked out the guards gave us a wide berth and followed at a suitably discreet distance. I waited until we were at the drekar again before I spoke, "He did know about the raid and he had made a pact with the Danes. I think that alliance may now be in jeopardy. Have your men light a fire on the shore and we will cook food. If we stay in darkness, they may fear we wish them harm."

Ráðulfr laughed, "Of that I am certain!"

Chapter 17

The voyage south from Alt Clut had been pleasant. The gods gave us good weather and a kind wind. We left the Stad on the Eden three days later. We had much to discuss before we returned to our home by the Water. Ráðulfr put into place a series of actions. I was now happier for Ráðulfr and his men would be crucial to the defence of my land. They could go to the aid of either Ketil or me. When I left and we rode south towards the Grassy Mere I felt that we had control once more. The Danes would come. They would attack but not for a while. The men who had fled would have to report to their leaders and then come north once more to speak to the Picts and the men of Strathclyde. If Ketil was attacked again then it would be the Picts. We had time.

I was in an expansive mood as I explained to my three companions the significance of all the features we passed. There were few people who lived in this valley. When we neared the Water at the Rye Dale I pointed to the rocky crag to the west, "And that is Myrddyn's cave. It is where my son, Wolf Killer, killed a wolf." I saw my two older warriors clutch their amulets and Erik just looked fearful.

We paused at old Arne's farm at the head of the dale. Arne was long dead but his great-grandson, Arnfasti, farmed the land now. We enjoyed some ale and rye bread before we pushed on to my home. It was dark when we arrived and the gates were barred. That was good. Karl and Cnut were doing what I had asked. They had heeded my warning and were being vigilant!

"How goes it, Jarl?"

"Better than we might have expected, Karl. My men will speak with you and tell the tale. Come, Erik. I will visit with Kara and then you can go to my hall and warn Atticus that we are home!"

Kara and Ylva had been expecting me. The horn of ale which was already poured told me that. They even knew of the battle but of Alt Clut and Dumnagual, they knew little. After I had explained what we had done Kara came to top up my ale. She kissed me on the cheek, "When other men your age are in their dotage your mind becomes sharper and sharper. You employed the perfect strategy. You think the Danes will still come?"

I wagged my finger and chided her, "Do not play games with me, daughter, you believe that they will still come, in fact, I think you know for certain that they will come."

She laughed, "I have been caught. Good, you are prepared. Then Ylva and I will do our best to give you fair warning of their attack but without Aiden, we are that much weaker."

I saw Ylva give her mother a strange look. "But we could become more powerful."

Kara shook her head, "Do not even think of that path. The power which might be unleashed would be hard to control. The land could be destroyed."

"I do not think so."

I shook my head, "I have a feeling that this is to do with the spirit world and volvas. I will let you two sort this out. I learned long ago to stay out of such matters."

My daughter smiled, "You cannot stay out of them for they are part of you, father, but you are right. Ylva and I must wrestle with these daemons ourselves."

I rose, "I have much to do. We will build signal towers. I spoke with Arnfasti at the Rye Dale. He will build one at the scar of Nab. I will have men build a line from there north to the Grassy Mere and the dale of Mungrise. That will just leave the land between here and the bridge of Skelwith."

Ylva shook her head. "There is a faster route. Build one at the head of Grize's Dale. They can be seen from Windar's Mere and the families who farm there can build and watch."

"It is good that you have a sharp mind."

I left them and headed for my hall. The food was being prepared by Atticus and the servants as I entered. The smell was exquisite. "It is good to be home. I should have sent Dagfinnr ahead and had the sweat hut lit. Tomorrow will have to do." I looked around, "Where is Germund?"

"He is over at Hawk's Roost helping Sámr and Baldr."

"Hawk's Roost?"

He shrugged, "They will explain. It seemed to make sense to them." I could tell the old Greek's logic had been ignored.

I waited until I had cleansed myself in the sweat hut before I ventured across the Water. Erik enjoyed the sweat hut and Atticus accompanied us so that he could begin to train Erik to use a strigil. It was not an easy task but Atticus was nothing if not patient. When we had done, I let Erik take the helm of the boat which we used to cross the water. He had a good eye for the wind. As he tied it up, I looked and saw that Sámr had a dozen men working under the watchful eyes of Germund. They were building a stone tower which was attached to the wooden hall. Germund had lived in Miklagård and knew how such towers were built. There was plenty of

139

stone around. Our farmers joked that the first crop they raised in their fields was a bountiful harvest of rocks.

We made our way to Germund, "It is good to see you back, Jarl. I did not think you would mind if I helped Sámr."

"Where is he?"

"He and Baldr are watching the hawks." Suddenly the name became a little clearer. He pointed to the north and we set off along the path which climbed towards the trees. We passed the outbuildings which Erika and I had built. We passed through the small vegetable plot which was now overgrown and we came to the palisade. There was a gate and we went across the ditch. We entered the dark world of the forest and walked along the old hunter's path which had been there when we had first come. Erik stepped on a twig and Baldr rose from the undergrowth and put his finger to his lips. He gestured for us to back off and we did. He and Sámr joined us.

"Sorry, Jarl Dragonheart but there is a hawk's nest yonder. We found it three days ago. There are three chicks and we are hoping to take one of the chicks and train it." I nodded. It was rare for a pair of hawks to be able to raise three chicks. Normally the runt would either die or be eaten by the others. "We are going to try to take the runt in the next few days."

"Good. I need to speak with Sámr."

Baldr nodded, "Would you like to watch with me, Erik?"

"Aye."

"Then be as silent as you can be. We are trying to work out the pattern of feeding so that when they are both gone from the nest, we can take the runt."

He nodded but looked sad, "That is what I was called by my mother, the runt. Can I help you feed the hawk? I would like to make it strong so that it can show the others that it is not a runt."

I knew then that the sisters had sent Sámr to find the hawks. *Wyrd*. It would help Erik to grow. The words used in his home had hurt him. The bird would be a symbol of the change in him. As we walked back to the palisade, I told Sámr what had happened and what I had done.

"I should have been there with you."

I shook my head, "There will be other times for you to learn to talk with kings. Now is the time to be with your wife and your unborn child. Now is the time for you to make your home strong." We had entered through the gate and I pointed at the tower. "This is good!"

"I saw all the stone and thought that a tower would be a refuge. It could be protected by a small number of warriors. The men who are building it with Germund are young warriors I have chosen to be my oathsworn. We will build a warrior hall. When I go to war then four will protect our wives in my tower."

When we reached his hall Aethelflaed came from the cooking area. She and Nanna had been baking and they were covered in flour. I saw that her bump and that of Nanna were more visible. "The servants said you were here, Jarl Dragonheart. I will fetch some ale."

I shook my head, "We will not disturb you. I need to talk with my great grandson." They left and Sámr and I headed for the table. All of the furniture was newly made. It smelled new. It was unspoiled as yet by ale and food stains, that would come. The table would become a map charting the family of my great grandson as they grew.

"Will you go to my father and ask for his men?"

"I will warn him that he may be needed. I will have towers built to link us with Whale Island."

"My father and Gruffyd, not to mention Raibeart, have more men than Ráðulfr. Surely, they would be the first that you would summon."

"And I will."

He heard the hesitancy in my voice. "You think that Ráðulfr and his men are better."

"I know that they are better. Gruffyd lost his best men during that raid on Om Walum. Your father's men are more like traders than raiders. Ráðulfr and his men are tempered blades. There may be fewer of them but they will have a greater impact on the battlefield."

One of Sámr's servants returned with the ale and poured it.

"Yet those who live at Whale Island have the better lives. They do not have to endure winters as bad as we or those further north. They do not have to suffer raids and battles. The taxes they charge for landing ships means that they are rich without raiding. It does not seem fair."

I supped my ale, "Now you are learning of the dilemmas of leading the clan. Each man has chosen his own path. Each thread, like a Norns' web, is interlinked. Arnfasti's family live at the Rye Dale because Arne chose to live there. Arnfasti could move to Whale Island but he chooses not to. Men make choices and live with them. I will call upon Ragnar and Gruffyd. Their men will fight for the clan but I fear they will lose more men and contribute less."

"And that is why the men of Cyninges-tūn are always your first choice in battle."

"Aye for at one time they were the Ulfheonar and now they are the sons and grandsons of Ulfheonar. You are already doing the same with those men who have chosen to follow you. I will have the miners who dig the iron to work harder. We need metal. I will have Ragnar trade for weapons and I will hire swords."

Sámr looked at me with questions in his eyes. I had surprised him but, in truth, I had been thinking about this for some time. Aðalsteinn and Dagfinnr had given me the idea. They were good warriors. As yet they had no families. I doubted that Aðalsteinn would want one but Dagfinnr might. They could live in Cyninges-tūn but instead of farming would be paid to serve me, initially, and then the clan.

"I have not lost my mind. I cannot recreate the Ulfheonar. Odin made those and sent them to me. They will not return. The blood of the Ulfheonar courses through the veins of the warriors of this valley but we need men like Karl Word Master and Cnut Cnutson. They protect my home but they are old wounded men. We pay them. Cyninges-tūn and its folk are happy to do so. I will merely choose men who wish to be warriors and do not wish to farm. There will be warriors like that at Whale Island."

Once Sámr knew my mind he helped me to formulate an idea of the sort of men I would like. Baldr joined us in the middle of the afternoon and we told him of our plans. He nodded but seemed distracted, "I have the pattern of the birds. If we are to take a chick, Sámr, then it must be soon. I climbed a nearby tree and peered in the nest. I have seen the runt. We should take it tomorrow."

"Then we will do so."

I saw Erik's face. It was bright with anticipation, "Would you wish to be here, Erik Shield Bearer?"

"I would."

"Then come with Germund when he returns in the morning."

"You would take Germund back?"

"I would for I need his mind. He was a sword for hire. Who better to ask for advice? He will just be away from you for one night."

Germund proved to be more than useful. He told me what made a good sword for hire and I was surprised. I had thought he would tell me to choose young single men who were hungry to fight but he advised me to choose older men who had either chosen not to have families or had lost them. He pointed out that as professional warriors they would work harder at their skills. Younger warriors were more likely to fall in battle. He was right. Our greatest losses on the raid to Portus Cale had been the younger warriors who had chosen to follow Sámr. By the time he and Erik left the next day, I had a better idea of what I wanted.

I know that I should have gone, almost immediately, to visit with my son and grandson but I was enjoying my valley too much. Many of my warriors had begun families years earlier and now their sons were training with Karl and Cnut. They wished to speak with the Dragonheart and I enjoyed being with the young boys who would soon become men and warriors. In addition, Baldr, Sámr and Erik had taken a chick and were hand rearing it. It had yet to fledge and they would train it. I had never managed to have a hawk. I envied Sámr. I visited Hawk's Roost as often as I could. The hawk was of the type called Goose Hawk. They were a brave bird and took on geese even though the goose was a larger bird. I had much to occupy me in Cyninges-tūn.

Haaken came to visit at the end of Sólmánuður. He was bored. He enjoyed playing with his grandchildren but just until they bored of hearing his stories. He only had granddaughters and so he came to stay with me. He and Atticus argued and debated much. I think they were great friends but they hid that friendship behind banter.

The consequence of all of this was that I did not get to visit with my son and grandson until the middle of Heyannir. By then we had all watched, somewhat nervously, as Sámr had released Hunter, the goose hawk, for the first time. The bird had been trained using a leash but this was the first time that he had been allowed to fly free. Of all of us, only Erik seemed unconcerned. Like the bird, he had grown in the month or so since we had been back. He had eaten well and trained hard. He was a handspan taller than he had been and his frail frame had filled out a little.

As Sámr stroked the bird's head Erik offered counsel, "Lord Sámr, what is the worst that could happen?"

"The bird could fly off and not return."

"Then that would be meant to be but you saved the runt of the brood. He would have died had you left him in the nest and yet you took him and you made him strong. If he flies free then his existence is down to you. It is the gods who give and permit life. Is that not enough power for you? If he chooses to return then that is even better but let him fly. Let him enjoy the freedom of the air."

Sámr looked at Erik, "How did you become so wise?"

Haaken was with us and he simply said, "He lives with the Dragonheart and Atticus. It should come as no surprise that he has picked up knowledge."

Sámr's fears proved groundless. Hunter took off like an arrow from a bow and disappeared. We had chosen the open ground by the Water but Hunter, after swooping dangerously close to the surface then soared and dived back into the forests to the east of the hall. We saw nothing. Had he returned to his family? The other two chicks had also fledged and gone to seek their own territory. Perhaps he had emulated them. Sámr began whirling the lure with the dead sparrow on it. He began whistling. I saw the fear in his eyes. He thought the bird had gone and then suddenly, the bird appeared and raced from the hall to land on Sámr's glove. It came at the speed of an arrow from a Saami bow. It proceeded to tear the dead bird to pieces. It was trained and it would not leave.

Erik, Haaken and I took that as a sign and we mounted horses the next day to ride to Whale Island. We would take all day to make the journey for I wished to see the signal towers which had been built already. We only needed two for the Water was straight and there were no trees along it to mask a signal fire. We would need more in the forest section. Luckily farmers had cleared many of the trees to make farms. This was fertile land. When the river flooded it deposited goodness onto their farms. I knew that some believed that they could grow wheat. I was not certain but I knew that many wished to grow that most luxurious of cereals.

I went to Ragnar's hall. He lived closer to Whale Island. Gruffyd now lived to the east of the river on which our ships were repaired. The land there had been farmed and occupied by our warriors but, over the years, raids from Mercia, our wars and an outbreak of a pestilence had left it empty. Some thought it lazy of my son to occupy the farms of the dead. I thought it showed sense. He would not raid as much and using the farms of those who had once been part of the clan did them honour. I would visit with him once I had spoken to Ragnar.

Ulla War Cry had grown into a warrior. He was no longer the frail young boy who had almost been taken by the Norns. As we had travelled south Haaken and I had told Erik, Ulla's story. I smiled as I saw Erik taking in the young warrior who had once been as small as he had been. "Ulla, take Erik to the stables."

"Aye, great grandfather."

"Where is your father?"

"There is a trial in the Great Hall. A man is accused of murder."

They left and I was alone with Astrid. Astrid was pleased to see me. She regarded me as a foster father and I was chastised for keeping apart for so long. My grandson had chosen the best of wives.

"It is good to see you, Astrid, and you are to be a grandmother soon. Aethelflaed is with child."

Her face fell briefly. She had not known. Sámr had forgotten to tell her. Then she recovered her composure, "Then Ragnar and I will visit with them soon."

"That would be good for he has done much work on his hall and they would be pleased to see you."

She gave me a shrewd look, "But not necessarily his father."

"I know that they grew apart and I cannot fathom the reason but he has changed. If you could take Ragnar and Ulla War Cry to see him then that would be a good beginning. Ragnar chose to live here."

144

"Just as Sámr chose to live close to you." She held up her hand, "I can understand why but I am his mother and it hurts."

I sighed, "And how is Elfrida?"

"She is grown older but the summer weather suits her and she aches less. I will take you to her for she will also be pleased to hear Sámr's news."

She was and I sat with the two women telling them of Sámr and Aethelflaed. I also spoke of the danger from the Danes. Elfrida was a Christian and her hand went to her cross. "My eldest and my husband lie there dead because of Danes. They are a plague on all humanity." Elfrida was a Saxon. Her people, the people of the East Angles and of Essex, were now under the heel of the Danes. She was a kind woman, a Christian woman, but she hated the Danes.

I left the two women and went to seek my grandson. He was still sitting in judgement on the man accused of murder. I entered the hall which was filled with the men of the settlement. They would have a say in the sentence.

I saw the accused. He was Beorn Sharp Tongue. I had met him many years earlier when he was a young man. He had had a high opinion of himself then. He had been belligerent as a youth. I saw him now as a man grown. He was massive and his whole manner reminded me of some of the Danish jarls I had met. I wondered if he had their blood in him.

My grandson was summing up, "Beorn Sharp Tongue, men have testified that you killed Arne Siggison and that he did not defend himself. Have you anything to say now that all the evidence has been collected?"

He almost snarled at my son and I did not think that he adopted the correct position. "I am a Viking. I told Arne Siggison that I wanted the corner of land which abutted mine and he would not sell it to me. I told him that I would take it if he would not sell it and he said he would appeal to the jarl. I said we should fight for it and he would not. He would have lived had he let me have the land."

My grandson said, "Then you are guilty by your own admission. You killed without cause."

He spread his hands and adopted a surprised expression, "I had cause. I wanted the land. Are we Vikings or are we the followers of the White Christ?" He looked around for support but none was forthcoming. "What justice can I expect from the son of a Christian. You are not a true Viking!"

My grandson's knuckles were white as he gripped the scabbard on his sword. He stood and I could feel him calming himself. He would have been well within his rights to have Beorn Sharp Tongue executed for his insult but he did not. "Beorn Sharp Tongue, you are banished from the

Land of the Wolf. You have seven days in which to leave. Your family may stay and farm your land but you must leave!" He turned to the assembled warriors. As he did, he caught sight of me, "What say the warriors here gathered?"

To a man, they shouted, "Aye!"

Beorn Sharp Tongue shouted, "I do not accept your judgement! You are the pup! I would speak to the Wolf himself. I would hear Jarl Dragonheart's judgement."

His back had been to me and he had not seen me. The men around me had and they parted. Haaken and I strode forward. I had my hand on Ragnar's Spirit. When he saw me his face fell. He had thought to humiliate my grandson.

"Then hear my judgement now! I confirm my grandson's judgement and more. If you utter one more insult, Beorn Sharp Tongue," I drew my sword, "then I will execute you myself, here and now! What do you say? Will you leave my land or shall I execute you as you deserve for your crime and your insult?"

His eyes glared at me but his voice was smaller, "My family and I will leave. I will take my snekke and find a land where there are real warriors. This was once the Land of the Wolf but it is now a toothless wolf! I will leave but I will have vengeance on this clan!"

I sheathed my sword and, as I turned, I backhanded him so hard across the side of his head that he fell to the floor, "Think yourself lucky that I did not kill you. You have but two days to leave. If you are still here when I return to my home then you will have the blood eagle!"

He rose and wiping the blood from his mouth left. The men began banging their feet on the wooden floor and chanting 'Dragonheart!" Over and over.

Haaken One Eye shook his head, "We should have gutted him where he stood. Nothing good will come of this, Dragonheart!"

146

Chapter 18

That evening I ate with my grandson and his family. "Ragnar, you need to be firmer with your people. This was murder. There was no question of mitigation. What of Arne Siggison's family?"

"He has a son. I was going to give them coin as weregeld."

"Give them Beorn's farm. That is only right and proper."

"Of course. I am sorry."

"Do not be sorry. Being a jarl has rights and responsibilities. You enjoy much but you must have a stronger hand. Did you hear his words? He was challenging you. You cannot allow any to challenge your position."

He shook his head, "I was going to ask if any had ever challenged you but I can see that it was a foolish question. Perhaps Beorn was right. I may be not strong enough to be jarl."

"You are strong enough." I turned to Ulla War Cry. "Ulla, you are now a man. Can you not help your father?"

"I will try but I am not Sámr."

"Sámr's thread is not yours but you do not choose your thread." I saw Erik Shield Bearer taking all of this in. He was learning. I changed the subject for I could see that Elfrida and Astrid were becoming upset. "I am having signal towers built for when the Danes come and come they will. When they do, Ragnar, I will need you to leave enough men to defend your homes but to bring the best to Cyninges-tūn. It will not be a warband which tries to kill me. It will be an army."

He nodded, "When will this stop?"

I sat back and said, simply, "When I am dead. I have angered and hurt too many Danes for them to forgive me. I have killed Saxon kings and Danish war chiefs. The Danes may control the eastern side of the land but the Land of the Wolf stands as a symbol of their failure. When I took the side of Athelstan and then destroyed their Dyflin home they were forced to do something."

He shook his head, "But why do you do such things? Why did you bring back Aethelflaed?"

I turned and said flatly, "Because the Norns had spun. If I did not do these things then you and your sons would never have been born." He gave me a blank look. He did not understand. "Aethelflaed is not the first Saxon who has married into my family. There was a Saxon Queen called Elfrida first. Think of the clan had she not joined it!"

He sank back into his chair and nodded, "Now I understand."

The murderer and his family left the next day. I saw him cursing the quay as he left. I was not worried. He was not a galdramenn and it had no power. I knew that we had another enemy and that did worry me. We should have executed him but it was too late for that. Had I intervened then my grandson would have had even less power. On such small mistakes do disasters grow.

I conferred with the hersir who lived in the land north of Whale Island before I left to travel east to meet with Gruffyd and his men. I wanted him to know the importance of the signal towers. He was an older warrior and he understood better than any. He would ensure that his farmers did as I had bid. I left with a rift between my grandson and myself.

I also had conference with Elfrida before I departed. I spoke to her of her son. She was understanding, "It must be something he inherited from Wolf Killer. The two of you seemed to have a problem speaking with each other."

"But not with you."

She smiled, "No, Dragonheart, not with me. We will visit Cyninges-tūn at Ýlir. We will stay with Sámr and make good the distance we have put between us. It will be good to see Cyninges-tūn and my grandson's home, Hawk's Roost."

I kissed her hand, "You will always be a queen to me."

We rode east and Haaken was able to speak freely. He had been restrained in Ragnar's Hall. "It is good that your grandson only commands Whale Island. He has Raibeart there in case of danger but he is not strong enough. He reminds me of a priest!" I had spoken at length with Raibeart and he knew my mind.

"Do not judge Ragnar so harshly. We have fought alongside him and there is none braver."

"Aye, but he has changed. Perhaps it was when he almost lost Ulla and Sámr or perhaps the fate of Gruffyd and Mordaf put doubts in his mind. A warrior can have no doubts or he is dead."

"He will be strong." My words belied my fears.

Gruffyd had built himself a stronghold which lay on a high piece of ground some twenty miles by road, east of Whale Island. It was a fertile piece of land and, now that the Mercians had been vanquished from the south of us, it was a safer place to live. We could, however, see the High Divide as we approached. When the Danes came there was a chance that they would come for Gruffyd too. The land through which we passed was heavily populated. There were animals grazing as well as crops growing.

My son had been clever. He had built the stronghold so that it was clearly visible from afar. He wanted an enemy to know where he was. He had used the stones he had found to build his wall. As we twisted and turned up the trail to get to it, I saw that he had built a number of ditches. Cleverly he had used the natural folds in the ground so that some of them were wider than others. The bridges which crossed the three ditches could all be easily removed. At the four corners of the walls and on the single gatehouse he had built small wooden towers for archers. If the Danes came then they would struggle to defeat the ditches and the walls.

There were just four men watching from the walls but that was all that was needed. They waved as we approached. Haaken nodded, "Your son has a good eye for defence. With mailed men on the walls then an enemy would never take this place."

"And it may be that he needs the defence."

Erik asked, "What do you mean, lord?"

"If the Danes come then this is a good way to reach the heart of my land unseen. North of here there are few people until the southern end of the Water."

Bronnen and Ebrel greeted us. Ebrel, Gruffyd's wife, said. "I am sorry, my lord, but our husbands are with our sons and they have taken men hunting."

I smiled, "Then I have the opportunity to wash and to change my clothes. We would stay the night if it is not inconvenient."

"Of course not." Servants were waved over and we were taken to a pair of rooms on the first floor. Gruffyd had had the foresight to have the sleeping quarters above the Great Hall. The stairs were points where an enemy could be held. He had had the floor made of wood too. His wife had been the daughter of the King of Om Walum. There was no longer a King but she was used to more than a hut with a dirt floor. Gruffyd had been aware of the shortcomings of his first hall. This new one reflected the former status of his wife. I realised that this had been the real reason for the raid he had made. The building could be built from what we had but furnishings, especially good ones, did not come cheap.

We heard the dogs barking and knew that my son and his hunters had arrived. We went down the stairs. The warrior in me noted that while they were well made, they were only three men wide. Three mailed men, at the top, could hold off an army. I heard noise as we descended and a bleeding Dane was dragged into the hall. I saw my son wave Ebrel and Bronnen from the hall. He looked up at me. "This is good timing, father. We caught some Danish spies. The rest died but we managed to save this one for questioning."

We hurried down. Two of my son's men held him. The Dane had a stomach wound and would not last long. "If you are going to question him then you ought to do it sooner rather than later. Already he is knocking at the door to the Otherworld."

Gruffyd nodded, "I bow to your knowledge and ask you to question him."

I lifted the man's chin. I saw anger and pain in equal measure. He was not a young warrior. I put his age at about forty. "I am the Dragonheart. Your entry to Valhalla rests in my hands. If you answer my questions, I will give you a sword and a warrior's death." He stared at me defiantly. I sighed, "I know almost all. You were sent when your attack in the north failed. Sven the Boneless was less than happy and told Ubba Ragnarsson that you needed to attack in the south instead!"

He looked at me in horror. I said nothing. "If you know all then give me a sword and my warrior's death."

I shook my head, "I need more than that. You are a spy and a Dane. I have no reason to be merciful. Where is the army gathering?"

"That cannot help you."

"Then telling me does not betray your leader." I saw the pain from the wound. A stomach wound was always fatal and rarely quick.

He nodded, "West of Jorvik there is a camp. The Land of the Wolf is doomed. Ubba Ragnarsson has the crews of thirty drekar gathered. All of those you have slighted are gathered; the men of Dyflin, the Skull takers, all of them. You cannot survive."

I laughed, "In which case why do they need to send an old warrior to scout out the land? Surely they could just walk in and slaughter us all!"

A sharp pain must have scythed through him for he doubled over. "Kill me now!" I waited. "Ubba Ragnarsson is in Sweden visiting his father. There is to be a raid on Paris. He has to ask his father's permission. When he returns then you will die."

I had enough information. I took a sword from one of the guards and nodded to Haaken One Eye. I handed the sword to him and said, "I will see you in Valhalla." Haaken slid his dagger across his throat the moment his bloody fingers wrapped around the sword.

As the body was dragged away Einar Fair Face shook his head, "How did you know so much already?"

"I dreamed and I guessed. I heard, from Ketil, that Ragnar Hairy Breeches and his sons were at the heart of the Danes in the East. Carr had gathered that information from Ada in Jorvik. Ubba was one of the lords whom Sven the Boneless had allegiance to. Ubba and Garðketill the Sly had raided together and were blood brothers. It was a guess and it saved time. The man had moments left to live."

While servants cleaned the floor Gruffyd and Einar led us to the table. Ebrel sent servants in with ale. "Is this the reason you are here?" I nodded and told them of the attack on Ketil. "This just tells us that they will attack. It also confirms your suspicion that they might try to come through me to get at you." The ale was poured and my son drank. I remained silent. I saw him ruminating.

Eventually, I asked, "Did any escape?"

He looked at Mordaf who nodded, "Aye, grandfather. My men and I were chasing three of them. One turned and went berserk. It took all four of us to kill him."

Haaken nodded, "That is berserkers for you! Olaf Leather Neck had the best technique to deal with them. He took their heads. A man cannot fight without his head!"

"It matters not, Mordaf. The attack cannot take place until after the new grass. If Ubba is in Sweden then he cannot be in Jorvik."

Mordaf asked, "Then what will the thirty crews be doing?"

"They will be ravaging Northumbria. They will practise their art for they know they will need all of their skills to defeat the Clan of the Wolf. Thirty crews mean they have more men than we can muster. They will know that we have to guard our borders. An attack on Ketil and scouts here tell them that we have to be prepared for an attack anywhere. They will hope that we relax our vigilance. We will not."

"What can we do, then father?"

"You need to build signal towers between here and Whale Island. They are in place from there to my home. Send the signal when you are attacked." I sighed, "They will come for me but if you cannot spare men to come to our aid then do not worry. Ráðulfr Ulfsson and his warband are my reserve. Raibeart and Ragnar can spare men."

Gruffyd smiled and put his hand on mine, "And you are my father. If I am able, I will bring men and still leave my walls defended. We, too, are Clan of the Wolf. It has taken me some time to realise that but I see it now. I would have questioned the Dane and discovered nothing. I would have dismissed it as a speculative raid by a band of bandits. We are not alone here. It is good that you have come. We can be one family once more and one clan again. We will defeat these Danes!"

The three of us stayed just a couple of days and then headed north. The ride home was of greater interest to us now. This might be the way the Danes came. Haaken and I cast our eyes over every piece of ground as we rode to our home. I saw many places where we could ambush or hold them up but, sadly, all were too far south. When we reached the Water, I knew that we would have to fight an enemy, for the first time, on the land around my hall. Thus far we had fought them some distance

151

from our homes. The only ones who had harmed us had been the witches who had abducted Kara. We would not be fighting witches this time, it would be Danes.

"Jarl, how many men are in a drekar?"

I looked at Erik Shield Bearer. It was good that he was paying attention and listening. "You are thinking of the Dane's words, thirty crews?" He nodded. "A drekar can be as small as a snekke or almost half as big again as a threttanessa. If you take an average of forty men for each crew then we would be facing more than a thousand men."

Haaken added, "Well over a thousand for there will be those who live close by Jorvik and wish to seize the opportunity to raid our land. It could be nearer fourteen hundred men."

"And how many men can we muster, Jarl?"

"If we took every man and every boy from every farm and settlement then we might raise twelve hundred men."

"But we cannot do that can we, Jarl?"

"No. There are two probable ways they will come. Either through Windar's Mere or Gruffyd's Stad. We can draw on the men of Cyninges-tūn and the dales which are close by. That would give us more than four hundred men. Ráðulfr Ulfsson can bring a hundred. Raibeart and Ragnar could field another two hundred. Asbjorn would give us another one hundred. We would have to face them with four hundred and hope that we could hold out until our reinforcements arrived."

Erik was silent. "Then," said Haaken One Eye, "you need to hire as many swords as you can."

Chapter 19

It seemed that my days back in Cyninges-tūn were filled from early morning until dusk with tasks. Getting old did not mean that I slowed down. These were the longest days of the year. I was just glad that I was an old man. Thanks to an old man's bladder I did not expect as much sleep as I once had. I slept less than any now that Uhtric had gone to the Otherworld. I was constantly planning and helping Sámr to train the warriors who would be needed to fight the Danes. When I was not doing that, we were strengthening the defences. Haaken moved into my hall to help me. I think he believed this would be his last war. I hoped it would not be. Atticus was worked harder than any. His clever mind and his knowledge of the fortifications of the east helped us. We built a double gate. It did not inconvenience our people during the day but when the gate closed at night it was a double barrier for axes. With men covering the two gates we could make the space between the two gates a killing zone. We had our slaves deepen the ditches and used the Roman idea of a shallow entrance and a steep exit. The Romans called them ankle breakers.

Sámr, Baldr and I also began to train every man who did not have mail to use a bow. I had two hundred men with mail of one sort or another. The other two hundred would use bows and slings. I sent for Rollo Thin Skin and Aðils Shape Shifter. I needed them with me to train the warriors. Until the crops were harvested, they trained each day. Haaken Bagsecgson had his forge working every hour he could to produce arrowheads and studs for leather. Our tanners produced jerkins of hide which were almost as good as mail.

All the time that we prepared for war life went on for my clan. Fishermen sailed my water, women produced bread and cheese. Mothers produced babies and my two volvas spun spells. Each banner we used would have a spell woven into it. All of my warriors had a woven piece of wool which contained magic. They each wore it beneath their helmet. The miners mined for stone, copper, slate and iron. The iron was almost worked out but we extracted every last piece of the precious ore. Nanna and Aethelflaed blossomed and grew larger. Erik Shield Bearer became bigger and stronger. He worked with Sámr and Hunter. It seemed to me that the two had a link which could not be seen but was there. Hunter was Sámr's bird but she flew better for Erik and returned with game each time he released her. Had he not had a baby due I think Sámr might have resented the affection the bird obviously had for Erik.

At Tvímánuður I went with Erik, Haaken, Atticus, Rollo and Aðils Shape Shifter to Dyflin. We did not take *'Heart'*; she was too big. We took a newer, smaller threttanessa, *'Black Dragon'*. I took just ten men with me to row. I hoped to hire men in Dyflin and they would row back. Two of the men I took were Aðalsteinn and Dagfinnr. They were now my shadows.

I took the steering board. I did not know how many more opportunities I would have and this short voyage seemed perfect. The men did not have to row for the winds were kind. It was not a fast passage but time was unimportant.

The jarl in Dyflin was a man I could trust, Bergil Hafþórrsson was the eldest of the three brothers who followed me. I had offered the title of Jarl of Dyflin to another but when he had refused Bergil had taken on the task. I had not seen him since then. I wondered how he had fared. King Conan mac Finbarr had also been one of my warriors and he ruled part of Hibernia. I hoped that between the two of them they could provide men for me.

A good sign was the longphort which had ten drekar already there. That was a great number of ships and it boded well. The men I had left with Bergil had all served me and I was welcomed warmly by them all. Haraldr Halfdansson greeted me at the quay, "The Jarl will be pleased to see you."

I waved a hand at the ships in the longphort, "Where have all these drekar come from? Is there war on the island?"

"It is Hrolf the Horseman. He has had such success that many ships are sailing to join him in a raid up the Frankish river. The Danes are also sending many ships. It is said that Guthrum, a mighty young leader, takes many ships there and that Ragnar Lodbrok will lead them."

Haaken shook his head, "Then they will not want to come and be a sword for hire."

Haraldr Halfdansson said, "Do not be certain. It is a long voyage to Frankia. They have to pass Wessex and their king is hunting Vikings. We have had many ships pass through who speak of drekar and knarr being attacked close to Wihtwara and it means sailing under a Dane."

"A Dane? I thought you said Hrolf the Horsemen led the Vikings."

"I did but he only commands the drekar of the Clan of the Horse and they have less than ten drekar. The jarl will tell you all. He is in the Great Hall."

Bergil Hafþórrsson and his brothers had come to me with nothing. Within a short time, they had proved themselves to be amongst the best of my warriors and when Mánagarmr Long Stride had declined my offer of the Jarldom of Dyflin Bergil had accepted. Consequently, when we

154

walked in, even though he was in the middle of a debate with the captains of the drekar in the longphort, he rose and walked over to me. He dropped to a knee and bowed his head, "Jarl Dragonheart, this is a great honour you do us!"

I lifted Bergil to his feet. I did not like subservience. "Rise, Bergil, I come seeking men."

He nodded, "As do these captains."

I did not know the warriors who sat around the table but their clothing and weapons told me where they came from. There were two Danes, a few from Orkneyjar and the rest were Norse. As soon as Bergil had said my name I was recognised.

"If you like, Bergil, I can wait beyond your hall. Perhaps I might send to King Conan."

He shook his head, "He is not yet King Conan. He and his brothers still fight for the crown. He will win but he has to subdue many smaller tribes first. Sit at my table and drink. There is room enough and you honour all of these captains with your presence."

I nodded and we sat. As we did so the two Danes looked at each other and then rose, "We will leave, Bergil Hafþórrsson. We have enough men and we did not know that the Clan of the Wolf would be here. We wish no trouble."

Bergil stood. He towered over most men, "Do not insult my guest, Ivar Black Tooth, or there will be trouble here in my hall."

The man he had addressed shook his head, "We wish no trouble but there is bad blood between my men and the Clan of the Wolf."

I nodded, "Let it go, Bergil. I do not come here to make war and the air will be fresher now." I could trade insults with any man. They left.

Their leaving, however, cast a damp atmosphere on the meeting, or perhaps I had clarified Bergil's thinking.

Jarl Finbarr of Ljoðhús spoke first, "Jarl Bergil, you have no drekar yet for they are being built and your men cannot raid. Let us speak with them and offer them oars on our ships."

"And what benefit would come to me? If you take my men who can defend my longphort?"

"It is known that Mánagarmr Long Stride is your ally and he has ships to help defend you." There was a pleading note to the warrior's voice.

"I say again, what benefit is there for me? You take my warriors away with no promise of returning them. Even if you are successful then we will not see any of the gold you take." Bergil knew his own mind.

"You wish payment?"

"I wish recompense for the warriors I might lose."

"They will come back better armed and richer."

"If they come back at all. It is many leagues between here and Frankia. They may stay. At least if they go with the Dragonheart they are a neck of water away is all and I know that they will return."

The faces of the captains darkened and they glared at me. None would risk my wrath but I knew that they harboured dark thoughts. It seems I either made firm friends or deadly enemies wherever I went.

Bergil rubbed his beard, "I tell you what I will do. We will speak with my men. You and the Dragonheart can make your offers to them. If any men sail with you, Jarl Finbarr of Ljoðhús, then I want ten silver shillings for each man before you take them and I will have them swear to return when the raid is over."

"That is robbery!"

"Be careful how you speak to me in my hall. As you say, I have no drekar. There are ten in my longphort which would begin to make me a fleet."

They were beaten and they knew it. "Let us go then. We have wasted enough time as it is."

We headed to the market square in the centre of Dyflin. Dyflin was a trading port. The market stalls were almost permanent. Around the sides had sprung up the tables and shelters of the alewives and warriors gathered there. Vikings are all sailors at heart and sharing news was something we all enjoyed. The crews of the drekar and the warriors of Dyflin mingled happily together sharing news and stories.

The entrance of Bergil and the rest of us made them part and become silent. Bergil found an empty table and climbed upon it. Then he held up his massive hands, "Warriors of Dyflin, we have been honoured. Drekar captains have heard of your prowess and wish to hire some of you to sail to Frankia and raid their mighty river." There was a cheer. He held up his hands, "While I am happy for that to happen, I am unwilling to lose my men permanently. Any who sail with Jarl Finbarr and the others will swear an oath to return to me when the raid is over."

I saw nods. One warrior shouted, "Why does not Jarl Dragonheart lead the fleet?"

"Because Jarl Dragonheart does not wish to sail to Frankia. He needs men but I know not why. Jarl, would you like to climb up next to me and tell us why you need men?"

"Aye, old friend!" I took his arm and he pulled me up. I saw many faces I knew. As I spoke, I looked at the Danes. They had left the hall but not Dyflin. The two captains were with their men. I saw the opportunity to warn the Danes of Sven the Boneless that I knew of their impending attack. Perhaps it would deter them. "I have heard of a raid which is planned on my land. Ubba Ragnarsson, the son of Ragnar Hairy

Breeches, is gathering Danes to fight me. They do not worry me." Some of those before me laughed. "However, there will be much mail and coin on these raiders when they come and I am offering warriors from Dyflin the opportunity to spend the winter with me and return to Dyflin richer and better armed. I have brought a half-empty drekar for I do not need many men." I smiled at the Danes, "I still have Ulfheonar!"

There was a cheer from those below me. I stepped down and Bergil held up his hands. "Those who wish to sail to Frankia will swear to me before they leave."

Finbarr shouted, "And what of those who follow the Dragonheart?"

Bergil smiled, "They need not swear for I trust the Dragonheart!"

In the end, just ten men wished to go to Frankia. They swore an oath. Twelve wished to serve with me. Haaken, Aðils and Rollo helped me to make the choice. The rest stayed with Bergil. As we headed to his hall for food and ale he said, "What you may not know, Jarl Dragonheart, is that we are building a fleet of drekar up the river. They are almost finished. My men will be able to raid next year. The ones who go to Frankia will not have returned but the twelve you take will. Your arrival was fortuitous, Jarl Dragonheart, for I did not want to lose too many of my men and I knew that the offer of Frankish gold was attractive. Come, we will feast and I will hear all that you have to say. How do my brothers fare?"

"Both have wives and soon will be fathers. They are now important men in the clan. When we go to war, they are the ones who stand beside me."

"Then that is true honour. I am pleased."

We sat at his table and he waved slaves to bring forth food and ale. I noticed that they were all Hibernians.

He turned to me, "Was it not dangerous to tell the Danes that you knew of their plans?"

I shrugged and drank the ale which was good. They had burned barley to make it black and rich. "They may not speak to Ubba or Sven the Boneless although, I confess, that they are likely to stop in Lundenwic in which case the Danes will know. If they know then they may change their plans and when a lord changes plans at the last moment, they are more likely to go awry. In addition, we know not where the direction of their attack. The more doubt I can sow in their minds about our preparations the better."

"Would you have more of my men come with you?"

"Your hold on this land is precarious enough. It is why I have hired men. They will be few in number but I have fought with these twelve. They are front rank warriors. My aim is to hold the initial attack until my other warriors can reach us. We have the winter months to prepare and to lay in food. With luck, the Danes will try a siege and hope to starve us out and then the land will come to our aid." It was good to know that he would aid us if we needed him.

While we were in Dyflin my men and I took the opportunity to make purchases. We had Moorish bows but we found and bought two Saami bows from a Saami trader. We stayed the night with Bergil. He seemed reluctant for us to leave. He had not heard of the death of Olaf Leather Neck and it upset him. He had admired him.

"I had hoped when my son becomes a man, that Olaf would teach him how to use the Danish axe."

"I fear that there is none now, save your brothers who use the axe."

He nodded, "And good as they are, they are not as good as Olaf and Rolf were. Will we see their like again?"

I shrugged, "Warriors come and they go. Each one is unique. Rolf was not the same axeman as Olaf. Who knows? The Norns spin their webs and play their games."

Bergil looked at me, "You sound weary, Jarl Dragonheart."

"I suppose I am. The three Ulfheonar you see with me now are the last. I have lost a son, a granddaughter, a grandson and a great-grandson. A man should not have so many losses."

Haaken said, "And this year Uhtric and Aiden have gone to the Otherworld."

Bergil clutched his Hammer of Thor, "Aiden too? The world changes, Jarl!"

"That it does."

We sailed back the next day. We had to row for the winds were against us and I did not bother raising the mast. I had wondered if the two Danes might wait for us to ambush us on the way home. Without a mast, we were as good as invisible and we reached Whale Island safely. I sent my men, new and old, home and Erik and I spent two days with Ragnar. I needed my son and grandson to work together. They needed to communicate with each other. If the Danes came by sea they could come at any time; even over the winter. Their drekar would have to patrol and give us warning.

As we headed north, I saw that the early crops were being harvested. It had been a good summer and our granaries would be full. Most of the beans we grew would be dried. We had fish in winter and plenty of game so that our winter diet of beans was not as dull as it sounded.

Erik was now a much more confident rider. He had grown a great deal and would soon need a bigger horse than the one he rode. I wondered if he might be ready for a byrnie when the new grass came. I would have

Haaken Bagsecgson make him a mail vest. Worn over leather it was very effective. It just left the arms exposed. That was why many Vikings wore battle bracelets. They gave protection to their arms. His sword was still a short sword but that was all that he would be able to manage. He had grown but not enough for a long sword.

"You must keep up the practice with the Moorish bow, Erik Shield Bearer."

"Will I not be fighting at your side, Jarl?"

"If we have to face them shield to shield in the first battle then we will lose. That is why half of our men will fight with bows. You will be needed on the walls. Your bow will be one of the forty best bows used by the two hundred archers. You and the other Saami and Moorish bow armed archers can send arrows further. You need to be able to send twenty arrows in quick succession and not tire."

"I could not do that yet, Jarl."

"I know. Each day you will spend an hour on your bow and an hour with Germund."

"And Hunter?"

"I fear that you will have little time for hunting with the hawk. We all need to make sacrifices and that must be yours. We do not choose our paths. They are chosen for us."

I could almost hear the Norns spinning or, perhaps, it was the spirits of the dead whispering across the water.

Chapter 20

The harvest came and all the men were busy. With Sámr's hall and tower built we could concentrate on finishing our defences. Men practised once a week with their bows. Boys collected the roundest stones they could from the Water and they practised with their slings. Sámr and Baldr spent part of each day riding with their men. They found game trails over the ground to the south and east. They took Hunter with them too and combined hunting with familiarising themselves with the land. It was as they were on the high ground to the west of Windar's Mere that Hunter discovered the Danish scout.

Sámr and Baldr came directly to my hall after the incident. Both were both shaken and awed by what they had seen. "We had seen signs of men or a man, in any event, and I had released Hunter to take down a pigeon we had seen. He did not go for the pigeon but, instead, swooped down into the woods. We heard a scream and branches breaking. When we rode towards the noise, we found the Dane. He was lying on the ground. His back had been broken. Hunter had ripped out one of his eyes and raked his head with his claws. He must have been high in the tree spying upon us. We searched around and found the trail of other Danes. The scream must have alerted them for we lost them at the southern end of Windar's Mere. There had been three others. We placed the Dane's head on a stake at the high point. We named it Hawk's Head in Hunter's honour. The bird was sent to us. Of that, I am convinced."

That night as I told the story to Atticus and Germund they showed contrasting emotions. Germund clutched his hammer and Atticus scoffed. "A bird is a bird and has no soul!"

"Then why did the hawk attack a man and not its prey?"

Atticus waved a dismissive hand, "Birds are stupid creatures! I know not why they do what they do! Disgusting creatures!"

Erik shook his head, "Hunter is not stupid, Atticus and animals can think. The Dragonheart told me of Úlfarr the Wolf. That story tells me that animals have a spirit."

I laughed, "Erik is right, Greek. I accept that you are a clever man but your religion and your science cannot explain the natural world. Believe what you will but I think that Aiden's spirit communicates with the hawk. He died when the hawk became an egg. I am not saying that Hunter is Aiden but Aiden speaks to it. Sámr and Baldr saved the runt from death. The bird has repaid us. We will redouble our vigilance. The Danes are here now. They are scouting and they are watching." I shook my head, "Asbjorn has let me down. They should never have been allowed to get as close to our land as they did. Erik, we will ride on the morrow with Aðalsteinn and Dagfinnr. We will speak with Asbjorn."

When we reached the head of Windar's Mere and Asbjorn's hall the faces of the men we saw did not bode well. They were grim and pained. Asbjorn's wife and son, Eystein, greeted us. "It is good that you have come, Jarl Dragonheart. We were going to send to you, my husband is dying."

"He was wounded? I did not know there had been a battle."

Eystein shook his head, "No, Jarl, there is something in him which eats at him. No matter how much he eats he loses weight. There is blood where there should not be blood. He had the coughing sickness last year and it has never left him."

My hand went to my wolf amulet. It sounded like the worm I had had. Thanks to Aiden we had caught it early and the doctor in Miklagård had saved me. It would be too late for Asbjorn. I put my chastisement from my mind. He had not been in a position to keep watch. They let me go into his chamber alone and they waited without.

When he saw me, he tried to rise from his bed. He was grey and his eyes looked close to death already, "Do not rise, old friend. I hear you have been ill."

"We both know that I am dying." He touched his belly. "Is this where you had your worm?"

I lifted my tunic and showed him the scar. He nodded, "Then I am honoured, I have been afflicted by the same dragon which tried to kill the Dragonheart." He closed his eyes as some paroxysm of pain coursed through his body. He opened them and nodded towards his sword. "I keep that close by me. Soon I will see Eystein the Rock, Olaf and the others. You will watch over my son and my people?"

"I will." I leaned in. "Is he ready to lead them?"

"He is except..." he shook his head, "Dragonheart, he has not fought in great battles. That is my fault. I did not do as you did with Sámr. I did not go to war enough. I sat and enjoyed my family and this beautiful valley. I thought I had all the time in the world."

"Then I will speak with him. War is coming and I fear that here, in Windar's Mere, will be fought a battle against great numbers of Danes. We need a leader for your people. The leader must be strong. I will look in Eystein Asbjornson's eyes and I will see into his heart. I promise that your people will be safe." He looked in pain. "I will send Erik back to Kara. Aiden had a potion. It eased my pain and made sleep easy when I was ill. He said that if I took too much then I would sleep forever."

Our eyes met and I saw understanding. "Then I will be grateful if you can help me to ease the pain. It upsets my wife, son and daughters. I have caused them enough worry."

"Rest, my friend, and I will return." I stood and took out Ragnar's Spirit, "Until the potion is here then hold the hilt. This has power too." I took off the necklet of Odin's Stones and laid them on his chest. "And the Allfather can help too."

I went outside and led his wife and son away from the door, "You should have told me sooner."

Eystein said, "He would not let us."

"Eystein, if you are to lead these people then you need to be strong. I needed to know! This stad is vital to the security of our land! I will speak with you later. Erik, go with Dagfinnr and ride to Kara's Hall. Tell her that Asbjorn has the worm and I need Aiden's potion. She will understand and Erik?"

"Aye, lord?"

"Do not tarry. I would have you back here as quickly as you can. Change horses."

"I will, lord, and I will not let Asbjorn down."

Asbjorn's wife said, "I will have ale fetched."

"No, go to your husband and I will speak with your son."

Eystein had trained as a warrior. I could see that he was well muscled. His sword was a good one. However, he had no scars. That either bespoke a great warrior or one who had not been in many battles. My face and body were like one of Atticus' charts. They were covered in lines. I decided not to judge. We left the hall and went out among the people. All had slumped shoulders and downcast faces.

"Eystein, the words I speak now are for you and no other." He nodded. "I came here to reprimand your father."

He looked shocked, "But why?"

Instead of answering I looked over to where warriors were practising, "How many men have you on patrol today?"

"Patrol?"

"Riding the borders to look for Danes."

His head dropped. He shook his head and then looked up at me, "We did so for a few days after you had been. We saw no one and then father became ill. I thought it a waste of time."

"Three days since four Danes crossed your land and were west of Grize's Dale. How many others have there been?" He had no answer. "War is coming and you are not ready. Your father wished you to be the jarl when he dies. I am not sure that you are the warrior who is up to the task."

162

He looked at me and I saw steel in his eyes, "I am ready, Jarl Dragonheart!"

"Then why did you not order men to watch the borders of our land? What were you doing? Is this because you are not yet a warrior?" He looked shocked and recoiled. "Where are your battle scars? How can you lead men when you have not fought!"

"That is not my fault!"

I shook my head, "I see steel in your eyes but hear whining in your voice. This is not the way to impress me." I had to be harsh with him for the sake of my people.

"Tell me what is and I will do it!"

"When I leave here, I will return to my home. I have men there who could lead the people of Windar's Mere. I will return in one moon. I will judge you then."

"Judge me? You make it sound as though I have committed a crime!"

"And you have committed a crime! Negligence! It is such crimes that can lead to the destruction of the clan. Windar, who was jarl here before your father, was guilty of that crime and he paid for it with his life when the town was attacked. Sadly, many others also suffered and died. Your father was vigilant until he was stricken and instead of taking on his mantle you wallowed in self-pity. Lead, Eystein! Lead!" I knew I was being harsh but in our world, a man had no time for self-pity.

His eyes were hard as he nodded and said, "I will, Jarl Dragonheart." As if to make the point he walked over to the warriors and began to give instructions. They nodded and twenty of them went to the stables. Like all of my settlements, we had bred small horses. They were hardy and could carry heavy warriors for long distances. It was the best way to search a large area. I doubted that they would find any Danes; to do that they should have been on the trails before dawn. The presence of them and their horses would, however, make the Danes warier.

I went back into the hall and found Aðalsteinn. "We will be staying the night. Ensure that our horses are cared for."

My warrior had been standing close enough to hear the words between Eystein and myself. "It must be hard for him, Jarl. His father is dying."

"And if this was a battlefield, would he have time to grieve or would he not fight even harder?"

"I suppose he would."

"Life is hard, my friend. You of all people know that. You can grieve for the dead and worry about the sick but only when peace reigns. This is the Land of the Wolf and peace is a luxury we rarely enjoy."

163

I went back inside. Asbjorn's wife was just leaving the bedchamber, "He is sleeping and that is a mercy." She threw herself in my arms, "I cannot bear to see him in pain. He is a good man and does not deserve it."

"I know. I have sent to Kara for medicine."

She brightened, "Then there is hope."

I did not spoil her dream. The medicine would ease the pain. It would not cure him.

Eystein busied himself away from me. His wife and young son came into the hall and sat with us. The boy was little more than two years old. Asbjorn's wife sat him on her knee. "I am just pleased that Asbjorn got to meet his grandson."

I nodded, "Our children and their offspring are a great comfort to us all."

The two women questioned me about my family but especially about Ylva and Kara. The two were also spinners of clothes and understood the art of the volva. The afternoon slipped away. The servants prepared the evening meal. Eystein returned not long before it was served. He looked contrite. His wife and mother, sensing he needed to speak alone with me, took the child away and left us alone.

"You have something to say, Eystein?"

"You were right, Jarl Dragonheart. The Danes have been on our borders."

"Your men found them?"

He shook his head, "We found their camp. It was a cold one." He shook his head, "It was less than four miles from the edge of the Mere. They came from the east." He realised the inherent danger of Danes camping so close and remaining unseen.

"Then it is not too late to become vigilant. You know now what to look for. As winter draws on it will become easier to find their trails and the evidence of their presence. Hunt them down and kill them. Leave their heads as a warning. Your father promised me watchtowers. Are they built?"

He hung his head.

I sighed, "Then you must take men away from the harvest and have them search for Danes and build watchtowers. Come, have some ale brought and I will tell you what will be required when the Danes come. You may well be the one leading the men of Windar's Mere. It will not be a time for indecision."

We continued our talk throughout the meal. After we had eaten the two of us went to speak with Asbjorn who had woken some time earlier. His wife had been sat with him and when she came out, she was distraught. "If he was a horse in that condition, we would end his misery."

I shook my head, "That is not our choice. When Erik returns his pain will lessen. I took this potion and can swear that it made my life easier."

"But it did not cure you."

"No, Eystein. That needed a doctor who cut me open and took out the dragon!"

When we went in to the chamber, we did not speak of the illness. Instead, I told him what I had had Eystein do. He nodded, "The fault was mine, Jarl Dragonheart, and not my son's." I said nothing. He turned to his son. "Where did you find the sign?" Eystein told him. "Then they know the land well for there is a hunter's trail which comes over the ridge from the northeast. Cent's Mere is a good place from which to watch. Since Cent's son was killed by wolves no one has lived there. They fear his ghost. Have men stay there for four days at a time. They can watch across the valley and they will see the Danes if they come. Then they can use the signal towers which we have yet to build to warn the Dragonheart."

He lay back, exhausted by his own words. Eventually, he opened his eyes, "Is that good enough for you, Jarl?"

"Aye, Asbjorn, that will do."

Erik arrived well after dark. He and Dagfinnr looked exhausted. He handed me the small amphora jug. "Kara reminded you to be careful of the dose, Jarl."

I smiled, "I know and you have done well. The two of you go and eat." I took the jug and a horn of ale. I poured in a small amount and entered the chamber. "I have put the potion in the ale. Drink it, Asbjorn and you shall sleep."

"And will I wake, Jarl Dragonheart?"

"You will and we shall see what the morrow brings." I leaned in and said, "One of the side effects is that you dream. You may well enter the spirit world. Do not be afraid. They will not harm you."

He nodded and drank the whole horn of ale. It would take a few moments for the liquid to enter his body and the drug to take effect but I saw his face relax and he smiled, "Kara is a great witch. I feel no pain. Thank you."

"I will see you on the morrow."

That night was one in which I was denied sleep. The Danes had sent at least three parties over to scout out my land. Would they come sooner than I expected? I began to doubt myself. Eystein was older than Sámr but he was barely ready to take over from Asbjorn. I could not die yet. My work was unfinished. After what seemed like moments asleep, I

165

woke. It was almost dawn. The hall was quiet although I could detect when I had gone outside to make water, the first signs of dawn. I went to see Asbjorn. He looked better. His wife lay asleep on the other side of the bed.

He held out the empty horn, "This is indeed a miracle potion. Later, Jarl Dragonheart, I would administer my own dose."

We both knew what he meant, "Are you certain?"

"Aye, Jarl, I cannot bear to see my wife so distraught. She is becoming ill and she has a grandson, Asbjorn, named after me who needs her attention. My work on this earth is done. Eystein has spoken with me. Your harsh words were just what he needed. He has been hiding in the shadow of his father. It may well be that he dies in the battle with the Danes but if so then it is *wyrd*. He has a son. He has a future."

I realised that the potion had, indeed, worked, "You dreamed?"

"Aye, I dreamed. Aiden came to me and spoke. I am content. Do not tell my family. I will see them all to say goodbye and then take the potion. I pray you make certain that my fingers grip my sword."

"I will do that, Asbjorn the Strong." I clasped his arm in mine and felt his thin, bony fingers grip my arm. The dragon inside him had almost consumed him.

His wife stirred and Asbjorn leaned over to kiss her, "Wake up sleepy head. I feel better and the Jarl needs food!"

There was joy in her eyes at his voice and she leapt to her feet, "Aye, Jarl."

He winked at me and held out his hand. I slipped him the jug. I knew he would not take it until I was next to him. He needed me to ensure that the sword was in his hand.

The news that Asbjorn was a little better, brightened everyone. After we had eaten, I said, "Let us take his grandson to see his grandfather. It will be good for both of them."

I stood back as the four of them sat on Asbjorn's bed and my warrior made his grandson laugh. He tickled him and the boy giggled. He played for quite a while. When his wife saw pain flicker on his face she said, "Come, let us leave him. He is tired."

Asbjorn gave the slightest of nods to me and said, "No, I will have some of my ale. There is some potion in it and it will ease my pain." As his wife handed it to him, he kissed her, "You have been the best wife a man could have. I am honoured that you chose me. Eystein, you will be a great leader and young Asbjorn will be a warrior too." He raised the horn, "I raise this horn to you all and my friend, Jarl Dragonheart. It has been a journey I could not have imagined when first I met him. Thank you, Dragonheart." He swallowed the ale and then reached for the sword.

166

It fell to the floor and I quickly picked it up and placed the hilt in his hand.

I said quietly, in his ear, "Farewell, my friend. I will not be far behind you."

He smiled and closed his eyes. His wife screamed, "No!" And threw herself on him. "Do not leave me! I am not yet ready to part!" She held his hand and sobbed on his chest. I watched his chest rise and fall and then stop. He must have emptied the whole jug into the ale. "No!" He could not hear her. His spirit was already hovering above our heads. I could feel him. I let her sob while Eystein cradled his wife and son in his arms.

Tears coursed down Eystein's face. "I did not tell him that which I should."

"He knew what was in your heart and you will see him again. He will come to your dreams. take comfort in that. Few warriors get to choose the time and place of their death. Asbjorn the Strong's was a good one. He was with his family and in his home. He had his sword in his hand. What more can a warrior ask?"

Chapter 21

Autumn came early as I headed home and the world seemed darker. Erik Shield Bearer and my two men were aware of my mood. Aðalsteinn said, as we neared the Bridge of Skelwith, "My death, Jarl, will be in battle. I have neither wife nor child any longer. It will be a good death."

Dagfinnr shook his head, "Do not be so keen to go so quickly, uncle. I have yet to take a bride and when I do then my children will need someone like you. You shall be the grandfather that was denied them."

I shook my head. My mood was affecting the others. "Asbjorn is in Valhalla. He was a warrior and we do not grieve. Let us put our minds to defeating these Danes. You are both new to my hall. How could we make that stronger?"

That changed the mood for we spent the last hours of the journey coming up with ideas to make it hard for the Danes to attack me in my own home. I knew that despite all the precautions we might take Danes could still sneak over my palisade. I was Ulfheonar and I had done it before. It was Aðalsteinn who came up with one idea I had never even thought of.

"When we raided the Franks, we attacked a town in the middle of the night. The warriors who ascended the walls were skilful and they made not a sound. We should have gained entry save that there were geese in a pen by the gate and when they heard our men they began hissing and honking. If you had geese close to your hall then any who disturbed them would raise the alarm."

I nodded, "A good idea and if the men who tend them are the night guards the geese will not react to their presence."

"And you should bar your doors at night, Jarl Dragonheart."

Once again Dagfinnr was right. There had been no danger for so many years that we had long since stopped barring them. The servants came and went from the rear entrance. That would need to stop. I began to worry about those who lived in our walls. The clan I knew but what of the slaves? We had many. None were Danes but they could have been bought. As we rode over the col which led to my land, I shook my head. If I worried about everything then I would drive myself mad. The Norns had spun. What would be would be.

Sámr was sad that Asbjorn had died. He had sailed with him. A warrior's death was expected but not a worm eating him from within. It made all of us view our mortality and our end.

Sámr's hall and tower were finished and Ragnar had sent word that he and his mother would be visiting soon. This was an attempt to build a bridge. Aethelflaed and Nanna, despite the fact that they were both heavy with child, threw themselves into the business of making their new home something which would impress Astrid and Elfrida.

I visited with Kara. She and Ylva had been to the cave of Myrddyn and they had spent the night there to dream. It had been after Asbjorn had died. We all knew that it was significant. The dream confirmed it. As the three of us sat before a fire, watching the flames, dance, they told me of the dream. "The Danes will be here sooner rather than later, Jarl. In the dream, we saw Aethelflaed and Nanna. They had their bairns but they were newly born."

"Then before the new grass?"

"Perhaps. And they will come from two or three directions." Ylva shrugged, "Dreams are not precise. Some came over Úlfarrberg while others crossed the Hawk's Head."

"I will send word to Ketil, Eystein and Gruffyd. This helps us."

"There is more. We saw Ubba Ragnarsson. He had with him a witch. They know of our power and they seek to neutralise it with their own witch."

"One witch?"

"One witch was all that the spirits allowed us to see. There may be more. As I said, grandfather, dreams are imprecise and the Norns sometimes tell us truths which are half-truths. They are there to catch the unwary who do not use their minds. You have a plan and that will cover any threat the Danes make."

Kara patted my hand, "Do not fear, my father. We have other volvas. The women of the clan will not sit idly by while the men of the clan fight. We will fight too but we will use the spirit world."

Haaken had left me and my other two Ulfheonar had returned to their families. For a brief time, I had my hall to myself. I played chess with Atticus and I watched Erik grow from within and without.

When my grandson arrived, he brought news of Mordaf. My grandson had, apparently, married. When they had moved to their new home there had been some families who had been there when Sigtrygg had ruled. From what Ragnar told me Oda was a good choice for Mordaf. She and her family had learned to fight when they were left alone and attacked by Danish, Saxon and Hibernian bandits. My grandson appeared to have chosen well.

As Ragnar had arrived after dark, they stayed that first night with me. Atticus excelled himself and produced the best food we had eaten in some time. He used some of the spices from Tui. Germund and Erik helped to serve the food. My servants and slaves meant well but I was used to them and they could be clumsy. Kara and Ylva joined us. Astrid had seen little of my daughter and granddaughter. Elfrida was more comfortable with them. On the outside, Aiden's death did not appear to have affected my daughter much but I saw Astrid and Ragnar exchange meaningful looks and gentle touches of the hands as they passed their food, and I saw the sadness in Kara's eyes. Her dead husband might talk to her from the spirit world but that did not make up for the loss of his physical presence. It was as we ate that I began to see the change in the relationship between Kara and Ylva. Kara allowed Ylva to lead the conversation more. As I sat back and enjoyed the company of my family, I realised that the change had been coming since Aiden's death. It struck me then that Kara was preparing to join him. It had been brought home by Asbjorn's decision to save his family suffering. Ylva was now the more powerful volva and when Kara went to the Otherworld then she would gain power. I was sad but I could do nothing about it. The Norns had spun.

We did not take a boat across the water. The day was grey and filled with sleet flecked rain. It was a warning of a winter which would be hard. Instead, we rode around escorted by my new ten warriors as well as Aðalsteinn and Dagfinnr. They rode ahead and behind. We had seen no Danish scouts but such a prized party might tempt scouts who would be able to return to Sven the Boneless with Dragonheart trophies.

Aethelflaed and Nanna were both heavy with child. Ylva, who visited them once or twice a week, told me that their babies would be born at the end of Mörsugur. They both glowed. I had remembered when both of my wives had been with child. They had had the same glow. It was Sámr who showed the greatest change. I saw it in his father and brother's eyes. It was not a physical change. It was something from within. Perhaps it was fatherhood, I know not but he appeared like a leader. I had met Kings and Emperors. I had spoken with great Counts and Dukes. Sámr had that bearing.

After he had greeted his parents and grandmother, he took them on a tour of the hall. Ragnar remembered it as did Elfrida but the others had only seen the ruin I had left. When they returned Sámr had his servants bring ale which was warmed with a poker and infused with honey, butter and cinnamon. We had brought enough spice back from our raid on Portus Cale to indulge ourselves. While Astrid fussed over Sámr and Aethelflaed I sat with Ragnar and Ulla War Cry.

Ragnar said, "How have you wrought such a change in my son, grandfather?" He shook his head. "It is not just his size, it is his bearing. I feel as though he is the father and I am the child."

"Sámr has been chosen to lead the clan. Perhaps it is the spirit of my dead wife, Erika, now working with Aiden, or it may be that Odin has taken an interest. I have done little except to put around him those whom I trust and to offer encouragement when he needs it. He will lead the clan when I am gone."

Ragnar gave me a sharp look. "You are not leaving us! This is not the worm again is it?"

I laughed, "I have no reason to leave the Land of the Wolf. I have an unborn child of my blood and I wish to see him. As far as I am aware, I will be the only one with a great, great grandchild. I will be honoured by that title."

Ulla War Cry shook his head, "You have far greater titles!"

"No, Ulla, as I near the latter end of my life I see the world differently. The Land of the Wolf and the Clan are important but my blood, coursing through my family is more important. When I was in the cave by Wyddfa I saw the threads of time. I have blood in me that was here when the Romans built their wall. The sword that now lies with Aiden was wielded against the enemies of this land. Long after we are gone there will be someone with our blood and they will be fighting for the clan. I am a guardian of the clan and Sámr will be the next. Who knows, his unborn child may be the one after."

The visit, which lasted until the first baby was born, was a joyful time. Ragnar was healthy and my grandson looked pleased that his son had named his firstborn after him. Nanna had not yet given birth but Ragnar thought to stay just a short time and then go home to Whale Island. The extended visit was caused by the change in the weather. Ýlir brought winter. It was as though Odin himself had commanded ice. We had a three-day rainstorm and then woke to clear skies. That would have been the time for Ragnar and his family to leave but who could leave the Water when there were clear blue skies and Old Olaf looked as sharp as ever? The cold air felt invigorating after the rain and they did not leave.

The ice came in the night. My servants kept the fires banked up all night but, even so, the cold was so severe that we could see our breath before us while we were within our sleeping chambers. We woke to the Water beginning to freeze at the edges and the clear blue skies were replaced by white ones which were laden with snow. They came from the north and were harbingers of a harsh winter. Even as Ragnar prepared to leave a blizzard descended which stopped anyone from moving out of their homes. I only discovered this later on for I was in my hall with my people. The snow fell relentlessly for four days. I had not experienced such weather for many years. Atticus had never seen weather like it. The snow stopped at dusk. The skies cleared and the land froze. When we woke it was to a frozen Water. I waited two days to see if a thaw would come. Often, we had a freeze early in the winter and it thawed quickly. After two days it had hardened. It was getting colder.

"Erik, let us venture out. I would see how my people fare."

"Aye, Jarl."

"Atticus, I fear we will not have the opportunity to find fresh food. Are we prepared?"

"We are, lord. It was in anticipation of an attack by the Danes but it will help us with an attack by Nature."

"No, Atticus, nature does not attack us. She tests us."

We went, first, to my warrior hall. They were well but I ordered them to clear the snow in the settlement so that people could move around. I went to the older ones for I knew they would be in the greatest danger. We had prepared for hard times and all were healthy. Finally, I went to Kara and Ylva. Their faces warned me of trouble.

"What is it?"

"This will be a wolf winter."

"You are sure?" I spoke to Ylva for Kara looked deep in thought.

"We are. We dreamed but even without a dream this freeze so early means that the wolves will descend from their high passes. The she-wolves are heavy with young and the males will need to provide for them."

"Then we will have to hunt them." I did not relish a long march to the Dale of Lang or Úlfarrberg which was where they proliferated.

Ylva read my thoughts. "You will not need to go far. There is a reason I am named Ylva. I dreamed that they come. Sámr has a child and will be jarl of the Clan. His great grandfather was Wolf Killer. They will come… it is not just the Danes who will test Sámr. It is the wolves too."

By the time I returned to my hall it was dark. The days in Mörsugur were so short that if you blinked you missed them. It was the time when wolves could hunt under cover of darkness. I had Germund prepare spears so that we could hunt. "Erik, you have never hunted. If you wish to stay in my hall with Atticus there is no shame."

Atticus shook his fussy head, "Dragonheart, there will be no wolves! This freeze will keep every animal inside."

Just at that moment, from the Hawk's Head came the first howl. There were wolves and they were not far away. The freeze must have struck the high ground earlier. "What say you now, Atticus? That is a scout. He has come down and found food. The food will be our animals and, if we try to stop them, then us. On the morrow, we will visit with Sámr. He needs to know of the danger." I looked at Erik, "Well?"

"I will come. I have grown and I am your shield bearer. I will watch your back for you."

172

Atticus shook his head and mumbled. "A man who is nearly seventy hunting wolves! Has the world gone mad?"

The Water looked to be frozen enough to walk upon but I did not risk it. Before dawn, I rose and summoned my twelve men. I had Germund prepare horses and the fifteen of us rode around the Water to Hawk's Roost. The journey which was just a few miles, took until what passed for noon. The snow had drifted and the gate was barred. I had my men clear the snow while we shouted for it to be opened from within.

When it creaked and groaned open, I was greeted by Sámr, Ulla and Ragnar. Sámr said, simply, "The wolves?"

"It will be a wolf winter. I came to warn you. That wolf we heard last night was a scout."

Sámr nodded, "Aye, it caused Nanna to give birth. Baldr has a son, Úlfarr."

As we walked towards the hall, I clutched my amulet. *Wyrd.* That had been the name of the wolf which had saved my family. "Mother and child are well?"

"He has a good set of lungs on him. They are well. When do we hunt the wolves?"

"You do not. The clan will need a leader and you need to protect your mother, father and grandmother. None will venture forth for some time. The wolf was by the Hawk's Head and Grize's Dale. They have never been there before. When next we hear them howling, I will take my new warriors and we will hunt." He began to speak. "I am still the jarl. I will hunt."

He nodded, "As you wish. Who will you take?"

"The men I brought with me today. The wolves are not here yet. It was a lone wolf we heard. We have time."

I smiled at Elfrida and Astrid, "I think you will be stuck here for some time."

Elfrida laughed, "Stuck is the wrong word, Dragonheart. It is a joy to be around the babies. The men may be unhappy but we are content are we not, Astrid?"

"That we are." She looked as happy as I could remember.

We did not stay long. We needed to be back before dark and we had preparations to make. It was dark when we returned home. Our beards were rimed with frost. Our very breath froze before us. As my men took away the horses I said, "We will hunt without horses. If you have them then wear seal skin boots and if not then line your leather ones with the fur of animals or down. We may have to sleep in the open. Take cloaks and furs. Germund will arrange the spears. As soon as we hear the wolves howl close by then we leave. I care not if it is in dark of night."

173

"Aye, Jarl."

The wolves came in the middle of the night two days later. The cold had been unrelenting. No more snow had fallen but that mattered not for it had been so deep already that it was as solid as rocks. That made the insides of our homes a little warmer. Germund came to wake me but I was already awake.

"Go fetch the others. And Erik?"

"He is risen. Atticus makes porridge and he is preparing food for us to take."

I shook my head, "We take no food with us. That will alert the wolves."

I dressed and went outside. I listened. There was silence. Then I heard the wolves. They were across the Water close to Grize's Dale. There were a few families there. More worryingly the next home to the north of them would be Hawk's Roost. We had to stop them before they reached Sámr's hall. Erik and my men were already tucking into the honeyed porridge when I entered.

Atticus gave me a bowl, "I would say this is foolish but you would ignore me. Be careful, Jarl. You are no longer a young man nor even a man in middle age. You are old and your reactions will be slower."

I shook my head, "I am Dragonheart. You are a Greek and know not what my body can do. I take with me good warriors. All will be well." As we prepared to leave, I strapped on Ragnar's Spirit and Wolf's Blood.

When we stepped outside the cold hit us. It was so cold it hurt my mouth. Atticus had given me a woollen scarf and I wrapped it around my mouth. The wolf's head kept my head warm. I looked across the ice-covered Water. I heard, in my head, Aiden's voice. He told me to trust my Water.

I turned, "We cross the ice. I will go first. We walk in single file. I want five paces between each man. Walk in my footsteps. Erik, you will be last."

Germund said, "Let me go first, Jarl."

"This is my Water and my land. We will be safe. Trust me."

I stepped onto the ice. It felt solid but that could be an illusion. I took six steps. There was a slight creak as Germund stepped behind me on to the ice. He was a bigger man than me. I had to trust my dead galdramenn. Once I began to walk, I found it became easier. Unlike the land this was flat. There was no danger of slipping. I fixed a point in my mind and headed east. I settled into a rhythm. Germund had a leg which was lame. He was not slow but there was little point in rushing across the ice. When the wolves howled again, I changed direction slightly. They were moving north towards the Hawk's Head. I saw, to the south of me, the sparks from the fire at Sámr's Hall. We had to get between the wolves and my family.

Getting off the ice was harder than getting on. I had to grab hold of a straggly snow-covered branch and pull myself up. I turned to help Germund once I had secured a foothold. We made our way through the undergrowth to find where the trail had been. It was invisible. Only the lack of branches and bushes close by identified its course. It was covered in frozen snow. I did not intend to use the trail for long but it would be the quickest way to get to the wolves. As we listened for the wolves, I tried to remember who lived on the slopes above us. My heart sank when I realised that the next home was that of Sámr.

I had to make a decision and I headed up through the woods. There was a trail there. The last direction from which I had heard the wolves was to the east and north. As we moved along the trail, my spear held before me, I realised that the snow had been flattened and not by animals. Men had walked along it. It was not Sámr and his men. They had not been out of the hall and palisade since before the snow. That could only mean one thing: Danes. I turned and made the sign for danger. It was passed down the line. Dagfinnr was behind Erik. It was right that my shield bearer came to hunt the wolves but not that he should be in danger. He was too young to die on his first hunt. It had almost happened to Wolf Killer.

As we moved along the trail I began sniffing for wolves and also for Danes. As an Ulfheonar I knew that my sense of smell might be the difference between life and death. I could see why no one had colonised this part of the forest. There was rarely anywhere which was flat for more than four paces and the trail twisted and turned as it climbed up the gentle slope. It was as the footprints left the trail to head south that my nose picked up the pungent smell of wolf. I waved us into a long line and gestured for Erik and Dagfinnr to join Germund behind me. There was a clear sky but no moon. The snow and ice reflected light and made the path slightly easier to see but the undergrowth ahead, laden as it was with frozen snow, made visibility difficult. Then I heard the sound of animals gnawing and growling as they ate. It was wolves. I raised my spear and the others did the same.

I moved even more slowly. The men who had made this new path had made it easier for us. There was no frozen snow to crunch. As we moved ahead, I saw first, movement, and second, an open space. It was a camp. I waved my spear left and right for those on my flanks to move around. There were just four of us approaching what was obviously a man-made encampment.

One of the two wolves feasting on half-frozen human flesh saw us and turned to growl. The cold made their sense of smell less effective. It was why we hunted them in Þorri. Their eyesight, however, was faultless. A wolf's defence is to attack and the two of them saw the four of us and leapt at us. Aðalsteinn and the men on the flanks reacted quicker than Germund. Their spears were hurled into the flanks of the two lean animals. Even so, one still almost made Germund. He rammed his spear into its chest but it took Erik's spear to kill it. He rammed it in the wolf's eye and it fell dead. My men retrieved their spears and looked around. I saw what they did. These had been Danes. I counted the remains of, perhaps, ten men. I only worked that out by the swords and shields. As men they were unrecognisable.

Germund said, "Here is a puzzle, lord. These are well armed Danes and yet their swords are in their scabbards. Why did they not defend themselves?"

I looked at the snow in the centre. Using my boot, I cleared it. There was no sign of a fire. "They froze to death. There is no fire. They were either scouting or coming here to take our lives. They did not light a fire for fear of alerting us. The cold came and they must have died." I knelt down and looked at the moustache of one whose body had been gnawed but whose face was intact. "These are members of the Skulltaker Clan. They were here to kill me." I took a knife from a scabbard. It had a long narrow point, almost like a needle used to sew leather. "These are assassin's weapons."

Gandálfr Snorrison, one of my new men said, "I can see ten swords but there are not ten bodies here. At least not ten whole bodies."

I stroked my beard as I tried to unravel this knot, "I think that the wolf scout we heard some nights ago found the Danes. They may not have been dead then. He fetched the males from the pack and when they arrived, they took the men. They were either asleep or dead. More likely dead, I think. They have females to feed. Notice that they have taken the parts which are easy to carry. They have taken legs and the innards. They left the heads, the hands and the feet. These two wolves are not from the same pack. Sometimes there are rogue wolves. They live in pairs or alone. They took advantage of the feast that was left."

I saw that Erik was opened mouthed.

"Erik Shield Bearer, your strike killed one of the wolves. You may have the pelt. Help the rest of my men to put spears through their bodies and we will take them back. Germund, rest your leg. Have the weapons and mail collected. Dagfinnr and Aðalsteinn, come with me and we will make certain that they are all accounted for."

My spear was unbloodied as was Dagfinnr's. Aoalstein's had broken. He drew his sword. I led them beyond the camp. There were no Danish footprints. They had come from the path and made their camp. I turned, just before the tracks I followed descended. I saw sparks in the distance. It was Sámr's Hall. I turned and followed the wolf tracks. Wolves are very clever creatures. They follow in the leader's tracks. Specks of blood and small pieces of the corpses marked their trail. The trail began to rise again. I saw that the prints changed. One animal had left the pack and gone up the slope.

"Dagfinnr and Aðalsteinn, follow these prints and see where the wolf went. I will follow the pack." As I moved, now alone I felt the hairs on my neck begin to rise. I took my spear and rammed it into the ground. I drew my sword. Closing my eyes to enable me to smell the air better I put the blade to my lips. I heard Aiden's voice in my head, *'Beware Dragonheart. Walk the line between life and death. This is the land of the Wolf.'* And then the voice was gone

I opened my eyes. I could not smell wolf but my Ulfheonar senses told me that I was not alone. The path climbed. There was a large rock to my right and so I went to the left. As I neared the rock, I smelled wolf. Even as I turned the huge he-wolf leapt down upon me. It landed on me and knocked me on to my back. His huge paws were on my chest and he bared his teeth as his mouth came towards my throat. Aiden's words came to me.

I did not raise my sword, instead, I spoke, "Offspring of Úlfarr I am Jarl Dragonheart and this is my land. I beg you not to take my life."

Its mouth came closer to me. Saliva dripped onto my beard. It must have heard something for its head turned suddenly.

I said, "Hold your weapons! Do not strike the wolf!" I knew, without turning my head that it was Dagfinnr and Aðalsteinn. The wolf slowly turned its head and I stared into its eyes. In my head, I heard a voice. It was not Aiden's. *'You are the defender of this land. You have the spirit of the wolf yet you have the heart of a dragon.'*

I spoke, "The lands to the east are filled with our enemies. When your young are born take your pack there for I would not hurt you."

'We are hunters and this is our land. The Danes are enemies and we were sent to kill them. They feed our young.'

"And more men will fill this land. We have bright steel and weapons which kill. You cannot win."

I stared into its eyes and I saw wolves stretching back through eternity. The wolf's mouth closed and as he stepped off my chest, I heard, *'Winning and losing are your words, not ours.'* With that, he turned and loped off.

My two men ran to me to help me up. Aðalsteinn said, "If I had been told this I would have said that it was a lie. Why did he not kill you?"

"He spoke to me."

"We heard no words."

"They were in my head. Come, let us return. The threat of the wolf has eased. The Danes gave them a larder but it shows that the threat of the Dane is still real."

Chapter 22

We reached Sámr's hall as dawn was breaking. My two warriors soon told the others of what they called the miracle of the wolf. I knew that Aiden had interceded. I did not know if the wolf pack would head east but I suspected they would not bother my valley again. I had no reason other than a feeling in my heart. As we had walked back Erik said, "Hunter found the Dane close by. What does that signify, lord?"

"That the land and the animals are our allies. We are at one with the land and the Danes are not."

The sight of the two wolves produced such terror in Aethelflaed and Nanna that Elfrida and Astrid quickly took the two Saxons away. There were no longer any wolves in the land of the East Angles. To see a wolf for the first time was terrifying,

"Sámr, you need to watch the Hawk's Head. This is the second time we have found evidence of the Danes."

Baldr said, "Perhaps they will tire of losing men."

"None had mail. These were swords for hire. Skull Takers are killers. They also have witches who are as powerful as Kara and Ylva. Those witches will not travel in winter but come the new grass then they will."

Having crossed the ice once, the second time was easier and we reached my hall safely. My men began to skin the wolves. Erik would have a fur of which he could be proud. I spoke with Kara and Ylva. They knew all as I had expected. "It was my husband. He became a shape shifter and entered the mind of the wolf. It was he spoke the wolf's thoughts. You were lucky, father, but the Mother is on our side." She looked, wistfully, north. "Úlfarrberg and the cave of Myrddyn are both powerful allies." She smiled at me. "Have you not thought, father, that both lie at the heart of the Land of the Wolf yet few people live close to them? That is not a coincidence."

I had not thought of it before but now, as I walked back to my hall, I did. The farm at the Rye Dale and the farm at the foot of Úlfarrberg were among the only five farms in what should have been the most productive part of our land. My farmers chose other ground to farm. My jarls were spread out around the borders of our land but in the heart, the heart of the wolf, there were none to protect it. Perhaps it did not need protection. None had ever attacked us through the land twixt the cave and Úlfarrberg. This was not the time for such thoughts. We had an enemy to defeat who was human and voracious.

The cold spell lasted just ten days longer and then the snow and ice melted. It caused flooding to all of the low-lying areas. People endured miserable conditions for the whole of Gói. Ragnar and my family headed south when the road south was free of water and the road was safe for the women. Elfrida was no longer a young woman.

Ragnar now knew the scale of the problem. He understood that this was not a possibility any longer. It was a certainty. "I will warn Gruffyd of the danger and tell him of your encounter with the wolf. I see now that my son, Sámr, was well chosen. We have lost him but we have lost him to the clan and that is good. I swear, grandfather, that we will be vigilant. We have strong walls and good defences. I know I am lucky to have Raibeart ap Pasgen as a neighbour. We can hold out for at least ten days. Gruffyd, I am certain can last longer. Here is where the danger lies for they will come for you. They come for the heart of the Clan of the Wolf."

After they had gone, I began to work more closely with my new men. I had seen, on the hunt, that they were good warriors but that was only part of their role. They would have to fight in a shield wall. As the weather warmed, I began to work for an hour each day with my new men, the veterans and my town watch. This would be a battle in which all of us would take part. Haaken had rejoined me as soon as the weather had improved. We practised on the flat land between the walls and the Water. We combined the shield wall with our archers and slingers. The young boys of the town were keen to fight for the clan. They knew no fear. I had my shield bearer train them. He was older than they were and knew how to use a sling. Unlike them, he had used a sling to kill a man in battle. In the time Erik had been with me he had learned much. Atticus helped him for Atticus had read about ancient battles.

Haaken and Rollo helped me to make the shield wall as effective as it could be. I had my veterans and newly hired men in the front rank. The ones without mail, who had not fought in a battle, were in the second and my town watch was the third. Germund joined the town watch. They were the shortest of the three ranks. I knew that if they were involved in the fighting then we had lost. Their task was to give steel to the younger warriors before them. We practised locking shields. We showed the newer warriors how to add their spears from the second ranks. We had to teach them how to hold their shield above their heads to protect from arrows. Each day that the Danes did not come made us stronger.

I blamed myself for the injury. We had been practising moving from a shield wall to a boar's snout formation. I had been too concerned with looking down the line and did not see the rut in the earth. I tripped and fell forward. Sweyn Jorgenson, who was behind me, looked down and, as he did so, the tip of his spear gouged a line along my leg. I was more annoyed with myself than him but Aðalsteinn and Ráðgeir berated the poor youth until I stopped them. "It was an old man's carelessness.

Leave the boy alone. Erik, come and help me back to the hall. Germund, take over the drill." I saw Haaken trying to hide his laughter. He would tease me about this later.

Atticus, of course, had a self-satisfied look on his face, "I told you that you are too old for this."

I thought about going to Kara to be healed but this was not a serious wound and Atticus could deal with it. "Listen, old woman, stitch me up or do whatever you have to. It is nothing. Erik, ale!"

Despite my words, the wound hurt and it irritated me more than I would have believed thirty years earlier. I was unable to train for a few days. I made up for my lack of practice by walking around my walls each night to ensure that the gates were barred and the walls were manned. The Danes had not come yet but that did not mean they would not come! When I walked my walls Haaken One Eye was with me. He had one eye but it was a sharp one and he spotted things which I did not.

It was the end of Einmánuður. I had eaten well and I had drunk well. I should have slept all night but I did not. My wound no longer ached. It was almost healed but it itched. I rose to make water and, being up, decided to walk my fighting platform. The air felt damp despite the time of year. As I climbed the ladder, I felt a twinge in my leg. Another wound which would make my life difficult. When I reached the gate towers Karl Word Master was already there. He pointed down the Water. "Fog, Jarl, at this time of year who would have thought?"

I said, absent-mindedly, "Aye." The ale had dulled my wits. I looked down the Water and saw that the fog was coming quickly. Fog did not move quickly. It insinuated its way across the land. Then I remembered Kara's words. "It is the Danes! Sound the alarm! Light the signals!" In the time it took for me to say that the fog had closed to within a couple of hundred paces of the walls. This was not natural. It was witchcraft! "Alarm! Alarm!"

I raced down the ladder as quickly as I could. I ran into my hall and saw that I had roused them. "It is the Danes, arm and get to the walls! Erik, Atticus, help me with my mail!" Haaken ran for his mail while I dressed for war and battle much quicker than I had ever done before. Even so, I heard men dying as I ran, sword in hand and with Erik Shield Bearer and Haaken behind me, to the walls. When I saw a Danish head appear over the walls, I knew that they had brought ladders. Karl Word Master and Cnut Cnutson, along with the other old men, were holding off the enemy. I saw one Dane struck in the side of the head by Karl's sword and he fell. Men were racing up the ladder to reach the fighting platform. What we had not practised was where men would go when we were attacked and I saw that too many were heading for the main gate.

Slipping my shield over my back I shouted, "Beorn Hafþórrsson, take twenty men and go to the south wall!" The fog had come from the south. The odds were that they would be attacking there. I saw Kara, Ylva and another four volvas emerge. They stood hand in hand and began to chant. Kara and Ylva knew it was witchcraft and they were countering it. The fog was unnatural. There were witches with the Danes! They might defeat the witches but the warriors were a different matter. I began to clamber up the ladder. I saw that Siggi One Eye had already been felled by a Dane who had gained the fighting platform. Karl Word Master ran to end the threat. He had rarely had to run for many years and his lame leg became his bane. It gave way just as he reached the Dane with the axe and the Danish axe gouged first, into his neck and then, his body. Erik Shield Bearer's arrow went under the arm of Karl's killer. It emerged from his shoulder. He roared and turned to face us. I clambered up the ladder and he stood swinging his axe in anticipation of taking my head. I held Ragnar's Spirit behind me as I climbed, one-handed, up the ladder. I had to time it right. As he swung the axe, just a little too early, I climbed the next rung and, swinging my sword, hacked through his leg. He might have been a giant but even a giant needs two legs. He tumbled to the fighting platform and Cnut Cnutson hacked off his head and kicked his body to the ground.

When I reached Cnut, I swung my shield around. The Danes had managed to get a foothold in three places on the fighting platform. Beorn and his men would have to fight up ladders to clear the south wall. There was little point in bemoaning our fate. The sisters had spun.

"Erik and Germund, guard our backs. Cnut and Haaken, flank me. We will clear the fighting platform. "

We walked down the fighting platform three abreast. It was a tight fit but it meant none could get past us. Even as we moved, I saw another two of my men slain. They took two Danes with them but it meant that the east wall south of the gate was in their hands. If they were able to get down the ladder then they could open the gate and all would be lost. I spied hope for Ráðgeir had organised Dagfinnr and my new men into a wedge. They were heading for the gate. If the gate was breached, they would attack whoever came through. I was confident that Beorn could reach and take the south wall. Already the rest of my men were hurrying to help us. The town watch had bought us time. It was up to me to use that time well.

We did not run down the fighting platform. We needed to hit them together but we had to reach them before they could descend the ladder. The boys trained by Erik came into their own. They began pelting the Danes, who had attained the platform, with their deadly pebbles. I saw

182

one man struck in the head. Even though he had a helmet he plummeted to the ground. Others were struck on the arms, legs and bodies. They would hurt. The stones could break limbs but, most importantly, while they were protecting themselves, the Danes could not climb down the ladder and take the gate. Cnut was on the left and Haaken on my right. He had free rein to swing his sword.

As we neared the boys, I heard Erik Shield Bearer shout, "Now target those on the south wall!" Erik had grown since he had become my shield bearer.

When the barrage of stones stopped the Danes tried to move towards the ladder. As Haaken One Eye swung his sword into the side of the nearest Dane, I brought my sword over my head to strike the helmet of a second Dane who ran at me with his sword. His sword struck my shield and he was stunned. Cnut used a back-hand swing to hack into his neck. He fell to the fighting platform and we stepped over his body.

Cnut made a fatal error as he did so. He did not look down to see if there was a ladder at the wall next to him. There was and a warrior emerged and a Danish spear was rammed up under the edge of Cnut's helmet into his skull. He died instantly. Germund swung his sword so hard that he knocked the Dane and the ladder to crash into the stake filled ditch. He and his companions were all impaled. We had no time to see to our comrade's body and we moved down the fighting platform. More men had now joined us on the fighting platform and it looked like it was just the south wall where the Danes had made any progress. They could no longer take the gate and I shouted, "Ráðgeir, take your men and reinforce Beorn!"

"Aye, Jarl!"

The archers had now joined the slingers and were busy thinning out the enemy ranks. Ráðgeir led his men along the west fighting platform so that we were approaching them from two sides. I could hear my daughter and her women chanting. They were fighting the battle as hard as we were. Beorn and Benni, along with Aðalsteinn, had lost men but they were now hacking at the legs of the Danes on the fighting platform. When the Danes lowered their shields arrows and stones struck their heads.

I raised my sword and shouted, "Charge!" I wanted this ending quickly. Haaken and I, with Germund and Erik close behind us, ran at the side of the Danes. We hit the side of the Danes where they held their swords. Our shields took the blows from their blades but they could not defend against our weapons which hacked up and into them. An axe was swung from on high. I moved my head to the left and it slid down my helmet towards my shoulder. It did not reach my shoulder for Germund's

183

sword lunged over me and slid into the cheek and head of the Dane. My Varangian tore it out sideways. The Danes were doomed but they were not going to surrender and it became a bloody battle which they could not win. They were now outnumbered by over three to one and they all died without hurting any more of us.

"Archers and slingers, to the walls!"

I noticed that the fog had completely dissipated. I saw a huddle of women by the water. They were holding their ears and screaming. I could not see what was attacking them but something was. Glancing to my right I saw that Kara, Ylva and their women were still dancing in a circle and chanting. Their magic was stronger than the Danes.

The sky to the east was lightening. I saw, across the water, flames. Hawk's Roost was under attack. It was only then I thought to look north and then south. Karl, before he had been slain, had lit the signals. Ragnar and Ráðulfr Ulfsson would know of our danger. I saw no signals to the east. Sámr and his people had not had time to light theirs. Was the fire a sign that they had been defeated? Were they lying dead?

I went to the gatehouse, "Erik, climb into the arrow tower. You have good eyes. What can you see at Hawk's Roost?"

I clambered up as I looked over at the Danes. Our archers and slingers were now sending arrows and stones at them as some of the survivors of the failed attack on the walls fled south. They held up shields but some were still hit. There were still thirty or so Danes who were close to the walls. I heard a horn and they began to head south.

Erik Shield Bearer shouted down to me, "Lord, they are outside Hawk's Roost's walls and they have lit fires."

The Danes who had been attacking us were fleeing. I saw that the eight fishing boats we used were still drawn up on the beach. The Danes had not been able to destroy them for fear of making a noise.

"Germund, take command here. Haaken, Ráðgeir, Beorn. Fetch men. We will sail the boats to aid Sámr."

We descended the ladder and unbarred the gate. I could see that at least fifteen Danes lay dead outside the walls. A trail of dead and wounded men lay on the beach heading south. Germund would dispose of them. The sky was becoming lighter and I could see a little better. The Danes had ladders with them. It begged the question of how so many men had managed to get close to us when Eystein Asbjornson and his men were watching the trails from the south and east. The wind was from the south and we had to tack but the boats were quick enough and we drew close to the Danes. I had the leading boat and I headed further south. I wanted to destroy as many Danes as I could and they would be fleeing south to join the survivors of the attack on Cyninges-tūn. Were they attacking my son and grandson?

Only Erik had a bow. I turned to him. "When we land, I want you to send your arrows at the Danes as soon as you can. We must divert their attention from the walls of Hawk's Roost."

"Aye, Jarl. I am sorry about Karl and Cnut."

"They died like warriors. Asbjorn wished for such a death. We will not grieve for them but we will honour and remember them."

As well as Haaken, Haraldr Leifsson and Arne Ship Sealer were in my boat. I said, "When we land the four of us run at the Danes as though we are a warband." We could now see that there were almost fifty men assaulting the walls. The defenders were giving a good account of themselves but Sámr had less than twenty men to defend his walls. Our only chance was to make them think that the twenty-odd men I brought were more.

We landed fifty paces from them. I could see that the fire had been started with kindling and brush but although it had burned brightly it had not harmed the walls for the bottom three paces were made of stone. The timber above would be charred only. We dragged the boats onto the beach and I drew my sword. Even as I was running and screaming, "Clan of the Wolf!" Erik had nocked an arrow and sent it into the mailed back of a Dane who was less than thirty paces from us. The Danes saw us and reacted. They turned and ran at us. There were twenty Danes close to us. Erik sent two more arrows at them before they had covered ten paces and then they hit us. I could hear Sámr shouting for the gates to be opened and I heard Ráðgeir urging the rest of my men on.

I blocked the first sword with my shield and deflected a sword with Ragnar's Spirit. Erik was five paces away and the arrow he sent at the warrior with the axe who swung it at my head tore through the side of his head spattering blood and brains on the two swordsmen.

I swung my sword sideways as Arne Ship Sealer slashed his sword against one of the Danish swordsmen's legs. I punched with my shield into the other's face and then brought up Ragnar's Spirit under his neck. Beorn and the others crashed into the Danes. I stepped over the two bodies before me. I saw Sámr and Baldr leading men out of the gates to attack the Danes in the rear. Erik sent his last two arrows into the bodies of two more men before he drew his sword to join us. It was unnecessary. The last Dane was butchered as Sámr and Baldr's men hit them from behind.

Sheathing my sword and then taking off my helmet I said, as the first rays of a new dawn lit up Old Olaf, "The women and the children are well?"

185

Sámr took off his helmet, "Aye, Dragonheart and it was thanks to the bird."

"The bird?"

"Hunter the Hawk; he began screeching in the night. As I went to see why I spied the Danes and I saw the fog on your side of the river. I remembered what you had dreamed and I woke our men."

"Good. The hawk was sent by Aiden. I see that now."

"And you?"

"They managed to get over the walls. They had witches. Had they used them against you then things might have gone badly for us but Kara, Ylva and the other women managed to defeat them." He nodded. "Karl and Cnut died."

His face became as cold as ice. "Then we end this. We end this now."

I shook my head, "We do but we do not rush off. You cannot leave your families undefended. We have lost men. We know not what has happened to the east of us. They have fled south. I believe that means that Ragnar and Gruffyd are in danger. They will have warning for we lit the signal towers." I pointed south. The smoke could still be seen rising in the sky. If Ragnar knew then Gruffyd would know. They would bar their gates as I had commanded and they would sit tight. If Ráðulfr Ulfsson and Ketil Windarsson could then they would send help. "We have to trust that our men will come from the north but it could be two days before they reach us.

Sámr said, "You are, as always, right. Baldr, have the dead stripped and the bodies burned. Make sure our fires are extinguished."

I turned, "Arne, fetch two horses from Hawk's Roost. I want you and Haraldr to ride to Windar's Mere. I need to know if the Danes went there first. If there is peace then tell Eystein Asbjornson that I need half of his men and they should return with you!"

"Aye, Jarl. And if Windar's Mere is also a burned-out shell with the people slaughtered?"

"Then we will know!"

We began to pile up the Danish bodies. They would be burned. Sámr had lost men too. We had to bury them.

"Sámr, your family and Baldr's cannot stay here now. When we go south there will be too few to care for them. You must bring them to Cyninges-tūn." I saw, from his face, that he was not convinced. "Sámr, this was not just a vengeance raid. Sven and Ubba were not here to collect weregeld. There was planning. They were trying to take our land. They attacked two strongholds at once. They had ladders! They brought an army unseen into the heartland of the clan!" Turning to Haaken I pointed to the ladders. "Have you ever known Danes to bring ladders to a raid?"

Haaken looked at Sámr, "Dragonheart is right. They sent many men to scout us out. They knew that we were prepared and they still came." He pointed down the Water. "The men who attacked us fled south. These tried to flee south. There are more men there and I suspect that your father and Gruffyd are, even now, under attack. There will be burned out farms between here and Whale Island."

It was as though scales had been lifted from his eyes, He nodded, "And there may be other bands still at large. We will bury our dead and then I will bring all my people to Cyninges-tūn."

We sailed our boats back. Arne Ship Sealer had been wounded. He would not be marching south. He was in my boat and I spoke with him. "Arne, you will be one we leave in Cyninges-tūn. Germund, you will also be the guardian of my home. This is one of the most dangerous attacks I can remember. I think Ubba went to see his father for a reason. Ubba Ragnarsson wishes this for his land. I am not a king but I think Ubba sees himself as a king. There may be many more men than we expect."

When we reached my walls, I saw that Atticus and Kara had begun to organise our people. The Danish ladders had been used to make a pyre on the place where the witches had stood. The Danish bodies were already there and, as we stepped ashore, I saw the first flames lick the bodies of the enemy dead. Our dead were laid out at the cemetery. Kara and Ylva were tending to the wounded. Even as we walked through the gate, I saw Aðils Shape Shifter and his family coming from Lang's Dale. He led other warriors too. From the south came Rollo Thin Skin with his family and the bondi from the south and west.

I could not expect Ráðulfr Ulfsson until the middle of the next day at the earliest. I had a dilemma. Did I wait or did I march south to save my family? Aiden's voice came into my head. He told me that which I knew, I had to wait. I had done all that I could to impress upon my son and grandson the dangers they faced. If they were unprepared, as Windar had been all those years ago, then it was *wyrd*.

I went over to Kara and Ylva. The ones they tended had a chance of life. Those who had had no chance had already been given a warrior's death. They looked up as I approached. Kara said, "Had Karl remembered your words about the fog then he might be alive and many of these would not have been wounded."

Ylva shook her head, "No, mother, for this was the work of the Norns. Why did we not see the threat? The witches cast a spell across our Water. We have destroyed their power but they were clever. They brought

187

enough witches to break down our defences." She looked north, "We should have been in the cave of Myrddyn. There we could have harnessed the power of Úlfarrberg and the land."

Kara looked sad and weary, "You may be right, Ylva. I am loath to leave my hall and my home."

"Yet one day we will have to leave and the cave will become our home. Perhaps not yet but," she looked at me, "when Sámr rules then that will be the time."

I did not know what their words meant and, perhaps, I should have questioned them more, but I was too concerned with planning the battle I would have to fight; the battle to save the land and the Clan of the Wolf.

Chapter 23

I could see that Atticus was shaken. I was in my hall preparing what we would need for the battle to come. He shook his head, "This is a strange land! Fog moves and then disappears! Where is the logic?"

"It was not logic, it was magic."

For the first time, he did not argue with me. I had glimpsed him during the battle. He had seen my volvas chanting and he had clutched his cross. He did not understand it. My granddaughter had explained to me what she had meant by breaking the power of the witches. The Danish volvas had underestimated the effect of the spirits. The chanting of Ylva and Kara had summoned the dead and they had entered the minds of the witches. They would not flee south. They would head home to the east and hope to mend their shattered minds.

"We will be leaving as soon as Ráðulfr Ulfsson gets here. I will leave enough men to guard my walls but you will need to arm the women and yourself. There is a chance that this is a ploy to draw me hence and then devour my home. I leave it in your hands."

"I am not a warrior."

"No, but, since Aiden's death, you are the cleverest man I know. My men trust you. You can lead, for Kara and Ylva will help you. They know magic but, with your knowledge of tactics, you can help the men to defend. I give you and Germund full power to do as you see fit."

He bowed, "I am honoured. Come, Erik, you have much to prepare."

Haaken, unusually, looked worried, "My family live south of here."

"Aye they do but they live on the fells south of Old Olaf. They will only be in danger if we lose and I do not intend to lose to a warband of savage Danes." Haaken nodded. The Danes were not here to raid and take slaves. They were here to conquer a land, my land.

Sámr arrived at noon. He had used wagons to carry the women and their babes. I saw that he had brought Hunter with him. The hawk had saved my great-grandson and his family. Like Úlfarr the Wolf, he would be honoured. He was now part of the clan. The women were housed in Kara's Hall. Sámr and Baldr would spend the night with me.

As we shared a most welcome horn of ale with Rollo and Aðils Shape Shifter I said, "We do not have enough horses to take us all but we have enough to send you, Aðils Shape Shifter and you Rollo Thin Skin, to scout out the enemy. We are blind. I would have you leave as soon as you can. I cannot see that we will be able to march until the day after tomorrow. Ráðulfr Ulfsson will arrive tomorrow and there are still bondi who saw the signals and are joining us. We need all the men that we can get."

"Then we leave when we have supped this ale. I will take my son, Beorn Aðilsson. He has seen nine summers and he has skills. I will send him back with news."

Arne Ship Sealer and Haraldr did not reach us until after dark. They came with Eystein Asbjornson and thirty warriors. They had used every horse from Windar's Mere and the farms nearby. While the warriors went to the warrior hall Eystein came into my hall. There were four faces with questions on them and they all examined Eystein. Atticus poured some ale and then whisked Erik away, "Come, we have food to bring in and the jarl has words he wishes to say."

I looked at Eystein, "The Danes came from the south and east. Why did we not have warning?"

He looked up at me and I saw that he had aged. "Because my men were not good enough. I was not good enough. I had grown complacent. In all the years I was growing I never once had to endure an attack on our home. Our men lost the edge which a good sword needs."

"You have not yet answered me. Oathsworn died on my walls and their spirits and your jarl need answers."

"My men who were watching the trails were ambushed and slaughtered. They did not return by dusk yesterday. I led men out to discover the reason and we were ambushed. I lost another twelve men before we made our walls and by then we were under attack. We were surrounded."

Haaken shook his head, "You should have sent word when your men did not return. You should have barred your gates and prepared for an attack. Those twelve men you lost would still be alive."

I waved my hand to silence Haaken. Recriminations would help no one. "Did you defeat them?"

"No, Jarl, we stood to all night and we saw their fires burning but when we woke, they had gone. Arne and Haraldr saw their trail heading south."

As I mulled over his words Sámr said, "And thirty men are all that you bring to the aid of the clan?"

Eystein looked sad, "The thirty men are the best that I have. The ones who were watching for the Danes and the twelve I lost were my best men. Five of my thirty have mail and the rest have none. Sámr Ship Killer, my mother and my people need protection too. We come to the aid of the clan knowing that it is likely that we will die. We are a sacrifice and I am willing to make that sacrifice but I will not sacrifice my people."

I smiled, "There will be no sacrifice. We will not go berserk! The three attacks were all a diversion. Perhaps the one here was prosecuted a little more forcefully because they thought to end my life."

"How do you know that, great grandfather?"

"Because they used witches and they had Skull Taker warriors with them. That clan does not forget that I took their leader's head. It now makes sense to me. Their real targets are Whale Island and Gruffyd's stad. If they have those then they have our fleet of drekar. We know that Bergil Hafþórrsson in Dyflin has few ships. This would give Sven the Boneless Dyflin too. Ubba Ragnarsson could then sweep north and take all of this land. He is like his father, he is devious. He does not waste his men. He uses superior numbers to win! Ubba thinks that we will hunker down in our homes for he has hurt us. We will show him otherwise."

Sámr said, "Then let us leave now! We need not wait for Ráðulfr Ulfsson. How many men does he bring? A handful! If we get there too late then my father and my people will all be destroyed!"

"Do you not remember your father's words as he left? He told us that he could hold out for ten days. They could not have attacked them before they attacked us or we would have seen the signals. They attacked on the same day. Ubba Ragnarsson is a clever warrior. His father, Hairy Breeks, is a cunning man. They will have planned all of this. We still have time. My fear is that all those who live south of us will have suffered. The clan will have paid the price for our lack of vigilance." I did not look at him but Eystein knew that it was his mistake and, perhaps, his father's. One did not speak ill of the dead.

Ráðulfr Ulfsson arrived after dark. He had with him Ketil Windarsson and forty men from Ketil's Stad. Altogether we had more than a hundred fresh men. After the disasters of the last two days, it was uplifting. Sámr had underestimated my jarls. He had learned another lesson. He had learned to trust.

"Ketil?" I wondered what had brought my jarl from the north. I was pleased he had come but there were still questions in my mind.

"Windar caught two Danes the day before yesterday. They were not far from the head of Úlfarr's Water. He questioned them before he slew them. They had been sent to keep watch on our men. They told us of the attack on Cyninges-tūn. Windar sent to me and I brought my men as soon as I could. Windar will guard my land. I met Ráðulfr north of the Grassy Mere. We saw the signal fires and came as quickly as we could."

"Windar's Mere has been attacked also."

"We might have gone by Úlfarr's Water." He looked at Eystein.

Eystein shook his head, "You could not have aided us. The damage had already been done."

Ketil gave me a questioning look. I shook my head. I would explain on the road. "Your men will be tired. We will feed them and march at dawn."

Ketil said, "We are the Clan of the Wolf. We can march now to help our clan."

I shook my head and said, "Aðils and Rollo are scouting out the enemy. I would rather fresh men marched and knew what lay ahead. This is not a single warband. It looks to me as though they have scoured the lands of the east for swords." I emptied the clan amulets we had taken from the dead onto the table. "There are at least ten clans here. Ubba Ragnarsson is from a powerful family. His father, Ragnar Hairy Breeks, has ambitions. He would be a king."

Erik Shield Bearer had been listening. He said, "Gandálfr who came from Dyflin told me that the ships in Dyflin were headed for a gathering and it was led by Ragnar Lodbrok."

"That is Ragnar Hairy Breeks. Then he has many men at his command. He has, indeed, grown greedy if he thinks to take on Frankia and the Land of the Wolf. His son, Ubba, must be equally ambitious. Thank you for that knowledge, Erik, although that changes nothing. There are the crews of thirty drekar gathered. We have accounted for two crews, at the very least. With every warrior here and those in the two settlements south of here, we can muster less than twenty crews and that means taking farmers and boys."

Sámr nodded, "Aye, Dragonheart, but farmers and boys of the Clan of the Wolf."

I heard a shout from outside followed by the sound of hooves. The door opened and Gandálfr rushed in with Beorn Aðilsson. The boy looked exhausted. He had to have ridden at least thirty miles. Every face turned expectantly towards him. Before he spoke, we were in the dark. We hoped his words would enlighten us.

"Jarl Dragonheart, we have found the Danes. They have siege lines around Whale Island and Úlfarrston. They are ringed with fires. All of your drekar and the shipyards are burned. There are five drekar off Whale Island. My father and Rollo headed east and sent me here."

Haaken shook his head, "*'Heart of the Dragon'*, gone!" He shook his head. "They will pay."

"Now we know the size of the problem. They intend to make this land theirs and the five drekar stop us receiving help from the sea. We leave before dawn. We use every horse and pony we have. I will leave just the town watch, the wounded and the youngest of the boys. The rest of the clan goes to war. We relieve Whale Island and then Úlfarrston. Get rest, for you will need it."

When they had gone Sámr spoke with Haaken and myself, "Erik Short Toe? The ship's boys?"

"Speculation is idle, Sámr." I saw Erik Shield Bearer looking distraught. "Your imaginings will conjure a worse picture than the reality. We are warriors. We deal with that which we find." He nodded. In truth, I feared the worst. Erik Short Toe loved his drekar. If she was burned then, in all likelihood, he was dead too.

I rode with my leaders and the best of our warriors. That was not because we were any better than the men we led but we had to face the possibility of fighting a battle before we reached Whale Island. Each of the leaders carried with him a banner which had had a spell sewn onto it by Kara and her women. My whole wolf standard had been woven by them and Haraldr Leifsson did as his father had done. He carried my banner. Erik rode next to him with my shield. As we rode, I told Ketil of the disaster at Windar's Mere. He shook his head, "As lovely a place as that is I fear it is cursed. My father and many of my kin died there. My land is harsh and uncompromising but I would not swap it for I can defend it. My eagle's eyrie lets me sees enemies from afar.

It was in the early afternoon when Aðils and Rollo rode in. Their horses looked weary. "Gruffyd is also besieged, Dragonheart, but by fewer men. Had we been able to signal to him then we might have told him to sally forth for the Danes around his stronghold are thinly spread."

The Norns were spinning. My plan had been to go to the aid of Whale Island and Úlfarrston. We were seven miles from Úlfarrston and ten miles from the high ground where my son held out. A difference of three miles was nothing.

"We head east and defeat these Danes."

"But Whale Island?"

"Sámr, I know your family is there and you fear for their safety but think like the man who will lead this clan when I am in the Otherworld. If we destroy these Danes who besiege my son then we increase the size of our army. Aðils, how many men besiege Whale Island and Úlfarrston?"

"A thousand."

I looked at Sámr. I saw him become a leader in his answer. "We head east and you are right. I must use my mind as Atticus has taught me. My heart can lead me astray."

As we headed east, I reflected that his grandfather, Wolf Killer, had always thought with his heart and that had been his undoing.

We saw to the south and east burned out and ravaged farms. The Danes had come here. The southern end of Windar's Mere lay not far away. Eystein's patrols should have spotted the Danes. I knew now the path they had taken. Gruffyd's men were watching the High Divide to the south and east. There was a trail which led from the east and past the home my son, Wolf Killer, had made. After his death, the people left and it was uninhabited. The Danes knew it well. We would need to settle it again.

It was getting on to dark when we neared Gruffyd's home. I saw, in the dim light of dusk, the campfires ringing it. We dismounted a mile away. The wooden walls of my son's home had a gatehouse and towers. I saw men moving. My son had learned not to light fires which destroyed night vision. The men who had marched were tired. The men who had ridden, my leaders and my best men, were not.

"Rollo, take command here. Rest the men. The rest of you, we will follow Aðils. We spread out and kill as many Danes as we can. Eystein, take the south. Ráðulfr Ulfsson, you have the longest journey. You take the east. Ketil, your men can attack from the north and my men will follow me from the west. Do not make a battle cry. I would not have the Danes alerted." They nodded. "May the Allfather be with you."

Erik handed me my shield. I donned my helmet and then put my wolf cloak over the top. I drew my sword.

"Erik Shield Bearer, stay close to me and watch my back! I am getting old. Haraldr we will not need the banner." I moved my eyes towards Erik and Haraldr nodded. He would keep an eye on the young boy.

Raising my sword, I waved my men off. Aðils led the way. We were running through the ground which had not been cleared. We moved in a long and untidy line. We did not run quickly for a fall in heavy mail could alert the Danes. We passed over rough ground and small patches of pasture. We smelled the smoke from their fires and saw them moving. It was not long after dark and they were eating. Their sentries would be watching the stronghold. With the bulk of their army to the west, it was the one direction from which they would not expect an attack.

Aðils did not use a shield. He had a sword and a hand axe. The first two Danes died without even registering his presence. One was making water and one was emptying his bowels. They would not be going to Valhalla. As we ran towards the men around the fire one must have seen us and shouted, "The Wolf!"

They frantically reached for weapons. We were running and reached them quickly. I brought Ragnar's Spirit down on to the back of one Dane who was bending down to grab his sword. I split it open to the backbone. As I brought my blade back up, I backhanded a second Dane under the chin. I severed his throat. I saw Erik make his first kill with a sword as he blocked a Danish sword with his shield and rammed his blade up into the guts of the Dane. They were not mailed and not expecting an attack. All around was the sound of metal on metal. There were men shouting. Some were shouting in anger and others in pain as they died. The men I had brought with me, Erik apart, wore mail. The Danes we fought wore tunics and breeks. Few had had time to don their helmets. I knew that Ráðulfr and Eystein would have had a harder time as our noise would have alerted their camps but I knew, even as Danes tried to flee, that we had won. When the gates opened and Gruffyd led his warriors to sally forth then the battle was over.

It took a couple of hours to ensure that all the Danes were dead. We needed no prisoners and the wounded were despatched without the benefit of a sword in their hand. When Ráðulfr and Eystein brought their men and the booty they had collected I sent Erik to fetch the rest of our men.

"I knew you would come, father."

As we went into his stronghold, I told him of the three attacks and the situation further west. He nodded, "The first that we knew was when families began to flood into our walls. We had not watched to the north. We watched to the south and east. They came by Elfrida's Stad?"

"Aye, and that is my error." I looked at Sámr, "Hopefully, when you lead the clan you will not make as many mistakes as I have."

"No, great grandfather, these are not mistakes. This is the Norns. Your decisions are wise ones. I questioned this one and I was proved wrong."

We entered Gruffyd's walls. "How many men can you bring tomorrow when we go to Úlfarrston?"

"We lost some but I can leave enough to defend my walls and still bring fifty good warriors."

It would not be enough but it would have to do. "When Rollo arrives with the rest of the men, we will have a council of war and I will tell you my plans."

Gruffyd had plenty of food and we had taken much from the Danes. We ate well and I went through all my plans in detail. Our men rested for we would have a short sleep before we went to battle again. This time we knew where they were and we knew the land. We would use both to our advantage. I had men make rafts. They were crude but they would come in handy. I was not certain if the three Danish camps were communicating with each other. I planned on attacking at dawn but I had twenty fresh men I would use as a skirmish line to warn of any Dane who approached our camp. My plan involved precise timing. If I began at the wrong time then we were doomed to failure.

195

My leaders were happy with the plan. While those who had not seen each other for some time caught up on the battles they had fought I took Eystein to one side. "Are you happier now that you have bested the Danes?"

"I am but we all feel guilty about letting you down."

"A Viking does not regret his mistakes. Most of us make too many. I know that I have and it has cost me and my people dear. The secret is to learn from your mistakes. You have now fought in a battle. Tomorrow will be even harder for we will fight men who outnumber us. That is why Ráðulfr Ulfsson is on one flank and Ketil Windarsson on the other. You and your men are with Sámr and Baldr behind me and the men of Cyninges-tūn. You will be behind the banner. The Danes will come to take me and my banner. It will be your spears behind which will defend me."

"And we will. I have amends to make!"

My skirmishers found and killed three Danes who came east. I knew not if they were messengers or came to give orders. When they did not return to the main armies then Ubba Ragnarsson and Sven the Boneless would know that something was amiss. That could not be helped. My plan allowed for them to prepare for an attack. I would just surprise them with the direction from which we came. It would be our knowledge of the land and the moon which would give us the element of surprise.

We made the six miles to the river before dawn. We saw their campfires to the west and the sentries. We saw the shadows of their drekar lying off the mouth of the river. It was low tide. At this time of year, the tides were very low. We had learned that to our cost and lost some drekar to the sandbanks. Now we would use the low tide to cross where they did not expect us. We would ford the river. The rafts we had made were for the slingers, the bows, strings and the extra arrows we had brought from Gruffyd's Stad. It was my plan and I led. The ten men who were with me at the front each had a rope around his body. The water only came to our waists for most of the crossing. We did not rush for we did not want to alert the Danes. When we were within a hundred paces of the west bank the current became stronger and the water deeper. It was why the ten men at the front had mail. I felt the river fighting to push me over. I leaned forward as though I was in a shield wall and dug my feet in. At one point water washed over my head but it was brief and I was prepared. After that, the river became shallower and the current less strong.

I was not the first one to reach the other bank. That was Ráðulfr followed by Beorn and Ráðgeir. I struggled up through the mud. I had chosen this point because the first people who had built upon this river, in the time after the Romans, had built a quay. The wood structure had gone but the piles in the mud remained. I took the rope from around me and tied it off around one of the piles. I stood and waved my arm to the warband in the water. They could now pull themselves against the current.

Aðils had not crossed the river. My shape shifter had left before we did and had infiltrated the Danish lines. He now rose like a wraith from the dark and made his way towards me. He pointed and spoke in my ear as my men gradually emerged dripping, from the water. "They are gathering further north. They are trying to combine their two besieging armies. A few men wait at Whale Island. They expect us from the northeast. I had to slay two of their sentries. It will reinforce their belief that we come from Gruffyd's Stad across the land."

"And the other Danes?"

"There is a camp four hundred paces to the east of us. It is three hundred paces from Úlfarrston."

"You have done well. Go and find your son."

The low tide told me that we had another hour before dawn. That gave us the chance to form our lines and for the archers to string their bows. Knowing that they had an almost unguarded camp was a gift from the gods. We formed up as the sky over the High Divide lightened. I faced my line of spears and looked along. All were ready. I raised my sword and turned. We began to walk towards the camp which was just coming to life. They would have a rude awakening.

Once again, we made good progress before we were seen and, by then, it was too late. The first rays of the new day flashed into the eyes of the Danes. When we struck our blades would flash as they rose and fell. Our banners were flying and Raibeart ap Pasgen would know that I had come to his aid. Most of the Danes had decamped and were waiting for us to the north-west. There were still a hundred or so warriors in the camp. That would be just enough to keep the defenders occupied. This time there was no reason to be silent.

"Clan of the Wolf!" The words were roared out along the line. It was a ragged line. Sámr and Baldr, along with the younger warriors were running hard. It was they who tore into the camp. The Danes had not donned mail. Sámr and Baldr were like farmers harvesting barley. They scythed through bodies. I heard a shout from ahead as Raibeart led his men from behind their walls and between us we slew every Dane save for the handful who turned and fled to the sea. Their drekar still bobbed upon the water. Without mail, the survivors risked Ran to reach their drekar.

While my men finished off the wounded, Raibeart and I met and clasped arms. "I knew you would come but I did not expect you to walk on water. I would be careful, Jarl Dragonheart, lest the Christians think you are the White Christ reborn!"

I laughed, "And that will never happen! They have moved north to fight us. How many are there before your walls?"

"We counted five hundred but I know there are as many at Whale Island."

"And now I have given them a dilemma. They have combined their armies but, until they spy us, they are in the dark. When they spy us what do they do? Do they just try to hold us here? Are there crews on the drekar in the estuary and should they use them? If they take some time to attack us then they have combined their forces. It matters not what they do, I have made my plans. I will put my archers and slingers in your walls. Have your men with mail join our rear ranks. Your walls will be our bastion and I will put my best men on the right flank."

"I will make it so."

"Ráðgeir, have the archers and slingers go into Úlfarrston." I cupped my hands, "Form shield wall!" We were having to adapt our plans but they were improved rather than harmed. "Ráðgeir and Ketil, form your men on the right flank and angle them backwards!"

"Aye, Jarl."

To an untrained eye, it would have looked like chaos but men knew who was their shield brother. In many cases that had been their oar brother. They went to fight next to those with whom they felt comfortable. Haaken One Eye was on one side of me and Rollo Thin Skin on the other. Aðils Shape Shifter commanded the archers on Úlfarrston's walls. Raibeart's men were the third rank and they all had mail. They were not Viking. Most were of mixed blood but they all knew how to fight in a shield wall. They would add their weight if and when the Danes threw themselves at our shields.

They did not attack for some time and I knew that they had managed to combine all of their men. We could be facing almost a thousand men. The sun had risen by the time we saw the Danes advancing. The sun was getting higher and I saw it reflecting from the mail of the Danes. They would overlap us but they could not know that my archers and slingers would assault their right flank. Their left flank would, in all probability, push back Ketil and the others on our right flank. I had planned on that happening. I saw the pigtailed warrior that was Sven the Boneless. I recognised his shield which had a skull upon it. I recognised Ubba Ragnarsson's banner. It had an eagle tearing out the heart of a wolf. Was that why he felt the need to destroy me? Was I the wolf? The banners remained behind the lines of warriors who advanced. We had had no opportunity to spoil the ground before us or make it harder to cross. The Danes themselves had done a good job for the warriors now marched over the land which they themselves had used to empty their bowels when they had had their siege camp. They came steadily with their shields held before them. They knew of my archers and would be ready to lift their shields in a moment. Aðils Shape Shifter and my archers were facing the right-hand side of the Danes. They had no shields there. In the first shower of arrows, we could hurt their right flank. Sámr and Baldr now commanded the left flank with their younger warriors. I had given my great grandson the opportunity to win this battle. Would he take it?

Sven the Boneless was coming for me. I had thrown him from his home. I had killed his leader. I had humiliated him and he wanted vengeance. I had no doubt that Ubba Ragnarsson was using him. The fact that he allowed him to be in the front rank told me that. I had my sword resting on my shield. When they were one hundred paces from us, I shouted, "Lock shields!" That was a double signal. It made my men fix their shields together and place their right feet slightly behind their left. As they did so then the attention of every Dane was on us. I saw a subtle movement as they lifted their shields slightly. I had their attention. The second effect of the signal was that Aðils Shape Shifter ordered the slingers and archers to release. We had almost two hundred archers and slingers. The first flights and shower of stones wreaked havoc on their right flank. Even as someone shouted for them to swing around their shields the second and third flights had struck. When I heard stones rattling on shields and saw arrows sticking from shields, I knew that they had protected themselves. Before that had happened, we had hurt them. The Danish right flank had been badly hurt.

Sven the Boneless could not wait any longer and he shouted, "Charge!"

It was a mistake. The ones on the right were adjusting their shields and negotiating the bodies of their dead. Their centre and left hit us but not their right. Our archers sent arrows into the rear rank. The rear rank could not defend itself and there the men had no mail.

Then they hit us. These were not half-naked Picts. These were mailed warriors with shields as big as ours. They were backed by more men than we had. A spear came at my head and even as I moved my head out of the way a second rang off my shield and then my helmet. My head was jerked back. I held my sword out as the line hit us. I was pushed back as were Rollo and Haaken. The third rank behind us was also made up of mailed men and we did not move far.

Sven the Boneless' face was close to mine. Even as he opened his mouth to insult me, I head-butted him. I shattered his nose and broke most of the teeth in his mouth. I swung my sword overhand but he blocked it with his shield. I pulled my sword, which was now over his shoulder backwards across his mail coif. It was a not well-made byrnie for I severed ten links and a hole appeared. Eystein's spear jabbed out and, clanking off Sven the Boneless' helmet, it bounced into the eye of the warrior fighting Rollo. Even as the man began to fall Rollo's sword jerked forward and took the man in the second rank full in the mouth. He stepped into the gap and his body pressed against Sven the Boneless' arm. He could not move. Suddenly Erik Shield Bearer's short sword darted out and stabbed Sven in the thigh. He roared his anger and pain, I had my arm back and I lunged at his open mouth. Ragnar's Spirit came out of the back of his skull. As he fell, I stepped forward and the warrior next to Eystein took advantage, spearing Haaken One Eye's opponent in the right arm. Haaken finished him off and we moved forward. It was just one step but I could see that Sámr and Baldr had forced back the decimated men on the right. We were pushing back the Danes who outnumbered us.

Having space before me, I swung my sword sideways. I connected with a helmet. The distracted warrior was gutted by Haaken. A flurry of arrows descended. One was dangerously close to Rollo but they took out eight warriors in the third rank. There were now just seven Danes facing twelve of my men. Behind them, I saw Ubba Ragnarsson. He still had a reserve of over a hundred men. I saw his standard being waved. Was he ordering a retreat? Then I saw a face I knew amongst the hastily organised shield wall. It was Beorn Sharp Tongue. He was not only a murderer, but he was also a traitor! He had joined the Danes and helped them to infiltrate the Land of the Wolf. A red mist filled my head.

"Charge! Let us end this!"

Heading for the murderer, I punched with my shield and slashed with my sword. I had two shields in my back propelling me forward. Beorn Sharp Tongue was a bully. He had killed a man who was not a warrior. Even as his sword came up Odin aided me and Ragnar's Spirit shattered his blade in two and hacked deep into his neck. As he fell those around him tried to fall back in good order. The men we faced had nothing save the bodies of the dead behind them. There was no second rank providing support. When they tripped over their dead comrades they were slain.

Then, from the walls, I heard, "Dragonheart, the drekar are approaching the shore. They intend to land men!"

There was a beach behind Raibeart and his men. We were within touching distance of victory. Sven the Boneless was slain and his

200

oathsworn lay dead. Sámr and Baldr were driving towards Ubba and his reserve but if the drekar landed crews then we would be slaughtered.

"Raibeart, turn your men around and face the new threat."

"Aye, Jarl."

It was then that Ubba led his reserve. They formed a wedge and headed for our right flank. Ketil and Ráðgeir had been forced back by the sheer weight of numbers. The men who had been fighting against them had not been thinned by arrows and they had outflanked my finest of warriors. Already they were pushing against the men of Cyninges-tūn.

"Sámr, wheel right!"

"Aye, Dragonheart."

"Haaken, Rollo, let us show these young warriors how an Ulfheonar can fight." We turned, for we had space before us and we began to move towards the wedge which was moving quickly across the ground. Ubba was going to charge my men. He would hit them with his one hundred fresh men and they would plough through them. The swords of my men would be blunted. Ubba's men would have sharp blades and arms which had yet to swing a weapon. The rest of his men who had attacked Ketil and my men were still fighting. The reinforcements would swing the battle in Ubba's favour. If we were weary, we could not show it. I forced myself to run even the pain from my old wounds sent waves through my body. The three of us were together, others were slightly behind so that we made our own wedge. Sámr and Baldr had further to run and there were still groups of Danes fighting.

The hope we had was that we were going to hit the wedge at the side and we would hit their spear side. I raised my sword. I was aware that Haraldr and Erik were close behind. Eystein and his men were a heartbeat further back. There would be four of us with experience. The rest were novices. That thought spurred me and I ran faster. The Dane whom I hit saw me and tried to turn. My last burst of speed defeated his spear and I hit his hand with the boss of my shield as my sword stabbed the man before him in the back. Haaken then hacked into the side of the warrior who was next in line. A wedge works because every man is protected by at least two men. In our initial attack, we had slain three for Haraldr had stabbed the warrior who had dropped his spear when I had hit him.

We were driving deep into the soft side of the wedge. I drove my sword into the side of a warrior who was trying to turn his spear. He had good mail but my sword had a tip and I ripped through the mail. The wedge broke and the warriors turned to face us. Ketil and Ráðgeir had been saved but now the Danes faced a short line with just four veterans and the rest who were untried men.

It was then that two things happened at once. Sámr and Baldr's men reached the rear of the wedge and, from the north I heard a horn as Ragnar led the men of Whale Island. They were not on the battlefield yet but they soon would be. The horn was to tell me that they were coming.

"Shield wall!"

There was a crack like thunder as Sámr and his men hit the rear of the wedge. This was not a line against another line it was a confused maelstrom of bodies, blades and blood. You fought one man but another might stab you in the side or back. All men sought me. A Dane with an axe came at me. He had not been in the wedge. He must have been with the original attack. I saw one of Ketil's men hacked across the chest by the axeman and the giant lumbered towards me. I had time to take out Wolf's Blood and slip it into my left hand. He roared and launched himself at me. I tried to block his axe with my sword but it was such a powerful blow that it knocked it away and I barely managed to raise my shield. The axe knocked me to my knee. Ragnar's Spirit stopped me from falling. He roared with joy and taking the axe in two hands brought it down towards my head. I lunged up with the shield in my left hand. Wolf's Blood drove up between his legs and deep into his guts. I looked up and saw the look of surprise and then horror on his face. The axe fell to the ground. I ripped out the blade, bringing entrails and organs with it. As he fell, I stood and shouted, "Ragnar's' Spirit! Clan of the Wolf!"

My men all shouted but it merely drew the Danes towards me. I was not afraid. I had the joy of battle within me. If I was to die then Sámr could take over the clan. He had shown me that he was more than capable. I would end this Danish threat. I held my shield before me as I hacked at the spear of the Dane before me. I would fight my way to Ubba Ragnarsson and he would die. I might die reaching him but all attention would be on me and the best of the clan would live on.

Haaken One Eye had the same blood lust in his voice as he shouted, "Death to the Danes!"

He swung his sword so hard that he shattered the Danish shield before him. I backhanded my blade against the Dane's neck and he fell. A spear rammed into my shield and another into my side. My mail held but I felt a rib crack. I cared not.

Behind me, I heard Erik shouting, "Jarl Dragonheart! The ships!"

I was oblivious to all but the men before me. Ubba was just four men from Haaken and I. We would slay his oathsworn. Blows rained on my helmet and shield but the blue stones of Odin protected me. Ragnar's Spirit gave me power and strength beyond my years. I punched my sword at the face of a Dane and then used Wolf's Blood to rip across his throat.

And then suddenly Ubba Ragnarsson shouted, "Fall back! We are lost!"

The men before us seemed to melt away. They ran. We were so taken aback that we did not react quickly enough. They ran to a drekar which was floundering in the estuary, When I looked, I saw that blood ran down her side.

I turned to Erik Shield Bearer. He was grinning. "What happened?"

He pointed to the south. There were six ships there. They were fighting the last three of the Danish drekar. "It is Bergil Hafþórrsson, see his standard, Jarl Dragonheart. He has brought his ships to our aid. "

I saw Beorn and Benni. They were covered from head to toe in blood. Their shields were hacked and cut yet they banged their swords against their shields and cheered their brother. We had won. The Danes had come to take our land and the clan had prevailed.

Epilogue

It was two days after the battle that we finally cleared the last of the enemy dead and buried our own. Fifty of our warriors had died. Rollo had a wound to his leg. He would not be able to fight in a shield wall any longer. He had wanted to spend more time with his family and now he would. Eystein and his men had come of age and knew what it was to be a warrior.

As we made our way to the wrecked and blackened shipyard there was no joy in my heart in the victory. I had hoped beyond hope that Erik Short Toe or his family, at least, had somehow, survived. When we saw the burned homes and the bodies hacked so that they were almost unrecognisable we knew that my old navigator was gone. He had trained Sámr and then he had been taken from us. His hourglass, his charts, his compass were all burned. His head was atop a spear and his wife had been used and abused. I was just grateful that none of his sons and grandsons had been at home. They had been at sea in the family knarr. We gathered their bodies and buried them. The shipbuilders and sailors of the shipyard were all dead. My drekar was no more. I did not think that I would go to sea again. This vibrant community had gone. These were not warriors. They were shipbuilders and seafarers.

Erik Shield Bearer was the most distraught of all. Erik Short Toe and his wife had been as mother and father to him. They had given him a home and shown him kindness. Now all he had was me and my old men. I saw him changing before my eyes.

After we had buried the dead, we said farewell to those with whom we had fought. We said goodbye to the dead and to the skeletons that had been our drekar. We headed north to Cyninges-tūn. My work was finished. Sámr was now a leader. He had no ship yet but that meant he could build his own and that drekar would have Sámr's spirit within. I could stay in my home and be a counsellor for Sámr. I could advise him. I was no longer needed except by Erik. When he was a warrior then I could lay down my burden. I could go to Valhalla knowing that I had helped to save my clan.

The End

Norse Calendar

Gormánuður October 14th - November 13th
Ýlir November 14th - December 13th
Mörsugur December 14th - January 12th
Þorri - January 13th - February 11th
Gói - February 12th - March 13th
Einmánuður - March 14th - April 13th
Harpa April 14th - May 13th
Skerpla - May 14th - June 12th
Sólmánuður - June 13th - July 12th
Heyannir - July 13th - August 14th
Tvímánuður - August 15th - September 14th
Haustmánuður September 15th-October 13th

Glossary

Afen- River Avon
Afon Hafron- River Severn in Welsh
Àird Rosain – Ardrossan (On the Clyde Estuary)
Al-buhera -Albufeira, Portugal
Aledhorn- Althorn (Essex)
An Lysardh - Lizard Peninsula Cornwall
Balears- Balearic Islands
Balley Chashtal -Castleton (Isle of Man)
Bardas - Rebel Byzantine General
Beamfleote -Benfleet Essex
Bebbanburgh- Bamburgh Castle, Northumbria was also known as
Din Guardi in the ancient tongue
Beck- a stream
Beinn na bhFadhla- Benbecula in the Outer Hebrides
Beodericsworth- Bury St Edmunds
Belesduna – Basildon, Essex
Belisima -River Ribble
Blót – a blood sacrifice made by a jarl
Blue Sea- The Mediterranean
Bogeuurde – Forest of Bowland
Bondi- Viking farmers who fight
Bourde- Bordeaux
Bjarnarøy –Great Bernera (Bear Island)
Breguntford – Brentford
Brixges Stane – Brixton (South London)
Bruggas- Bruges
Brycgstow- Bristol
Burntwood- Brentwood Essex
Byrnie- a mail or leather shirt reaching down to the knees
Caerlleon- Welsh for Chester
Caer Ufra -South Shields
Caestir - Chester (old English)
Cantwareburh -Canterbury
Càrdainn Ros -Cardross (Argyll)
Carrum -Carhampton (Somerset)
Cas-gwent -Chepstow Monmouthshire
Casnewydd –Newport, Wales
Cephas- Greek for Simon Peter (St. Peter)
Chatacium -Catanzaro, Calabria
Chape- the tip of a scabbard

Charlemagne- Holy Roman Emperor at the end of the 8th and beginning of the 9th centuries
Celchyth - Chelsea
Cerro da Vila – Vilamoura, Portugal
Cherestanc- Garstang (Lancashire)
Cil-y-coed -Caldicot Monmouthshire
Colneceastre- Colchester
Corn Walum or Om Walum- Cornwall
Cymri- Welsh
Cymru- Wales
Cyninges-tūn – Coniston. It means the estate of the king (Cumbria)
Dùn Èideann –Edinburgh (Gaelic)
Din Guardi- Bamburgh castle
Drekar- a Dragon ship (a Viking warship) pl. drekar
Duboglassio –Douglas, Isle of Man
Dun Holme- Durham
Dún Lethglaise - Downpatrick (Northern Ireland)
Durdle- Durdle dor- the Jurassic coast in Dorset
Dwfr- Dover
Dyrøy –Jura (Inner Hebrides)
Dyflin- Old Norse for Dublin
Ēa Lōn - River Lune
Earhyth -Bexley (Kent)
Ein-mánuðr - middle of March to the middle of April
Eoforwic- Saxon for York
Falgrave- Scarborough (North Yorkshire)
Faro Bregancio- Corunna (Spain)
Ferneberga -Farnborough (Hampshire)
Fey- having second sight
Firkin- a barrel containing eight gallons (usually beer)
Fornibiyum-Formby (near Liverpool)
Fret-a sea mist
Frankia- France and part of Germany
Fyrd-the Saxon levy
Ganda- Ghent (Belgium)
Garth- Dragon Heart
Gaill- Irish for foreigners
Galdramenn- wizard
Gesith- A Saxon nobleman. After 850 A.D. they were known as thegns
Gippeswic -Ipswich
Glaesum –amber,

Glannoventa -Ravenglass
Gleawecastre- Gloucester
Gói- the end of February to the middle of March
Gormánuður- October to November (Slaughter month- the beginning of winter)
Grendel- the monster slain by Beowulf
Grenewic- Greenwich
Gulle - Goole (Humberside)
Halfdenby – Alston Cumbria
Hagustaldes ham -Hexham
Hamwic -Southampton
Hæstingaceaster- Hastings
Haughs- small hills in Norse (As in Tarn Hows)
Haustmánuður - September 16th- October 16th (cutting of the corn)
Hautwesel -Haltwhistle (Hadrian's Wall)
Hearth weru- The bodyguard or oathsworn of a jarl
Heels- when a ship leans to one side under the pressure of the wind
Hel - Queen of Niflheim, the Norse underworld.
Here Wic- Harwich
Hersey- Isle of Arran
Hersir- a Viking landowner and minor noble. It ranks below a jarl
Hetaereiarch – Byzantine general
Hí- Iona (Gaelic)
Hjáp - Shap- Cumbria (Norse for stone circle)
Hoggs or Hogging- when the pressure of the wind causes the stern or the bow to droop
Hrams-a – Ramsey, Isle of Man
Hrofecester -Rochester (Kent)
Hundred- Saxon military organisation. (One hundred men from an area-led by a thegn or gesith)
Hwitebi - Norse for Whitby, North Yorkshire
Hywel ap Rhodri Molwynog- King of Gwynedd 814-825
Icaunis- a British river god
Issicauna- Gaulish for the lower Seine
Itouna- River Eden Cumbria
Jarl- Norse earl or lord
Joro-goddess of the earth
kjerringa - Old Woman- the solid block in which the mast rested
Karrek Loos yn Koos -St Michael's Mount (Cornwall)
Kerkyra- Corfu
Knarr- a merchant ship or a coastal vessel
Kriti- Crete

Kyrtle-woven top
Lambehitha- Lambeth
Leathes Water- Thirlmere
Legacaestir- Anglo Saxon for Chester
Ljoðhús- Lewis
Lochlannach – Irish for Northerners (Vikings)
Lothuwistoft- Lowestoft
Lough- Irish lake
Louis the Pious- King of the Franks and son of Charlemagne
Lundenburh/Lundenburgh- the walled burh built around the old Roman fort
Lundenwic - London
Maeldun- Maldon Essex
Maeresea- River Mersey
Mammceaster- Manchester
Manau/Mann – The Isle of Man(n) (Saxon)
Marcia Hispanic- Spanish Marches (the land around Barcelona)
Mast fish- two large racks on a ship designed to store the mast when not required
Melita- Malta
Midden- a place where they dumped human waste
Miklagård - Constantinople
Mörsugur - December 13th -January 12th (the fat sucker month!)
Musselmen- the followers of Islam
Njörðr- God of the sea
Nithing- A man without honour (Saxon)
Odin - The "All Father" God of war, also associated with wisdom, poetry, and magic (The Ruler of the gods).
Olissipo- Lisbon
Orkneyjar-Orkney
Pecheham- Peckham
Peny-cwm-cuic -Falmouth
Pennryhd – Penrith Cumbria
Pennsans – Penzance (Cornwall)
Poor john- a dried and shrivelled fish (disparaging slang for a male member- Shakespeare)
Þorri -January 13th -February 12th- midwinter
Portesmūða -Portsmouth
Porth Ia- St. Ives
Portus Cale- Porto (Portugal)
Pillars of Hercules- Straits of Gibraltar

Prittleuuella- Prittwell in Essex. Southend was originally known as the South End of Prittwell

Pyrlweall -Thirwell, Cumbria

Qādis- Cadiz

Ran- Goddess of the sea

Roof rock- slate

Rinaz –The Rhine

Sabrina- Latin and Celtic for the River Severn. Also, the name of a female Celtic deity

Saami- the people who live in what is now Northern Norway/Sweden

Sabatton- Saturday in the Byzantine calendar

Samhain- a Celtic festival of the dead between 31st October and 1st November (Halloween)

St. Cybi- Holyhead

Scree- loose rocks in a glacial valley

Seax – short sword

Sennight- seven nights- a week

Sheerstrake- the uppermost strake in the hull

Sheet- a rope fastened to the lower corner of a sail

Shroud- a rope from the masthead to the hull amidships

Skeggox – an axe with a shorter beard on one side of the blade

Skreið- stockfish (any fish which is preserved)

Skutatos- Byzantine soldier armed with an oval shield, a spear, a sword and a short mail shirt

Seouenaca -Sevenoaks (Kent)

South Folk- Suffolk

Stad- Norse settlement

Stays- ropes running from the mast-head to the bow

Strake- the wood on the side of a drekar

Streanæshalc- Saxon for Whitby, North Yorkshire

Stybbanhype – Stepney (London)

Suthriganaworc - Southwark (London)

Syllingar Insula, Syllingar- Scilly Isles

Tarn- small lake (Norse)

Tella- River Béthune which empties near to Dieppe

Temese- River Thames

Theme- Provincial Army Corps

The Norns- The three sisters who weave webs of intrigue for men

Thing-Norse for a parliament or a debate (Tynwald)

Thor's day- Thursday

Threttanessa- a drekar with 13 oars on each side.

Thuni- Tunis
Tinea- Tyne
Tilaburg – Tilbury
Tintaieol- Tintagel (Cornwall)
Thrall- slave
Trenail- a round wooden peg used to secure strakes
Tynwald- the Parliament on the Isle of Man
Tvímánuður -Hay time August 15th -September 15th
Úlfarrberg- Helvellyn
Úlfarrland- Cumbria
Úlfarr- Wolf Warrior
Úlfarrston- Ulverston
Ullr-Norse God of Hunting
Ulfheonar-an elite Norse warrior who wore a wolf skin over his armour
Vectis- The Isle of Wight
Veisafjǫrðr – Wexford (Ireland)
Volva- a witch or healing woman in Norse culture
Waeclinga Straet- Watling Street (A5)
Walhaz -Norse for the Welsh (foreigners)
Windlesore-Windsor
Waite- a Viking word for farm
Werham -Wareham (Dorset)
Western Sea- the Atlantic
Wintan-ceastre -Winchester
Withy- the mechanism connecting the steering board to the ship
Wihtwara- Isle of White
Woden's day- Wednesday
Wulfhere-Old English for Wolf Army
Wyddfa-Snowdon
Wykinglo- Wicklow (Ireland)
Wyrd- Fate
Wyrme- Norse for Dragon
Yard- a timber from which the sail is suspended
Ynys Enlli- Bardsey Island
Ynys Môn -Anglesey

Maps and drawings

Stad on the Eden- a typical Viking settlement

A wedge formation (each circle represents a warrior)

0

0 0

0 0 0

0 0 0 0

0 0 0 0 0

0 0 0 0 0 0

The boar's snout formation

A boar's snout had two wedges and up to five ranks of men behind.

Historical note

My regular readers will notice that this section is much shorter than in previous novels. Some of my readers do not like the lengthy historical note section. You can find it on my website.

What I will say is that like them or hate them the Vikings were a unique race. Their descendants were the Normans but they were not the same as that hybrid of Norse and Frank. The true Vikings were pagans. They sailed further than any man. Columbus made the West Indies. The Vikings landed in New England and Canada! They were an uncompromising people and I hope that I have done them justice.

Some have questioned Jarl Dragonheart's longevity. There were examples of Vikings who lived as long. Harald Hadrada was one. They were hard men and their lives were violent. It was war which killed them and not the way they lived when at home. They were active and their diet seemed to make them live a little longer than might be expected. Meat, fish, cheese and ale must be a good combination! I think a vegan Viking would be a contradiction in terms!

The Vikings used foster fathers for younger warriors. When the first Vikings went across the Atlantic there was a German Viking who was a foster father to the leader of one the expeditions.

I used the following books for research:

- Vikings- Life and Legends -British Museum
- Saxon, Norman and Viking by Terence Wise (Osprey)
- The Vikings (Osprey) -Ian Heath
- Byzantine Armies 668-1118 (Osprey)-Ian Heath
- Romano-Byzantine Armies 4th- 9th Century (Osprey) - David Nicholle
- The Walls of Constantinople AD 324-1453 (Osprey) - Stephen Turnbull
- Viking Longship (Osprey) - Keith Durham
- The Vikings- David Wernick (Time-Life)
- The Vikings in England Anglo-Danish Project
- Anglo Saxon Thegn AD 449-1066- Mark Harrison (Osprey)
- Viking Hersir- 793-1066 AD - Mark Harrison (Osprey)
- Hadrian's Wall- David Breeze (English Heritage)
- National Geographic- March 2017
- The Tower of London – Lapper and Parnell (Osprey)

Other books by Griff Hosker

If you enjoyed reading this book, then why not read another one by the author?

Ancient History

The Sword of Cartimandua Series
(Germania and Britannia 50 A.D. – 128 A.D.)
Ulpius Felix- Roman Warrior (prequel)
The Sword of Cartimandua
The Horse Warriors
Invasion Caledonia
Roman Retreat
Revolt of the Red Witch
Druid's Gold
Trajan's Hunters
The Last Frontier
Hero of Rome
Roman Hawk
Roman Treachery
Roman Wall
Roman Courage

The Wolf Warrior series
(Britain in the late 6th Century)
Saxon Dawn
Saxon Revenge
Saxon England
Saxon Blood
Saxon Slayer
Saxon Slaughter
Saxon Bane
Saxon Fall: Rise of the Warlord
Saxon Throne
Saxon Sword

Medieval History

The Dragon Heart Series
Viking Slave

Viking Warrior
Viking Jarl
Viking Kingdom
Viking Wolf
Viking War
Viking Sword
Viking Wrath
Viking Raid
Viking Legend
Viking Vengeance
Viking Dragon
Viking Treasure
Viking Enemy
Viking Witch
Viking Blood
Viking Weregeld
Viking Storm
Viking Warband
Viking Shadow
Viking Legacy
Viking Clan
Viking Bravery

The Norman Genesis Series
Hrolf the Viking
Horseman
The Battle for a Home
Revenge of the Franks
The Land of the Northmen
Ragnvald Hrolfsson
Brothers in Blood
Lord of Rouen
Drekar in the Seine
Duke of Normandy
The Duke and the King

Danelaw
(England and Denmark in the 11th Century)
Dragon Sword
Oathsword
Bloodsword
Danish Sword

New World Series
Blood on the Blade
Across the Seas
The Savage Wilderness
The Bear and the Wolf
Erik The Navigator
Erik's Clan

The Vengeance Trail

The Reconquista Chronicles
Castilian Knight
El Campeador
The Lord of Valencia

The Aelfraed Series
(Britain and Byzantium 1050 A.D. - 1085 A.D.)
Housecarl
Outlaw
Varangian

The Anarchy Series England
1120-1180
English Knight
Knight of the Empress
Northern Knight
Baron of the North
Earl
King Henry's Champion
The King is Dead
Warlord of the North
Enemy at the Gate
The Fallen Crown
Warlord's War
Kingmaker
Henry II
Crusader
The Welsh Marches
Irish War
Poisonous Plots
The Princes' Revolt
217

Earl Marshal
The Perfect Knight

Border Knight
1182-1300
Sword for Hire
Return of the Knight
Baron's War
Magna Carta
Welsh Wars
Henry III
The Bloody Border
Baron's Crusade
Sentinel of the North
War in the West
Debt of Honour
The Blood of the Warlord
The Fettered King

Sir John Hawkwood Series
France and Italy 1339- 1387
Crécy: The Age of the Archer
Man At Arms
The White Company
Leader of Men
Tuscan Warlord

Lord Edward's Archer
Lord Edward's Archer
King in Waiting
An Archer's Crusade
Targets of Treachery
The Great Cause
Wallace's War

Struggle for a Crown
1360- 1485
Blood on the Crown
To Murder a King
The Throne
King Henry IV
The Road to Agincourt

St Crispin's Day
The Battle for France
The Last Knight
Queen's Knight

Tales from the Sword I
(Short stories from the Medieval period)

Tudor Warrior series
England and Scotland in the late 14th and early 15th century
Tudor Warrior
Tudor Spy

Conquistador
England and America in the 16th Century
Conquistador
The English Adventurer

Modern History

The Napoleonic Horseman Series
Chasseur à Cheval
Napoleon's Guard
British Light Dragoon
Soldier Spy
1808: The Road to Coruña
Talavera
The Lines of Torres Vedras
Bloody Badajoz
The Road to France
Waterloo

The Lucky Jack American Civil War series
Rebel Raiders
Confederate Rangers
The Road to Gettysburg

Soldier of the Queen series
Soldier of the Queen
Redcoat's Rifle

The British Ace Series
1914
1915 Fokker Scourge
1916 Angels over the Somme
1917 Eagles Fall
1918 We will remember them
From Arctic Snow to Desert Sand
Wings over Persia

Combined Operations series
1940-1945
Commando
Raider
Behind Enemy Lines
Dieppe
Toehold in Europe
Sword Beach
Breakout
The Battle for Antwerp
King Tiger
Beyond the Rhine
Korea
Korean Winter

Tales from the Sword II
(Short stories from the Modern period)

Other Books
Great Granny's Ghost (Aimed at 9-14-year-old young people)

For more information on all of the books then please visit the author's
website at www.griffhosker.com where there is a link to contact him or
visit his Facebook page: GriffHosker at Sword Books

Made in the USA
Las Vegas, NV
29 March 2023

69843111R00132